THE OVERNIGHTS

THE OVERNIGHTS

An Ashe Cayne Novel

IAN K. SMITH

AMISTAD

An Imprint of HarperCollinsPublishers

THE OVERNIGHTS. Copyright © 2023 by Ian K. Smith. All rights reserved. Printed in the United States of America. No part of this book may be used or reproduced in any manner whatsoever without written permission except in the case of brief quotations embodied in critical articles and reviews. For information, address HarperCollins Publishers, 195 Broadway, New York, NY 10007.

HarperCollins books may be purchased for educational, business, or sales promotional use. For information, please email the Special Markets Department at SPsales@harpercollins.com.

FIRST HARPERCOLLINS PAPERBACK PUBLISHED IN 2024

Designed by Nancy Singer

Library of Congress Cataloging-in-Publication Data is available upon request.

ISBN 978-0-06-325372-8

24 25 26 27 28 LBC 5 4 3 2 1

To Dashiell and Declan,

the oxygen in my life, the fire in my belly, the beat in my heart.

Never be thwarted in your pursuit of dreams.

Little hurts deeper than the raw death of an illusion.

—Ian K. Smith

PART I

1

She had agreed to meet at my office only if I had a back entrance through which she could discreetly enter and exit. It had been the first time anyone had ever made that request, but I was happy enough to oblige. Our phone conversation had been brief, and she had been in complete control. The office door swung open at precisely one minute before ten o'clock. Morgan Shaw, the prime evening anchor at the city's top-rated WLTV, sauntered in with dark oversize sunglasses and a mahogany sheared mink coat disguised well enough that only those of a certain ilk would know it was an expensive fur. She was more beautiful in person than she was on TV, if that were even possible. The fitted jeans and silk blouse with the matching Hermes handbag were exactly what I expected of a woman who commanded a seven-figure salary and a legion of fans throughout the city who had all but deified her.

"'Better three hours too soon than a minute too late,'" I said, standing as she walked in.

She didn't wait for me to offer her a seat. She relieved herself of the mink, flung it over one chair on the other side of my desk, and sat in the other. I felt like it wasn't inappropriate to stare. She had to be used to that.

"Three hours?" she said, looking down at her gold and diamond watch. "We agreed on ten o'clock."

"We did," I said. "You're early. Most people are late. That was just Shakespeare's way of emphasizing the importance of being punctual."

"They told me you quoted a lot of Shakespeare," she said.

"Did they tell you I like Thomas Kyd too?" I said.

"And who is that?"

"One of Shakespeare's lesser-known contemporaries. Wrote a play called *The Spanish Tragedy*. At the time, it was more popular than anything Shakespeare had ever written."

"What was it about?"

"Revenge. A Spanish nobleman is killed after having a secret affair with a beautiful woman who is beloved by many. The nobleman's ghost leaves the underworld with the spirit of revenge, and they go back to the world of the living to witness the murder of the prince who killed him."

"Maybe I should read it," she said. "I feel like my life is one big tragedy right now."

"You said on the phone this was urgent," I said.

"Very." She removed her sunglasses dramatically. Her eyes were a radiant topaz against flawless skin the color of warm cocoa butter. "I think someone is going to kill me. I need to hire you to be my bodyguard."

"Wrong man."

"I beg your pardon?"

"Not my line of work. I'm a private investigator."

"I know exactly who you are and what you do," she said. "That's why I'm here. I need you to investigate who is trying to harm me and why. But I also need someone who's going to protect me because I think they want to kill me."

"There are plenty of good private security companies around town. I can recommend several. A couple of ex-cops run one of the best in the city. Very professional. Very discreet."

"I don't want them," she said. "I want you."

"A common refrain," I said, offering my most alluring smile. "But alas, I'm not to be had."

"Are you playing hard to get?"

"As beautiful as you are, I can't imagine anyone ever doing that with you."

"And you're charming."

"Only after a good round of golf."

"So why won't you protect me or investigate who's trying to kill me?"

"Because I'm leaving town in two weeks for Arizona."

"Arizona? What's in Arizona? A bunch of octogenarians, scorching temperatures, and dry desert."

"You're forgetting the more than three hundred golf courses."

"Are you serious?"

"Very."

"Do you know who I am?" she said.

"Everyone in the city knows who you are from a mile away."

"And you're gonna turn me down?"

"Well, since you put it like that."

"I can pay you a lot of money," she said, unlatching a complicated-looking gold clasp on a bag that looked like it cost about as much as a sports car, maybe a little more.

"I don't need your money, Ms. Shaw."

"Call me Morgan."

I nodded.

"So if something happens to me, you would be all right knowing that you had the chance to prevent it from happening?"

"Depends."

"On what?"

"I'd have to weigh whatever that something is against my chances of getting my handicap below a ten."

"You're handicapped?"

"All decent golfers are."

"How can you play golf and have a physical impairment?"

"Tiger won the '08 US Open with a broken leg and torn ACL. But that's not the type of handicap I'm talking about. A handicap is basically a numerical measure of a golfer's potential ability. The lower the handicap, the better a player you are."

"And what does this have to do with you taking on my case?"

"My handicap currently stands at an even ten. Once you crack ten, you can be considered a good golfer. This year, I decided to spend some of the winter in Arizona so I can work on my game long after Lake Michigan freezes over."

"I only need you for two months," she said. "You can go to Arizona after that and play as much as you want."

"How do you know it will only be two months?"

"Because I heard you're the best and you always get results. Two months should be enough time."

I smiled. "If I were a marketer, I could work that nicely into a slogan."

"Can you ever be serious?"

"Sure, when I'm standing over a five-foot putt and it's worth three skins."

"Can you ever stop talking about golf? I've been here for close to ten minutes, and that's all you've talked about."

"You forgot about Shakespeare and Kyd."

She stood up and gathered her mink.

"Where are you going?" I asked.

"You're self-absorbed and condescending."

Before she walked through the door with great flare, I said, "You forgot to take the names of the security firms I mentioned."

And just like that, the stunning Morgan Shaw was gone.

2

What if something really happens to her?" Carolina Espinoza said to me as we sat in a corner booth at Beatrix staring down a rib eye steak and salade Niçoise. "I know how you're gonna feel, especially since you could've prevented it and she asked for help."

"I know," I said. "Me too. But I don't want to be some high-maintenance anchorwoman's bodyguard. No thank you."

"She's not just some anchor," Carolina said. "She is *the* anchor, and people worship the ground she walks on."

"Do you?"

"Do I what?"

"Worship the ground she walks on?"

"Of course not. I don't even watch local news."

"Well, there you have it."

"Did you at least talk about how long she's been in danger?"

"Nope."

"Did you find out who or why someone was trying to harm her?"

"Nope."

"Did you talk about what she could do to better protect herself?"

"Nope."

"Then what in the hell did you talk about?"

"Golf and Shakespeare."

"I should've known. Your two favorite topics."

"Only after you."

She moved her hand on top of mine and smiled softly.

"I have something for you," she said, reaching into her handbag and pulling out a large package.

I feigned surprise. "It's so perfect I almost don't want to open it," I said.

"Don't worry about it," she said. "Tons more ribbons and paper where that came from."

I carefully opened the taped seams of the paper and pulled out a glass frame. The two of us sat there with the sun setting behind us and the Koutoubia Mosque in Marrakech glowing in the background. It had been a perfect vacation in every way, and this captured all the fun and joy of that week whether it was riding camels, shopping at Jemaa el-Fnaa, or hiking into the Atlas Mountains. I looked up and was about to lean across the table to kiss her when I froze. It wasn't possible. I couldn't move at first. I scrunched my eyes. Why was I suddenly hallucinating? Julia, my ex-fiancée who had abandoned me three years ago and run away to Paris, was standing inside the doorway of the restaurant. What the hell was going on? Was the wine getting to me?

"What's wrong?" Carolina said, touching my arm. "Everything okay? Ashe?"

I kept staring and tightened my eyes. Everything started to look fuzzy. She wore a long charcoal-gray cashmere coat with her hands stuffed into the pockets. Her hair was slightly longer than I remembered, but she looked exactly the same as she did that last night she walked out of my apartment. She didn't have any expression on her face, but she was definitely looking at me. The waiters and other guests walked around her as she just stood there. Her bright red lipstick popped like neon against her caramel skin.

"You okay?" Carolina asked.

"I'm fine," I said, smiling at her. "I think it's the wine. I need to go to the bathroom. I'll be right back."

I stood and started walking toward the bathroom, which was not far from the front door. She was gone. I scanned the restaurant. She wasn't inside. I looked back at Carolina, who was looking down at the photograph. I quickly made my way to the door and ducked outside. I looked left and then right. I didn't see her. Then I spotted her coat a block farther north. She was moving quickly. I lost her between bodies on the crowded sidewalk. I yelled her name as I ran. She didn't turn around. I dodged and weaved until I was only yards away. I was about to call her again, but then I got a clear view of her. It wasn't Julia. The woman was shorter and had curlier hair. I stopped my pursuit. Passersby looked at me quizzically. My heart felt like it dropped a foot in my chest. My lungs worked to recover. How could I have made this mistake? But it had to be her. She was standing there looking at me.

I scanned the sidewalks in both directions, then looked across the street. Nothing. I turned and walked back toward the restaurant. It took me a couple of minutes to regain my composure. Why was my mind playing tricks on me like this after I had worked so hard to let go and move on with my life? I calmly walked back inside the restaurant, but the emotions swirling inside of me were anything but calm.

"I HAVEN'T SEEN YOU IN three weeks," my father said from his favorite winged chair, the reflection of the nearby roaring fire bouncing off his silk pajamas. He dangled a tumbler of dark cognac in his right hand. I was certain it was his Louis XIII. Dr. Wendell Cayne, retired psychiatrist and an expert in almost everything, only drank the best, especially when he was relaxing in his study in front of his elaborately constructed walk-in fireplace.

"You could always come to my place," I said. "I have plenty of room. We could have a nice dinner."

"You haven't invited me."

"Why do I need to invite my own father? You're always welcome."

"You're looking a little thin in the face," he said. It wasn't uncommon for him to change subjects when he felt like he was losing leverage in a conversation.

"Is that an observation or judgment?" I said.

"Just an observation. Have you been eating okay?"

"Like I've always been."

"And the trip to Marrakech?"

"One of the best ever. We had an amazing time."

"We?"

"I took a friend with me."

He raised his furry eyebrows. "Why am I always the last to know what's going on in your life?"

An answer immediately came to mind, but I thought better of speaking it. I didn't want another fight. It had taken a long time for us to recover from the last one. Our relationship had weathered its fair share of storms before and after my mother's passing, and I longed for calm. Despite the fact he knew how to push my buttons and sometimes annoy the hell out of me, I loved him deeply.

"It's not that serious," I said. "We're just feeling things out."

"Am I allowed to know her name?"

"Carolina."

"And what she does?"

"Works in BIS at headquarters. Administrative supervisor. So what's new in your life?"

My father swirled the cognac and took a sip. "I'm volunteering at the hospital now," he said. "I started last week."

"I thought you were enjoying retirement."

"I am. Tremendously. But I want to give back. I'm not seeing patients again. I want to help the medical residents. Unfortunately, there aren't a lot of Black and brown doctors on staff. These young residents need role models. Inspiration. The program director asked me if I'd help out." He waved his hand to highlight the expanse and opulence of the room. "Medicine has been very good to me. Paying it forward is the least I can do."

"And what's gonna happen to all your tennis matches?"

"I'm not volunteering *that* much." He smiled. "I meet with the young docs once or twice a week for about an hour. Maybe have some of them over to the house for dinner every couple of months. Impactful but not heavy lifting. My tennis schedule remains uninterrupted."

"When was the last time you spoke to Jules?"

He looked at the fire for a moment, then back at me. I knew the question would catch him off guard. He was smart and as good at answering questions as he was at asking them. Questioning had been the core of his skill set as a psychiatrist.

"I haven't spoken to Julia since you and I had our misunderstanding," he said.

"It wasn't a misunderstanding," I said. "You were secretly communicating with my ex-fiancée who just so happened to have abandoned me eight months before our wedding. You thought it was fine to secretly continue a relationship with a woman who practically ripped my heart out of my chest. There was no misunderstanding. What you did was wrong and hurtful. Plain and simple."

"I understand your feelings," he said, nodding. "I apologized for what I did. I understand the hurt that it caused you. I don't want to go back to that space. I haven't spoken to her since I saw her in Paris."

That wasn't good enough for me. Dr. Wendell Cayne could be extremely cunning when the need arose. Words and questions required great precision, or he would find small pockets of air and work his way to them and hide. "Has she reached out to you in any way?" I asked.

"None. Why are you asking me all this now?"

"Because I think I saw her."

My father sat up in his chair and rested his drink on a small marble table he had acquired on a trip to Turkey and proclaimed to be a relic of the Ottoman Empire. "What do you mean you saw her?"

"Today I was having lunch downtown, and I saw her standing in the door of the restaurant."

"What was she doing?"

"Just standing there looking at me."

"Are you certain it was her?"

"Of course. How could I not know what the woman I was supposed to marry looks like? Her hair was a little longer, but she looked exactly the same."

"Is it possible you were just thinking about her at that moment and you saw someone who looked like her, so you thought it was her?"

"I guess it's possible, but that's never happened to me before. Besides, I wasn't thinking about her. I was sitting there with Carolina, and I looked up, and there she was."

My father nodded his head confidently. "Did she do anything? Say anything? Make any gestures?"

"No, she just stood there."

"Did she smile?"

"No."

"Did you acknowledge her presence?"

"I got up to talk to her, but she was gone by the time I got to the door. I looked outside and thought I saw her, but it was someone else with a similar coat."

"Did you have anything to drink at lunch?"

"A glass of wine."

"You were likely hallucinating," he said calmly.

"You're saying that because I was drinking alcohol. Jesus Christ, Dad. I'm not a lightweight. And I wasn't even close to being drunk."

"You had a visual hallucination. Lots of things can cause them. People think hallucinations are always abnormal or a sign of a disease process. They're not. Sometimes they are part of the normal grieving process. People who are in emotional turmoil and have suffered a loss can see or hear things that really don't exist."

"But I'm not grieving anymore. I've accepted what happened and moved on with my life."

"Grieving can also be a subconscious process where it can last longer than you think. It's not always about external manifestations. Many people think they've reached closure when really, they haven't. This simply might be an instance where something triggered you to think about her, and your mind convinced you that she was there. This was an involuntary process. It happens all the time. I wouldn't give it much thought unless it happens again."

I heard and accepted what he said. But there was still that gnawing feeling somewhere in the dark recesses of my stomach along with the tiniest of voices in the back of my head insisting that it really had been Julia staring at me.

3

I stood on the sixth-hole tee box of the South Shore golf course staring down the 375-yard fairway with the expanse of Lake Michigan staring back at me. It was such a beautiful view, seeing the green perched above the water shrouded by the vast powder-blue sky. It was difficult not thinking about Walter Griffin, the highly connected former Chicago school board president whose body had been found a few years ago in a deserted, unseemly area called Wolf Point. This was one of the last holes of golf that Griffin had ever played before his life ended so abruptly and unceremoniously.

My phone buzzed and interrupted my thoughts. I had accidentally left it in my pocket, which was something I rarely did on the golf course for this very reason. I stepped back from the tee and answered it.

"They slashed all four of my tires and left a dead fish on my window," a woman's voice said. I knew right away it was Morgan Shaw. "Are you happy now?"

"What kind of fish was it?" I said.

"How the hell do I know? Does it matter?"

"Of course it does. If it's a Pacific bluefin tuna, someone just wasted a lot of money. That could be a clue to who did it."

"Do you know who this is?"

"Of course I do. There's that unmistakable beauty even in your voice." I looked at the foursome coming up the fairway on the hole behind me. They would be angry as hell if they finished their hole and drove up to find me talking on the phone, slowing down play.

"Had you taken my case, none of this would've happened to me," she said.

"But you didn't have a case. You had a premonition."

"Four slashed tires and a dead fish, tuna or not, is what I would call more than a premonition. Someone is after me."

I turned and saw the group behind me finishing up on the fifth green.

"I have to tee off," I said.

"Now you're drinking tea? I thought you were playing golf."

"I am. 'Tee off' means the first shot you take on a specific hole. Not the tea you drink at Claridge's."

"Is golf all you care about?"

"And a slab of ribs and fries with an ice-cold root beer to wash it down."

"If something happens to me, you're to blame."

"Well, since you put it like that, maybe we should meet up and discuss your premonitions."

"What time?"

"Six."

"Meet me at Swift & Sons over in Fulton Market," she said. "I have a table in the back."

"Impressive."

"Your sarcasm is wearing on me."

"I'll work on it."

"And I won't have a lot of time. I have a news meeting at seven. I'm on the air at ten."

"Try to stay alive til then."

AT PRECISELY ONE MINUTE BEFORE six, the stunning Morgan Shaw walked through the doors of Swift & Sons wearing sunglasses, wrapped snugly in a leopard-print dress, and carrying a handbag made of some exotic reptile. People gawked and whispered and nudged each other as she made her way through the restaurant. She acted as if she were oblivious to it all, but I was doubtful of that. She was the kind of person who proudly absorbed every glance and laudatory murmur.

As she arrived at the table, the host pulled out her seat. Morgan placed her handbag on it, then waited for him to pull out the seat next to it. She didn't take off her sunglasses until she had fully settled.

"You always make an entrance like that?" I said.

"Movie stars and starlets make entrances," she said. "I'm neither. I'm a primetime anchorwoman."

"Who many consider a celebrity."

"Well, that's different than a movie star. Any fifteen-year-old kid with a camera and a TikTok account can be a celebrity these days."

"But they don't have all your glitz and glamour," I said, nodding toward her handbag.

A lemon and lime wedge had already been set out for her on a small plate. She picked up the lemon first and squeezed it into her glass of Perrier, then squeezed in the lime and took a small sip.

"So are you going to figure out who's doing this to me?" she said.

"Maybe I should first understand what exactly is being done," I said.

"It started a couple of weeks ago," she said. "I got a small envelope in the mail. It had one sentence on it. 'Stop what you're doing before something bad happens to you.'"

"That's it?"

"Just that one sentence."

"Handwritten?"

"No, it was typed."

"Do you still have the letter?"

"No, I threw it away. I thought it was someone trying to pull a prank."

"I assume there was no return address."

"None."

"Where did you get the envelope?"

"My new apartment. I had just moved in a month ago."

"Where do you live?"

"Nine West Walton."

I knew the address. It was right down the street from another swanky doorman building where Sophia Caballé lived, an equally beautiful woman I had met while investigating Walter Griffin's death last year. I wondered if Morgan and Sophia ever passed each other walking to the nearby designer shops on Michigan Avenue.

"Do you remember if there was postage on the envelope?" I asked.

"I don't. I assume there was."

"But you're not sure?"

She nodded her head and took another sip.

The waiter brought over a basket of warm bread neatly wrapped in a linen napkin. He poured olive oil on a small dish between us, then promptly left.

"This bread is worth its weight in gold," she said, grabbing a piece and dipping it in the oil. "I'm not supposed to be eating these kinds of carbs, but I can't help myself."

"A meal without bread is like a cake without frosting," I said. "You can manage without it, but there's still that feeling something is missing." I took two slices and dipped them in the oil. Carb counting was no concern for me.

Two women walked by the table, slowing down as they got near before quickly passing to the other side of the room.

"Did you tell anyone about this letter?" I asked.

"Not at first," she said. "I didn't think much of it. But then two weeks later I got a box in the mail. Someone sent it to me at work. No return address. But it was stamped."

"What was inside?"

"A pair of braided leather floggers."

"Floggers?"

"Bondage floggers."

"Flog as in hit?"

"Exactly."

"Was there any message inside the box with them?"

"They *were* the message."

"Which was?"

"I don't know."

"Had you seen them before?"

"Not that exact pair, but I've seen one similar."

"Where was that?"

"In the nightstand next to my bed."

The waiter delivered a platter of grilled shrimp cocktail, king crab, and clams.

"I took the liberty of ordering ahead for us," she said. "Since you were so interested in the fish on my windshield, I chose seafood. The Spanish clams are in a white wine sauce with spicy chorizo."

"You like being in charge," I said.

"I like it when things are done properly," she said. "I don't rely on others when I can do things myself."

"Why would someone send you a pair of leather floggers?" I asked.

"Because they want to intimidate me."

"Are they that painful?"

"Not physical intimidation. They are letting me know that they know things about me."

"And these things would embarrass you?"

"I'm not embarrassed by anything," she said. "I make choices and live with the consequences. Life is too short to be embarrassed."

"Then how are they going to intimidate you?"

"I don't know," she said. "That's what you need to figure out. But it's no coincidence that my tires were slashed today, and that fish was on my car. Someone is after me."

"Maybe an ex who didn't want to become your ex, but you made him one anyway?"

"Maybe."

"What kind of car do you drive?"

"Today it was my G-Wagon."

"Where was it parked?"

"In the garage at work."

"And no one saw anything suspicious? What did security say?"

"They didn't see anyone."

"Surveillance cameras?"

"None of them faced the area of the garage I was parked in."

"Did they report it to CPD?"

"Of course, but that doesn't mean anything. They'll send some officer who will take a report, meet me, then ask for my personal phone number."

"I'll go and take a look."

"So finally you realize it's more than just a premonition?"

"I do. I also realize I have a flight to Arizona in two weeks, and I don't plan on missing it."

4

I barely kept up as Morgan Shaw raced her tinted-window midnight-blue Bentley back to the station on Michigan Avenue just north of the Chicago River. She drove like someone trying to avoid gunfire. We pulled into a garage underneath the building. Mechanic's black Viper pulled in behind me. The enclosed garage made the grumble of his exhaust sound like a rhino trying to clear its throat.

Morgan parked in the corner of the first level. I was surprised there were no assigned spots. Other late-model cars sat nearby. I pulled in a spot behind her. I had called Mechanic earlier for backup and asked him to follow us from the restaurant and keep a lookout to see if anyone else might be tailing us. He kept a safe distance and parked several rows behind us.

"Is this where the G-Wagon was parked when the tires were slashed?" I asked as she got out of her car.

"No, it was over there." She pointed to an adjacent row. "Up against the wall."

I quickly scanned the area. There weren't a lot of cars in that part of the garage—maybe fifteen or less. Most of the spots were empty. I noticed two cameras on the other side of the garage. Neither of them seemed to be pointing toward the area where she had parked.

"Not a lot of cars down here," I said.

"Most people have gone home," she said. "The cars you see now are mostly talent and management working late."

"I'm surprised they don't provide you with an assigned spot with your name on a fancy placard."

"Like I told you before, I'm not a Hollywood star. I'm an anchorwoman. Years ago, top talent had assigned parking. That doesn't fly these days. The optics aren't good. I make the big money with all the lights and attention, then you have news writers and associate producers who have to take the bus to work or rent a Zipcar. They don't need to see my name on some placard as a reminder of how much they work for so little money."

"I get that, but I'd think there at least would be a dedicated area for the on-air personalities for security reasons."

"There is one unofficially," she said. "The parking attendants usually keep this area reserved for us. They keep everyone else more along the outside rows. I park in this spot all the time. My name's not on it, but everyone knows it's for me."

"Why wasn't the G-Wagon parked here earlier?"

"One of the new cameramen parked a news truck there. He didn't know any better."

I looked around again. I was impressed by how unsecure it felt. Anyone could take a run at her. We were the only two on the floor along with Mechanic, still sitting quietly in his car. Save for the cameras, it would be an easy location to do some bad things.

"Show me the exact route you take every day from here to get to the studio," I said.

"Follow me," she said. "Even though it's only one flight up, I don't use the stairs because I don't like enclosed stairwells. Creeps me out."

She started walking toward a single elevator door. I turned and nodded my head at Mechanic before following her.

We rode up two flights, and the door opened to a large hallway that had a LensCrafters along one wall and a Japanese restaurant along the other. We took a left and walked about twenty yards until we reached a bright lobby with lots of potted plants. A large neon sign announced the station. A female security guard sat at a small white desk behind glass. The doors buzzed as she reached for the handle.

"He's with me, Keisha," Morgan said to the guard.

Keisha nodded her head full of thick maroon braids that had been twisted and piled on top of her head. Her uniform was two sizes too big for her tiny frame. She slid a sticker with the station's logo underneath the security window. Morgan grabbed it and handed it to me.

Keisha buzzed another door, we walked through, and we entered a long corridor in the station.

"I have to run to the news meeting," she said. "You can have a look around. I'll be done in about thirty minutes. I only stay for the first part, then I go to my office and read through the scripts. The newsroom is down the hall to the right. Anyone asks, just tell them you're my guest."

"Is Keisha the only security guard here?" I asked.

"No, there are two more. Keisha just works the front. Jimmy is in the security office, and Brandon is probably walking around."

"Will they have a problem with me walking unescorted?"

"Not after you mention my name."

I watched Morgan make her way down the hall and disappear into the newsroom. I decided to walk in the opposite direction. I passed by a couple of open doors and a few edit bays. No one paid me much attention. I turned the corner and walked into a large control room full of monitors and a long low-sitting desk with an enormous panel of buttons and knobs and other complicated machinery. I had never been inside a control room, but I had seen one many times on TV while watching Michael Strahan and the guys on Fox NFL Sunday. I always wanted to see what it looked like in real life. It was even bigger than I expected.

"You need a GPS?" I heard a voice say.

I turned around to see a short woman with dyed black hair, large square glasses, and a small box of memory cards in her hands. She wore cuffed jeans with a long beige sweater that draped to her knees.

"Just looking around," I said.

"And they let you back here?"

"I'm with Morgan," I said.

She rolled her eyes. "Figures."

"What does that mean?"

"Well, a cute guy like you could only be here for two reasons. Either they were looking at you for an on-air position, or you had some connection to Morgan. That girl is a piece of work."

She stepped to the desk and pushed a few buttons that brought up a live shot of downtown Chicago on several of the center monitors. The rush-hour traffic on Michigan Avenue had all but disappeared.

"Make yourself useful," she said. "Hand me that box on the desk behind you."

I did as instructed.

"I'm Heddy," she said as I handed her the box. "What's your name?"

"Ashe."

"Like the Egyptian Hawk God?"

"No, mine is spelled with an *e*."

"Like the tennis player, but your parents gave you his last name as your first."

"We can't choose our parents."

"But you can choose the company you keep. Why the hell are you with Morgan? You're cute and smart. You're wasting your time with that one. She's bold and beautiful and nice to jump in the sack with, but she's a career woman. Her job is all that matters. You'll be a distant third at best."

"What's second?"

"Her shoes. The girl puts Imelda Marcos to shame." She read the puzzled expression on my face, then waved me off. "I'm dating myself. You probably don't even know who Marcos is."

I shrugged.

"The First Lady of the Philippines way back when. She and Ferdinand embezzled billions of dollars. She was famous for her shoe collection. Owned more shoes than anyone in the world. Someone asked her about the collection once and she said, 'I did not have three thousand pairs of shoes. I had one thousand and sixty.' That's Imelda Marcos."

Heddy turned back to the instrument panel and hit more buttons, which brought up a running time code on several of the monitors.

"Sounds like Morgan isn't your favorite person," I said.

"Don't put words into my mouth. I've done a damn good job of doing that for myself all these years. She's a bitch, but I love her. Everyone loves her. What's there not to love about her? Gorgeous. Smart. Hardworking. Competitive as hell. The cheap sons of bitches upstairs ain't putting a whole bunch of zeroes on her checks for nothing. And she's worth every penny of it."

"How long have you worked here?"

"Since before your mother's ovary decided you might be a good idea. I've seen them all come and go. One pretty face after another until the makeup can't hide the wrinkles in the corners of the eyes or the surgery starts looking too obvious. This high-def technology has shortened a lot of careers."

"You ever hear of anyone who wanted to harm Morgan since she's been here?"

"Ha!" She laughed. "Trick question, right?"

"Actually, it's a very serious one."

"They put that nut job Haley Diggs away for two years downstate at Lincoln Correctional. He almost got her coming out of a restaurant on Oak Street one night. Lucky the valet was there to step in." Heddy shrugged her shoulders. "But that comes with the job. Lots of sickos out there with all kinds of fantasies. Common as diarrhea."

"Is the guy still locked up?"

"Nope. They let him walk about two months ago."

I couldn't help but wonder why Morgan hadn't shared this with me. It seemed like that would've been the first thing she would tell me. I was intrigued. I'd wait to see how long it took for her to bring it up.

5

"You guys fighting or dancing the damn tango?" Arnold "The Hammer" Scazzi yelled as he stood just outside the ring. Mechanic and I were lightly sparring. We were in the final minutes of our thirty-minute workout.

Mechanic stepped back, dropped his hands, then looked at Hammer. "Jesus Christ," he said. "Leave us alone or get your old ass in here and do something."

I took advantage of the distraction, stepped in, and quickly tapped Mechanic twice on the chest and once on the side of the head. Mechanic stood his ground.

"That's what you get," Hammer grumbled. "Stay focused and stop talking shit. I'm seventy and arthritic and can still beat the piss outta you." He waved his hand and walked away, still light on his feet, biceps a little wrinkled, but still bulging under his shirt.

Mechanic and I walked to the corner and took a seat on our stools. Just as we took out our mouthpieces and grabbed water bottles, Ruqsania "Rox" Begume—all five foot three inches of her and a touch over a hundred pounds—walked into the gym. Lithe, muscular, and wearing that smile on her face bright enough to light up a football stadium, she was the best female boxer I had ever seen. She was born and raised in Bangladesh, then moved to London for several years before finding her way to the States. After winning countless fights and titles, she hung up the gloves a year ago and of all things opened a small flower shop in Roscoe Village.

"You boys look like you've been through a war," she said, stepping up into the ring. "Hope you're not losing your touch."

Mechanic tapped her chiseled abs three times from his seated position. She stood there and took it.

"Hands still fast," she said.

"So is my gun," Mechanic said.

"Which one?"

"Both."

"Why don't the two of you save it for the bedroom," I said. "Let's talk about the business at hand. Morgan Shaw."

Rox pulled up a stool and sat beside us.

"I thought you were leaving for Arizona in a couple of weeks," Rox said.

"I am."

"How are you gonna do that and protect this prima donna?"

"I'm not protecting her. The two of you are."

Mechanic and Rox exchanged glances.

"You'll work in seven-hour shifts," I said. "The other ten hours she's either sleeping or at the station. She gets up at eight o'clock, then three mornings a week she runs a couple of miles on the lake. Two mornings she takes a swim in the pool in her building. Saturday mornings around ten she does Pilates. Sunday is her rest day. So the first shift should start at nine when she heads out for her run. You'll change shifts at four when she's at the studio prepping for the five o'clock news. She typically goes out to get dinner around six, then she needs to be back at the station for a seven o'clock meeting that preps her for the ten o'clock news. She's off air at eleven. She goes to the garage, gets in her car, then drives home. Once she's safely inside, the second shift ends."

"What does her building security look like?" Mechanic asked.

"Very tight. Three doormen at all times, one positioned at the door, the other stationed at the desk. They also have a security guard stationed in the lobby. There's a private garage underneath the building. Each tenant has a unique code to gain access so they can keep a log of which tenant enters and exits the garage. Deliveries are made in the rear of the building at a locked loading dock that's monitored by cameras and a security guard."

"But didn't you say someone got her car at work?" Rox said.

"They did. That garage is a problem. The security is sloppy and loose. You guys will need to park down there and walk her to the lobby. You can then hand her off to the station's security team."

"Is she really as big a prima donna as they say she is?" Rox asked.

"More," I said. "She's been the highest-rated anchorwoman in the city the last five years. She's beautiful, rich, and famous. She loves being under the lights. It's who she is."

"Does she have any idea who might be doing this?" Rox asked.

"I think she does, but she's not saying. A guy named Haley Diggs stalked her a couple of years ago and just got out of prison. But she didn't tell me that. I found out from a woman who works at the station."

"Sounds like that little piece of information is something you'd want to share with a guy you just hired to protect you," Rox said.

I shrugged my shoulders. "You'd think."

"What do you know about this Diggs guy?" Mechanic asked.

"Right now, just his name and a photo of what he looked like when he went away. Haley Diggs. White male. Six foot four, two hundred thirty pounds. Used to be a driver for UPS. Never married. Family lives in Hammond, Indiana. He played middle linebacker on his high school football team and never went to college. I don't know where he is now or what he looks like. But I'm working on it."

"Does she know he's been released?"

"That's what we'll find out at eleven o'clock. We're all meeting in her apartment."

COMMANDER RORY BURKE TRUDGED HIS two-hundred-fifty-pound block frame through the door of West Egg and made a beeline in my direction. He promptly ordered almost one side of the breakfast menu, then leaned back in his chair. His crisp white shirt stretched at the buttons.

"So what in the hell have your gotten yourself into now?" he grumbled.

"Morgan Shaw," I said.

Burke raised his eyebrows. "She's quite something to get into," he said.

"Not like that. She's hired me to protect her."

"Since when did you get into the protection business?"

"Broadening my offerings."

"And I thought you were heading to Arizona in two weeks to whack around the white ball at some fancy country club."

"I am."

"Is she going with you? 'Cause you sure in hell can't protect her from down there."

"Mechanic and Rox will watch her for me."

"That's right, the rest of the triumphant triad. How could I forget?"

"Don't be jealous because we have a hundred-percent close rate, and your men are hovering around forty."

"We can't just do anything we want to close a case," he said. "We have something called legal restraints and due process. Boundaries."

"Boundaries? Such as beating the shit outta somebody or exposing your secret witnesses when you're trying to flip someone to catch the bigger fish?"

"I'm the first to admit it ain't a perfect system. That's for damn sure. But it doesn't mean we can't keep working to change things. Besides, Robinson is gonna retire in two years. Cleaning out the rot at the top means there'll be less shit at the bottom."

"Morgan Shaw had a stalker named Haley Diggs who just finished a two-year bid down in Lincoln. About the time of his release, she got a letter in the mail warning her to stop what she was doing or face consequences."

"What was she doing?"

"No idea. But obviously something that someone yet to be identified is not overly thrilled about."

"Did she call it in?"

"Nope. She threw the letter away and didn't think much about it until she got a package in the mail. It contained a pair of leather bondage floggers."

Burke took a big gulp of black coffee. "What the hell is that?"

"Part of the adult play world."

"So she's a sex freak."

"'There are no facts, only interpretations.'"

"This another one of your goddamn poetry quotes?"

"Friedrich Nietzsche was a philosopher, not a poet."

Burke waved me off. "So somebody wants her to stop what she's doing, then sends her these flogger things. I don't know how the hell people get off like that."

"I've been told the pain increases the arousal."

"Weird shit."

"Gets a lot weirder than that. Straps and chains and metal prongs that scratch your skin and cause you to bleed."

"All in the name of kinky sex?"

"'That which does not kill us makes us stronger.'"

"I happen to know that one, smart ass. The German again."

I smiled.

"Speaking of Germans, you might ask her about Reinhard Schmidt," Burke said.

"The state senator?"

"Yes, that pompous ass."

Reinhard Schmidt was the influential state senator from the Tenth District who had just been elected majority leader. He owned a very lucrative chain of discount appliance stores throughout the city. He was married to the youngest daughter of Melvin Reardon, the powerful alderman in the city's Thirty-Third Ward.

"What's the connection between Shaw and Schmidt?"

A wide smile creased Burke's meaty face. "Probably those leather floggers she was sent in the mail."

Mechanic and Rox stood patiently outside Nine West Walton when I arrived, and a doorman stood nearby in the ornate lobby watching them with a heavy dose of skepticism. He stepped in front of me as I attempted to enter. He had me by at least two inches and fifty pounds.

"How can I help you?" he said. There was a hint of Boston in his accent but maybe some place closer like Bridgeport on the city's southwest side.

"Getting out of my way would be a great start," I said.

The doorman pulled his shoulders back, puffed up his chest, and glared at me.

"You get that move watching Nat Geo?" I said.

"What move?" he returned.

"Shoulders back, chest open. Making yourself look bigger. Animals in the wild do it all the time to intimidate a predator."

"I'm not an animal, asshole," he said.

I looked back at Mechanic and Rox. They shrugged their shoulders.

"Let me try this differently," I said. "If you don't get out of my way, I'm gonna step to the side and watch that little lady pulverize your fat, ugly ass."

He looked over my shoulder at Rox who offered the most pleasant of smiles. I could tell by the twitch in his right eye that he was seriously assessing the situation.

I leaned into him. "Tough guy, if you have a family at home, you might wanna call and tell them not to wait up for you tonight. When she's finished, and it will only take a matter of seconds, you'll be spending the night over at Northwestern getting most of the bones in your face reconstructed."

"They're here to see me," a voice called out from the depths of the lobby.

Morgan Shaw walked toward us in a pair of skin-tight jeans and an equally snug cashmere sweater. Her feet were squeezed into a pair of heels that made my toes hurt just looking at them. Of course, her makeup and hair were camera ready.

"I'm sorry, Ms. Shaw," the doorman said, stepping to the side obsequiously.

"No worries, Harry," she said, gesturing for us to enter.

I stepped close to Harry and said to him as I passed, "Today was your lucky day. She would've rearranged both of your jaws first, then smashed your nose to the other side of your right ear. Would've been really bloody and not very pretty."

Mechanic and Rox followed behind me. Morgan led us through the bright lobby and into the fanciest elevator I had ever seen with museum-quality artwork hanging on two of the walls inside the car. She didn't have to push any buttons. The doorman sitting at the desk had already taken care of that.

The light was almost blinding the second the doors opened into her apartment. The view of Lake Michigan appeared immediately and expansively. An entire wall of windows opened east, drawing the eye above the jagged skyline and out to the water where a few boats bobbed in the chop. Navy Pier, the Hancock, Lake Point Tower—they were postcard perfect.

Morgan led us down a long hall into a room that shared the same set of windows. Everything was clean and spacious and expensive looking. We fell into a cluster of deep-seated chairs. A pitcher of water and tall glasses of ice with lemon wedges had been set out for us. Introductions were made.

"So this is home," I said, scanning more of Chicago's famous landmarks.

"It'll do for now," she said.

"Meaning . . ."

"Meaning nothing is permanent. One day I won't be at WLTV, and I'll be somewhere on a beach waking up in the middle of January with temperatures in the midsixties."

"The desire is mutual," I said. "I'll be there in two weeks. It's in the eighties in Scottsdale right now."

"You think you'll have this solved in two weeks?"

"Maybe. If not, these two will look after you while I'm gone."

Morgan's disappointment quickly registered on her face.

"They're more than capable of taking care of you," I said.

She looked at Mechanic. "No offense, but what kind of name is 'Mechanic'?" she said.

"One that fits the bill."

"Meaning?"

"I take care of things."

"Like broken-down cars?"

"Like people's problems."

"What kinds of problems?"

"You name it."

"You carry a gun?"

"Two."

Morgan's eyes widened. "Why do you need two?"

"Sometimes I like to shoot both bad guys at the same time. Efficiency."

Morgan looked at Rox. "No offense, but how are you going to help me if some two-hundred-pound man comes running after me?"

Rox smiled. "That doesn't worry me at all."

"Well, it should," Morgan said. "It worries the hell outta me."

"It shouldn't. Before he even got near you, splinters from his right jaw would be lying on the sidewalk, and he wouldn't be able to see out of his left eye for about three weeks."

"You speak very violently for someone so small."

"I'm a very violent person," Rox said. "When I need to be."

"Rox has a thirty-five-to-one record in the ring," I said. "She fought professionally for ten years. Hands faster than lightning."

Morgan examined Rox a little more. "So what do you do now?"

"Run a floral shop in Roscoe Village."

"You were a boxer, and now you sell flowers?"

"All those roses men send you have to come from somewhere."

Morgan smiled.

We discussed Morgan's schedule and the shift work and what some of the exceptions might be should she need to leave her apartment unexpectedly when no one was on duty. Then I asked her about Diggs since it didn't seem like she was going to bring it up.

"He's a sick man," she said. "He was about to assault me outside Del Frisco's a few years ago. The valet grabbed him before he could get to me."

"Why didn't you tell me about him at dinner the other night?"

"I try to block him out of my mind as much as possible."

"But if someone is sending you threatening notes and slashing your tires, wouldn't he be the first person to come to mind?"

"Of course, but I try to stop my mind from going there. It's hard to explain. It's almost like if I can block him out, then he won't exist. I don't want it to be him. I want it to be someone else. If it's him, then that really scares me because after all he's been through, he hasn't changed his intentions or determination, which makes him even crazier and more dangerous."

"Do you know where he is right now?"

"Department of Corrections won't tell me specifically where he lives. They would only give me a general vicinity."

"Which is?"

"Chicago."

"Neighborhood?"

"They won't say."

"Did they give you a photo of what he looked like when he was released?"

"I asked. They told me they couldn't do that."

"I'll find him," I said.

"How will you do that?"

"Means and methods." I shot a glance at Mechanic, who didn't smile, but I could see his acknowledgment with the flicker in his eyes. We had met one summer working construction for the city. We came from opposite sides of town but quickly bonded under the hot Chicago sun over a love of cars and the gym. Our chain-smoking foreman was always barking the construction term "means and methods" to describe techniques and tactics used to complete construction of a permanent project or structure.

"Has anyone seen him near the station or here at your building?" Rox asked.

"No," Morgan said. "Everyone's on high alert."

"Which explains Acne Man's attitude at the door," Rox said.

"His name is Harry, and he's genuinely nice. He works really hard to look after me. He didn't mean anything by it."

"What about Reinhard Schmidt?" I said.

She turned and looked directly at me. "I'd rather discuss that in private."

"This is private," I said.

"I mean private as in you and me."

"There's nothing you say to me that you can't say in front of them. They're gonna be with you almost around the clock."

"Let's take a walk," she said, standing.

I stood also, shrugged my shoulders at Mechanic and Rox, then followed her down a hall and into a breakfast room that had a wall of windows facing north. I could see Wrigley Field in the distance.

"Reinhard and I quietly had a thing," she said matter-of-factly. "We ended it about six months ago."

"Amicably."

"As amicable as those things go."

"Who ended it?"

"I did. He was becoming too attached. Too demanding. When we first met, he told me he was calling off his engagement. It wasn't working. We started seeing each other secretly because I didn't want to have any drama. I was giving him time to dissolve his other relationship peacefully."

"Did he?"

"Not at all. She was already pregnant. He wasn't going to leave. I told him I was done. He wasn't happy. They got married a couple of months after. He still calls me."

"And what does he say?"

"Nothing. I won't answer his calls."

"Maybe you should answer and tell him to leave you alone."

"I've already done that. You don't know Reinhard. He's used to getting what he wants."

"'One man scorned and covered with scars still strove with his last ounce of courage to reach the unreachable stars.'"

"Who said that?"

"The great Cervantes."

"How do you remember all these lines?"

"I practice."

"You must practice a lot."

"Not as much as I practice my golf swing."

Morgan scrunched up her forehead, and even then still looked like a million bucks.

"I don't know how people have patience for all that. Seems like it would get pretty boring after a few minutes. I mean, how many times can you get excited swinging at a tiny white ball, then walking up to it and swinging again?"

"As many times as you can get excited walking into one of those shops on Oak Street and leaving with two thousand dollars' worth of shoes in a leather-strapped bag."

She delivered that perfect smile.

"You think Schmidt could be the one threatening you?" I asked.

"Possible. Those floggers that were sent to me were exactly like the ones he liked me to use."

"Was he the only one you used them on?"

Morgan folded her arms across her chest. "This is getting rather personal."

"It's probably going to get a lot more personal than this. If it makes you uncomfortable now, then you might need to hire someone else. But if someone is really trying to hurt you and it's as serious as you say it is, then I need to know everything. The more I know the better I can do my job."

"Are you going to share it with the two of them?" she said.

"Only the parts they need to know," I said.

"I like floggers," she said. "It adds spice. Most guys get really aroused by it. Helps them perform better. Reinhard wanted to use them all the time. But there have been others."

"Others?"

"Previous relationships."

"Any of them end badly or make you feel threatened?"

"Not at all."

"Jealous girlfriends or wives?"

"I don't make it a habit of getting involved with otherwise involved men," she said. "But men tend to lie about things like that and then you find out after the fact."

"Any other names come to mind?"

"None that would worry me like Reinhard."

"I'll take care of Reinhard," I said.

"What are you going to do? He's a very powerful man. And he has a really bad temper when he gets upset."

"How bad?"

"I've seen him make other men shake."

"Then my plan will work."

"Which is?"

"Punch him in the face and get him to tell me the truth."

"Seriously?"

I nodded.

"You're just gonna punch the majority leader in the face? He's six-five and extremely intimidating when he gets angry. You have to be either foolish or courageous to try something like punching him."

"'He who loses wealth loses much; he who loses a friend loses more; but he that loses his courage loses all.'"

"Cervantes again?"

"You're a quick study."

7

"S he's a piece of work. That's for sure."

Penny Packer and I sat at one end of a table long enough to seat twenty-four. Her cook, Balzac, fussed over the stove about ten yards away in a kitchen bigger than most hotels. She and her family's cosmetics empire had just taken over the second slot on Illinois's billionaires list. The guy who had been above her tumbled a couple of spots after getting burned on his short position on Tesla. We had been friends for several years after meeting on a golf course when one of the players in her group canceled at the last minute and they needed a fourth. I was playing alone that day and someone in the clubhouse suggested me to her. In the request that was made for me to join them, it was made very clear that Penny wasn't looking to socialize. She took golf extremely seriously and wanted someone who not only knew how to play the game but was equally determined to win. After grinding out a one-stroke victory on the last hole that morning and the requisite loser-pays lunch, our friendship had been quickly sealed. I had just told her about Morgan Shaw.

"How well do you know her?" I asked.

"Well enough. I know that she loves being Morgan Shaw."

"Can't blame her. What's not to like?"

Penny shrugged her shoulders. "Sometimes there's such a thing as too much attention," she said. "Can lead to bad things."

"You're talking about her stalker?"

"And Reinhard."

"You knew about them?"

"If it was meant to be a secret, it was badly kept."

"She thinks he might be the one harassing her."

"Reinhard likes his power," Penny said. "And he doesn't like when his power doesn't get him what he wants."

"You'd think a guy who has as much as he has would figure he has enough."

"Never. Men always want more. They don't think about what they already have. They think in terms of what they don't have."

Balzac brought over a plate of charred cauliflower salad with feta cheese, green olives, and winter citrus. He followed that with a plate of lemon bucatini pasta with salted black pepper berries and cacio.

Penny's insight into Schmidt came honestly. She also liked to have what she wanted. Balzac had been the head chef at the fashionable restaurant Avec. Penny loved the food so much she offered him three times what he was earning, better hours, a kitchen double the size, and expenses to have him cook for her privately.

"Morgan is an interesting person," Penny said between bites of salad. "She comes from a small town in Wisconsin. Her father was a pharmacist and her mother a seamstress. But you look at her and listen to her and you'd think she was brought up behind the gates of some estate up on the North Shore."

"I don't have a real handle on her yet," I said.

"And you might never get one. There are a lot of cracks underneath the veneer. Cracks she works really hard to keep hidden."

"Such as?"

"Her first marriage."

"Marriage?"

Penny smiled. "I'm not surprised. Very few know she was married many years ago to a football player out East. She never talks about it."

"How long ago?"

"At least ten years. Maybe more. Didn't last long. Six months or so."

"What happened?"

"I don't know this for sure, but I heard that he hit her a couple of times. She got out before it got worse. She's a tough girl and pretty as hell. Bounced back, and look at her now."

"You'd think someone hiring you to protect them would tell you the relevant information that might help you help them. She hired me three days ago, and this is already the third big piece of information she's conveniently forgotten to tell me."

"And it probably won't be the last. As much of a public figure as she is, Morgan guards her privacy fiercely. She's great at finding out things about others but keeps her personal cards very close to her chest."

"What else have you heard?"

"Besides the fact she returns some of her ball gowns to stores after wearing them, armpit stains and all?"

I smiled. Penny tended not to take these kinds of shots, but I could tell she relished revealing that little detail.

"She's obsessed with Reinhard Schmidt," Penny said.

"What do you mean?" I said. "I have it the other way around."

"I'm sure you do. You better do some fact checking on that. I've known Mel, Reinhard's father-in-law, and his family for many years. We see each other from time to time. Morgan Shaw is not a very popular topic of conversation."

"There are three sides to every story," I said.

"Well, you've got two of them now. Maybe it's time to find out the truth."

Penny's sources and information tended to be incredibly reliable and rarely wrong. Given Morgan's status, I already had a hankering this case was going to be tricky, but now I was convinced it would be a real challenge. It's difficult solving someone's problems when they're holding back information that could help you do the job. I understood her obsession with privacy and discretion, but this was downright obstruction.

"Why would she lie about Schmidt?" I wondered aloud.

Balzac returned and filled our wine glasses with a Conterno Monfortino Barolo Riserva that costs more than most people's monthly mortgage payment.

"We all have pride," Penny said. "And no matter how we like to pretend certain things don't matter, when it comes to relationships and sex and emotions, it always matters. Sometimes we feel better when we ignore rejection."

"'Reject your sense of injury and the injury itself disappears.'"

"Chaucer?"

"Marcus Aurelius."

Penny smiled. "Talking to you always feels like another hour sitting in my college English lit class. Except you make it a lot more fun."

"HOW WAS DINNER WITH PENNY?" Carolina asked.

I was driving home from Lincoln Park. I could tell by her voice that she was deliciously wrapped under her covers.

"The food was amazing as always," I said. "I can't imagine being able to eat every meal of my life like that."

"That's the power of five billion dollars."

"Morgan had a stalker who was sent downstate for a couple of years. He just got out a couple months ago," I said.

"That's scary with a capital *S*."

"IDOC would only tell her that he was living in Chicago. They wouldn't give up his address."

"What's it worth to you?"

"A homecooked meal with a bottle of Tignanello."

"And those tight blue gym shorts I like?"

"That can be arranged."

"You have a deal."

8

The office of State Senator Reinhard Schmidt covered the entire first floor of a small faded-yellow brick building on Devon Avenue, one of the busiest streets along the northern border of the Pulaski Park neighborhood. I found a parking spot in the back of a small lot. A long black Mercedes with the license plate RMS1 sat in the reserved space closest to the door. Its shiny chrome grill stood inches away from a posted sign ostentatiously painted with the words *MAJORITY LEADER*. I stepped into the lobby of the building, then through another set of glass doors with Schmidt's name and title stenciled in large letters just in case one needed to be reminded who occupied this suite of offices.

A young woman with short blond hair and bright emerald eyes sat behind an elevated metal desk typing furiously on her computer keypad. She stopped as I approached.

"Welcome to the office of the majority leader," she said. "How can I help you?"

"I'd like a few minutes of his time," I said.

"Do you have an appointment?"

"I didn't know I needed one."

"Unfortunately, you do." She smiled. She opened the binder sitting next to her monitor. "The majority leader is quite busy, but let's see if we can find a time when he's back in the office next week."

"You sure you can't squeeze me in today for just a few minutes?" I tried matching her smile.

"I really wish I could." She frowned. "But I'm sure we can find a date next week that works."

I took out one of my business cards, turned it over, and wrote the name *MORGAN SHAW* in capital letters. I handed it to her. "Maybe you can give him this and see if he'll squeeze me into his busy schedule."

She looked at the card and Morgan's name. I could see the recognition quickly settle on her face.

"One moment," she said. She stood and disappeared behind an enormous metal divider and down a busy hall. I watched as several people carrying papers and files as they opened and closed office doors crossed the hall. This was my first time ever visiting a state senator's office. I was expecting something more drab with cheap furniture and fake potted plants. What I had seen so far was anything but that.

Emerald Eyes reappeared. "Follow me," she said with that perfect smile.

I wondered how many times a day she smiled like that. Had to be exhausting.

We walked down the hallway, through another set of doors, and then down another short hallway until we arrived at second reception area. This part of the office had been carpeted and the walls built of solid mahogany. Two women sat at similar desks across from each other, flanking an open door. I could see Schmidt in the depths of the office leaning back in a swivel chair talking on his cell phone. The two women nodded at Emerald Eyes, who walked me through the door, then turned and left, closing the door behind her.

Schmidt finished his call and stood. He was tall with tapered chestnut-colored hair that set off his angular face. He had the body of a guy who swam in college or rowed crew. His clothes looked expensively tailored, embellished by the gold cuff links that matched the heavy Rolex shining on his wrist. He gave me a firm handshake and offered me a seat at a large round table on the other side of the office. A pitcher of water and several highball glasses sat neatly on a silver tray.

"How can I help you, Mr. Cayne?" he said.

"I don't want to take up too much of your time," I said. "But I just wanted to ask you a few questions about Morgan Shaw."

"Is she in trouble?"

"That's exactly what I wanted to ask you."

"I wouldn't know. We haven't spoken in months."

"Morgan has hired me to find out who's threatening her," I said.

"Why is someone threatening her?"

"Another question I wanted to ask you."

"Mr. Cayne, I'm not sure what Morgan did or didn't tell you, but our relationship ended almost a year ago. We had what we had, it ended, I'm married, and Morgan is doing whatever it is she's doing."

I decided to jump right into it since I knew my time would be limited. "You had fun when you dated her," I said.

"Is that a question, or are you making a statement?"

"Both, I guess. I guess the fun I was referring to was the leather floggers."

Schmidt absorbed the question with another smile. "Why exactly are you here, Mr. Cayne?"

"I want to know if you are harassing Morgan Shaw."

Schmidt leaned back and clasped his hands behind his head and laughed softly. "I am *the* majority leader of the Illinois Senate," he said.

"How could I miss that? It's plastered on almost every door."

"Why in hell would I harass someone given my position and risk my career? And better yet, harass the leading anchorwoman in the country's third largest city. Would be pretty stupid of me."

"*Amor vincit omnia*."

Schmidt stared back with a blank expression.

"Latin," I said. "Love conquers all."

"So you're a polyglot and a private investigator all wrapped in one," he said. "Well, let me say this in plain English. I was never in love with Morgan Shaw, nor do I desire harming her. She was a different chapter of my life—a good chapter but one that ended. Morgan was never happy that I moved on. She's not someone accustomed to rejection. She wasn't happy that she didn't have control and even more upset when I started dating Laura. I'm very content with my life. I have no need to stalk or bother or even contact Morgan."

I believed most of what he said, but I also knew that love and sex and breakups could be really complicated. Even if his interpretations didn't coalesce with the facts, a person's perception was still their reality.

9

Mechanic and I walked into my office and settled into our normal positions. I sat behind the desk while he took a seat across from me in his favorite low-sitting chair with a matching footrest. I plucked out a couple cans of cold root beer from the fridge. I kept the lights off and let the sun work its way through the large window that overlooked Grant Park. The cooler temperatures had scared away most of the boats, which were now parked and wrapped in various warehouses and boatyards in preparation for another harsh Chicago winter. I thought about Arizona and how nice it would be to wake up in the middle of October with my lined bomber jacket still back in Chicago and play a round of golf in a short-sleeved shirt.

We sat there quietly for several minutes like we often did, absorbed in our individual thoughts.

"She's gonna be a problem," I said. "She's not being upfront about everything."

I explained to Mechanic my conversation with Schmidt and how different a version he had offered regarding his breakup with Morgan.

"Who do you believe?" Mechanic said.

"The majority leader," I said. "Mostly."

"So why would she lie about something like that?"

"Beats the hell outta me. People lie about stuff they don't really need to. Or they lie about stuff because they're hiding something."

"What do you think?"

"I think she's hiding something."

"What makes you say that?"

"She didn't tell me about her stalker. She's not being straight about Schmidt and how all that went down. I feel like there's something more at play."

"Something good? Bad?"

"I have no idea." I continued to look out at the calm waters of Lake Michigan. "I have no idea at all."

"What are you going to do?"

"Keep asking questions. Keep looking around the corners."

"Are you gonna confront her?"

"Not yet. I need to piece more of this together."

There was a loud knock on the front door, then the sound of something dragging on the tile floor. I got up and retrieved an envelope that had been slid underneath the door. I knew right away it was from Burke. It was a large manila envelope without any writing or markings. I took the envelope back to the office and opened it. I pulled out a large black-and-white photograph and two pages that had been stapled together. Haley Diggs. He had close-cropped hair, a tattoo of an anchor on the left side of his neck, and a large mole just under the right side of his mouth. These prison-release photos were never glamorous, but he looked even more menacing than most. I handed the photo to Mechanic, who examined it with little interest.

I read the biographical report aloud. "He's originally from Muncie, Indiana. Mother and father killed in a car accident when he was in high school. Lots of priors—burglary, drugs, several assault and batteries. He has a younger brother living in San Diego. They're not close. The brother is an electrical engineer. Diggs lives alone in a one-bedroom apartment on West Agatite Avenue in Uptown, just north of Wrigleyville. He works at Abel's Car Wash in River North."

"Sounds like a winner," Mechanic said.

"Sounds like trouble to me. I think we need to pay him a visit."

"We?"

"Negotiations tend to be more effective when you're around."

Mechanic released a rare smile. My phone buzzed. It was Penny Packer.

"Hope I didn't catch you at a bad time," she said.

"Not at all," I said. "Just sitting here thinking about how great my life will be on that golf course in Scottsdale in less than two weeks."

"Well, that's exactly why I called. I've had a change of plans. I'm going to Albany in the Bahamas with my boys. They'll spend a couple weeks down there with me, then I fly over to the South of France. So I probably won't make it to Arizona, but don't worry—you'll have plenty of fun. The staff has everything set up for you. The club knows you may be down there through the first of the year. If you decide to stay longer, let me know, and I'll have the arrangements made."

"I can't tell you how much I'm looking forward to this and how grateful I am for you doing this."

"Well, I'm sorry I won't make it down there, but we'll get together soon. How's the bodyguard business going?"

"I'm not really sure," I said. "Sometimes I feel like we're on different teams. She comes to me for help, but then she doesn't help me help her."

"Welcome to the world of Morgan Shaw. Everything you see isn't always as it appears."

10

Abel's Car Wash was a small affair on Superior Street sandwiched between two luxury high-rise apartment buildings in the trendy River North neighborhood. We drove up to find a long line of expensive cars, hazard lights blinking, extending west almost to the courthouse on the next block. Two large empty wicker chairs sat outside the car wash. Two men in slim-fit jeans stood adjacent to the front door, smoking cigarettes and laughing. I pulled up next to a fire hydrant and turned off the car.

We were met with the loud sounds of vacuum cleaners, water hoses, and lively reggaeton music piping in overhead. Customers seated in large leather chairs packed the elevated waiting room to the right of the entrance. Fashionable men and women sat with their phones texting and watching videos as tiny dogs peeped from pricey Italian tote bags. A short olive-skinned man stood at a small counter rifling through papers and giving orders. We approached.

"We're looking for Haley Diggs," I said.

"Who are you?" the man replied with a slight Spanish accent.

"I'm a private investigator," I said, taking out my card and handing it to him. "Are you the manager?"

He looked it over cautiously and said, "I'm Abel, the owner. Is something wrong?"

"That's what I want to find out," I said.

"Is Haley in trouble?"

"Depends if he's been a good boy or bad boy."

Abel turned to Mechanic. "Who are you?"

"The invisible man."

"What does that mean?"

"I'm only seen when I need to be."

"Listen, I don't want any trouble," Abel said, placing my card on the small countertop. "I run an honest business. I have good customers. I don't want any problems."

"Where's Haley?" I asked.

"He's out on break right now," Abel said.

"When will he be back?"

Abel looked down at his watch. "In about fifteen minutes."

"You know where he went?"

"Probably to get something to eat."

"We'll wait for him."

"I don't want any trouble," Abel said.

I looked at Mechanic, then back at Abel. "I'll try to keep him under control," I said, nodding toward Mechanic.

We walked out the door, sat in the car, and waited. Two women in tights and sweatshirts walked by.

"Perfect view to pass the time," Mechanic said as he leaned back and tightened his eyes.

After ten minutes of silence and lots of well-coiffed dogs strutting on shiny leashes, I spotted him in my rearview mirror. He wore a pair of black Carhartt pants and a gray hoodie. He was eating from a bag of chips. He looked a lot more normal than his release photo.

"Approaching from the east," I said. "Fifteen yards on your right."

We opened our doors at the same time. Diggs stopped immediately, five feet away from us.

"Haley Diggs," I said.

"Who the fuck are you?" he said, lowering the bag of chips.

"One of your biggest fans."

"What the fuck?"

"Pretty extensive vocabulary."

"You're a wiseass," he said. "Add that to my vocabulary."

"You know what rectal prolapse is?"

Diggs scrunched his face, then looked at Mechanic quizzically. Mechanic looked straight ahead without flinching.

"A rectal prolapse is when the rectum drops outside of your anus," I said.

"Jesus Christ, man. That's sick."

"No, that's gonna be you if you keep talking shit to me."

"I ain't got no beef with you," Diggs said. "I'm minding my own business. You're the one approaching me."

Diggs started to walk by us. Mechanic stepped in his way. They stood apart for a moment, staring at each other. Mechanic had him by a quarter of an inch. Diggs had him by twenty pounds.

"Not a good idea," I said. "I know you have all that prison muscle under your sweatshirt, but that won't be enough."

Diggs looked at me, then back at Mechanic, and took a step back. "What the hell you guys want?" he said.

"To find out why you're trying to re-create scenes from *The Godfather*," I said.

"What the hell are you talking about?"

"You know *The Godfather* movies?"

"Of course I do."

"Luca Brasi sleeps with the fishes," I said.

"*The Godfather, Part I*," Diggs said. "So what?"

"The mobster Sollozzo killed Brasi, then sent the Corleone family Brasi's bulletproof vest stuffed with a dead fish. A Sicilian message that he was dead."

"Thanks for the recap," Diggs said. "What the fuck that got to do with me?"

"The message you sent Morgan Shaw."

"I ain't sent no message to Morgan."

"The dead fish on her car windshield and the slashed tires."

"Man, you're talking crazy. I ain't been anywhere near her or her car."

"You sure?"

"I know where I've been, and it's not near her. I don't have any reason to be anywhere near Walton Street. Way too fancy for me. I lost enough of my life. I don't want to lose any more."

"She's trouble? You're the one who was stalking her."

"I wasn't stalking her. I was trying to meet her. It was a misunderstanding. She took my intentions the wrong way."

I laughed. "Well I guess the judge took it the wrong way too."

"He did. But I served my time and didn't complain about it. I'm out, and I don't want any problems."

"Morgan Shaw is off limits," I said. "We catch you within a mile of her, and you'll have to grind up those chips and eat them through a plastic tube sewn into your stomach for the rest of your life."

Mechanic stepped to the side and let Diggs walk by. We watched him enter the car wash before returning to my car.

"What do you think?" Mechanic said after I had started the car.

"He's lying."

"What makes you say that?"

"Because he knew she lived on Walton, and I never mentioned that. She just moved there a month ago. Her address isn't public information. He found out some way, and it wasn't from her."

11

A couple of days had passed without incident. Mechanic and Rox rotated their protection. Morgan didn't have any complaints. I continued my plans to leave for Arizona. The temperature had taken a dramatic dip, which brought out skull caps and puffy jackets. I happily counted down the days. I was on my way to Hammer's gym when Rox called.

"We have a problem," Rox said.

"Are you with her?" I said.

"I'm at the station. She's in her office. Another letter arrived today."

"What did it say?"

"'Watch your back, bitch!'"

"Where was it delivered?"

"To the station."

"Was it in the mail?"

"Yup. With a postmark."

"Who knows about it?"

"Everyone. They want you to come to a security meeting in an hour."

"I'm going for a quick workout at Hammer's, then I'll be right over."

———◇———

WE SAT IN A LARGE conference room with an oval table. Several monitors hung on the walls broadcasting programming from other stations. Morgan sat in the middle of the table in a red silk top that perfectly matched her lips. A tall blond with angular features and small horn-rimmed glasses sat to her right. A handsome, well-appointed middle-aged man sat on Morgan's left. A stocky dark-skinned man in an ill-fitting suit sat at one end of the table with his walkie-talkie resting next to his hands. I sat at the other end. The blond took charge.

"I'm Rebecca Karlson," she said. "This is Blake Stein, our executive producer for the ten o'clock." She pointed to the man seated to Morgan's left. "Isaac Johnson is our head of security."

Johnson nodded sternly.

"Morgan has told us that she's hired your firm to help with protective services," Karlson said.

"'Firm' is a bit grandiose." I smiled. "We're a small shop, but what we lack in numbers we make up for in effort."

"Any suggestions on next steps?"

"Can I see the letter?"

Karlson opened the binder in front of her and took out a large Ziploc bag that contained the letter and envelope. She slid it down the table. I examined the contents, then took pictures with my phone. *WATCH YOUR BACK BITCH* was in different letters of various sizes and looked like it had been cut from magazine articles. The address on the envelope had been typed from a computer and printed. There was no return address, but there was a postmark. I zoomed in and took a picture of it. Carol Stream, IL 60188.

"Have you called the police?" I said.

"Already done," Johnson said. "They're coming by this afternoon. For obvious reasons, Morgan is our top priority. We called in the first letter, then the car damage, and now this. A Detective Torres from the Eighteenth District is lead on the case."

I made a mental note to reach out to him.

"We're all concerned for Morgan's safety," Karlson said. "We know that Diggs has gotten out of jail and is back in the area. I'm not saying he's behind all this, but he's obviously top of the list. Do you have any ideas?"

"It's really difficult to know," I said. "I had a conversation with Diggs a couple days ago. It would be pretty stupid of him to start doing all this less than a month after getting out, but he's definitely a person of interest."

"We're tightening things up here," Johnson said. "The building is putting several cameras up in the garage, and we've doubled our security efforts at front reception and the loading dock. Our efforts here combined with what your team is doing should provide full protection."

"Are you still going to Arizona?" Morgan asked me.

"Six days and three hours," I said.

"Do you think this is the best time to go?"

"Temperatures are in the low eighties. No rain in the forecast for the next ten days."

"I mean, is it the best time considering this recent letter?"

"You're in good hands here," I said, nodding to Johnson. "Mechanic and Rox will call me with daily updates."

"How long will you be gone?" Karlson asked.

"About six weeks."

Stein and Karlson immediately looked at each other. "We'll be in the middle of sweeps," Stein said.

"What's sweeps?" I asked.

"Our ratings period," Stein said.

"Relevance?"

"There are only four periods throughout the year when Nielsen, the media monitoring company, collects detailed demographic information about who's watching TV and what they're watching. This information is compiled into ratings, and these ratings are what matter most to advertisers. The higher your ratings, the more money a station can charge for advertisements. November is the most critical of these four ratings periods."

"And our ten o'clock news is the most important of our newscasts," Karlson said. "It's the flagship. We've been number one for the last five years, and we intend to stay there."

"Who's number two?" I asked.

"Alicia Roscati at WMTQ."

I didn't watch local news much, but I knew Roscati. She was very blond, very beautiful, and very smooth.

"When do these ratings get reported?" I asked.

"Every morning," Karlson said. "The company tabulates everything overnight so the ratings can be distributed the next morning. There's a lot riding on this November. We're only half a point ahead of WMTQ. Everyone will be monitoring the overnights very carefully."

"Someone's gotta come in second," I said.

"True," Morgan said. "But number one comes more natural to me."

We spent the next fifteen minutes reviewing Morgan's security detail. Then Karlson had to leave for a meeting, and Stein needed to start working on the ten o'clock show. Johnson went to check on the progress of the security cameras. Once everyone had left, Morgan closed the door and sat back down but this time next to me.

"I need you to go with me on a story," she said quietly.

"Why are you whispering?" I said. "It's only the two of us here."

"Habit. I need to do this tomorrow. Can you come?"

"What time?"

"After I get off the show."

"Isn't eleven o'clock late to be going out doing interviews?"

"Not this kind of story."

I lifted my eyebrows.

"It's gonna be a blockbuster. Three-parter, maybe five if I can get enough sources. If I pull this off, we will win November."

"Sounds big."

"As big as they come."

"Am I allowed to know who you're interviewing?"

She shook her head.

"Am I allowed to know what the story is about?"

"Only if you swear not to say a word to anyone."

I nodded.

She leaned in to me and locked eyes. "Kevin Fitzpatrick, superintendent of police."

12

The next morning, I pulled out of the garage and made my way toward Michigan Ave. I wanted to stop by a couple of stores and pick up some clothes for my trip to Arizona. I was two blocks away from the station when I noticed the tail three cars back. It was a silver four-door sedan. There was no license plate in the front, so it was likely an out-of-state vehicle. I couldn't tell if the driver was a man or woman, but they mirrored every move I made. I drove in the left lane, lowered my speed until I reached the library, then I quickly accelerated and dipped all the way to the right lane across two lanes of traffic and turned onto Madison. I stopped at a red light. Seconds later, the silver sedan made a turn onto Madison. It was now only two cars behind. However, I still couldn't see the driver. The light turned green. I slowly traveled west.

I dialed Mechanic's number.

"Where are you?" I said when he answered.

"Just leaving the gym. Heading to my apartment to change. What's going on?"

"I wanted you to come do a flank maneuver if you were nearby. Somebody's sniffing."

"I can be there in about fifteen," Mechanic said.

"Too late. I'll figure something out."

I had a plan. I drove at a steady pace so I wouldn't lose the car, then I pulled into the right lane. The silver sedan did the same without using its blinkers. I continued driving toward the intersection at Dearborn Avenue. The light was green, but I wanted it to be red. I slowed down and made sure just to approach the light as it turned red. I stopped quickly, jumped out of the car, and started running toward the silver sedan. I was a car length away when it accelerated, darted left, then sped by me. I could see it was a woman, but that was it. She moved too fast. She raced forward, then turned in front of my car and took a right on Dearborn. I caught the license plate. The tags were from Missouri. I ran back and jumped into my car, but a long line of people crossing the street blocked me from making the turn. By the time I found a gap big enough to squeeze through, the silver sedan was gone.

I texted the license plate number to Carolina, then I dialed Burke's number. I wanted to ask him about Torres from the Eighteenth District. He didn't pick up, so I left a voice message. Then I had an idea. I dialed my father's landline. He was one of the last people in Chicago to have one.

"I haven't heard from you in a week," he said. "It's good to know you're still alive."

"Why can't you just surprise me one time and say something nice to me when I call," I said. "Just once."

"Every time you call me it's a surprise," he said. "So I guess I could return the favor."

"How's your knee?" I asked.

"Better. I haven't played tennis for two weeks. The rest is letting the inflammation settle."

"I wanted to ask you about Mr. Lewis from the post office," I said. "Do you still keep in touch with him?"

"I hear from him every once in a while. They had to finally commit his daughter to a long-term inpatient facility. Her schizophrenia just wasn't getting any better."

"You still have his number?"

"Sure. I have it somewhere in my office. Why do you need to talk to him?"

"I want to ask him some questions about postal tracking of a letter. Figured he might be able to help."

"Well, he worked there for almost forty years. If anyone knows the ins and outs of that place, he would. I'll text you his number."

"I'd appreciate it."

"When are you coming over for dinner?"

"Before I leave for Arizona."

"Are you done with that anchorwoman?"

"Not at all. Which is why I need to speak with Mr. Lewis. I need help with a letter she received."

"Give me fifteen minutes. I just got out of the shower. I'll text you his number once I'm dressed."

I walked into the shops at Nine Hundred North Michigan looking for whatever they had left of summer apparel.

MY PHONE RANG THE MINUTE I pulled into my garage. It was Burke.

"How's your celebrity client?" he said.

"Still alive."

"That's setting the world on fire. Meet me in the parking lot over at Thirty-First Street Beach. I'll be there in thirty minutes."

He was gone before I could answer.

I ran up to my apartment, gave Stryker a treat and a new bowl of water, then ran back to the car and headed over to meet Burke. He was parked at the back of the near-empty lot in an unmarked car. His driver wasn't with him. I turned off my car and joined him.

"What's this business with Torres?" he said, looking straight ahead. Our vantage point allowed us to observe any cars entering or exiting the lot.

"He's lead on the Morgan case out of the Eighteenth."

"That's bad luck he drew the case."

"Why?"

"Because he's dead weight. Six months before retirement."

"Then why would he take the case? Doesn't make sense. He retires and this thing goes to trial for some reason, he has to come back and testify and not get a dime for his time."

"The call came through as a major. They knew it was a high-profile case, but whoever called first didn't identify it was Morgan Shaw. They were trying to keep a lid on it. Torres works day shift. The desk assigned it to him."

"Didn't someone upstairs know the guy was about to fly in six months?"

"They knew it all right. The sergeant over there moved to reassign it, but he got overruled."

"By whom?"

"Lieutenant. Told him to keep everything the way it was."

"You don't find that strange?"

"Damn right I do, but I've stopped trying to figure out how they make decisions upstairs."

"Did Torres try to pass it off?"

"From what I hear, he didn't make much fuss about it."

None of it made sense. A senior detective six months from retirement typically wouldn't want to lead a major. Lots of eyes and ears would be on a case with the stakes so high. This would be a big aggravation with a lot of people looking over his shoulder. Only a young officer would want this kind of case. It was a perfect way to make waves and earn some stripes. But a guy like Torres would punt it as far away from his end zone as possible. It was also strange that someone upstairs wanted to keep him on a case like that given the circumstances.

"You think I could talk to him?" I asked.

"Probably. I need to put a call in over there, but it should be all right."

I decided to offer Burke something from my side because that's the way our relationship worked.

"Anything going on with Fitzpatrick lately?" I asked.

"Beyond the usual bullshit?"

"Beyond that."

"I haven't heard anything. Why?"

"I don't need to tell you to keep this between us."

Burke turned to me, his face fire red. "Jesus fuckin' Christ! Like you really need to say that to me."

I smiled. "Morgan is going on some big story tonight that she insists will be a blockbuster. She won't tell me who she's interviewing, but she did say Fitzpatrick is the focus of the story."

"Holy shit. I hope she knows what she's getting herself into. Fitz is one vindictive sonuvabitch."

"I didn't have the heart to tell her. She was so excited about the story and what it would do for her ratings."

Burke turned to me and said, "Ashe, I can't tell you what to do. But as your friend, I'm warning you to stay away from this shit. Fitz has wanted to get even with you for the last five years. He'll find any excuse to nail your ass."

"Not if Morgan nails him first."

13

Morgan Shaw stepped off her studio throne, slipped into a long coat, and made her way toward the back exit. I followed closely behind her as she chatted away on the phone. Just before she stepped into the garage, she turned to me and said, "This is for all the marbles tonight. If we get this right, everyone in the city will be watching."

"And the overnights will show you in first place," I said.

"You're a fast learner."

"I try not to disappoint."

"Only three other people know about this story. Duane, my photographer, Rebecca Karlson, and now you. I've decided to let you sit in on the interview."

I raised my eyebrows.

"I trust you," she said. "And I think you'll appreciate how explosive this is."

I followed her through the door. Duane waited for her in a dark SUV that didn't have any signage or indication it was a news vehicle. I jumped in my car and followed them out of the garage. We drove south a few blocks, then turned west onto Madison. I thought about the woman who had been following me, then looked in my rearview mirror. No other cars were on the road for at least several blocks.

We drove all the way out past the towering United Center and the Michael Jordan statue. A few quick turns and we found ourselves in a quiet block of small, neatly arranged townhouses. The garage door to one of the townhouses opened, and I followed the truck inside. The door quickly closed behind us. The three of us stood in the tiny garage.

"Duane Muhammad, this is Ashe Cayne," Morgan said.

Duane was a slight man, short with glasses and close-cropped curly black hair. He extended his hand, and we shook firmly. "Nice to meet you brutha," he said. "Big fan. Much respect for what you did with Marquan's shooting."

"Nothing more than what anyone else should've done," I said.

"Yeah, but you were the only one who had the balls to do it." He bowed his head and tapped his chest twice.

"We have to hurry," Morgan said. "He'll be here in twenty minutes."

Duane went to work pulling bags and cables out of the back of the truck, into the house, and up the stairs. I offered to help, but he declined. "I have to handle everything myself," he said. "Union rules."

The townhouse had been sparsely decorated, and the small living room had already been outfitted with a couple of chairs facing each other and two cameras behind each chair. Duane went to work setting up a camera positioned on the side of the chairs to get a wide view. A couple of potted plants and a few cheap prints hanging on the wall, and this was the magic of TV.

"When we start, you'll be fine over there," Morgan said, pointing to an area just behind Duane and closer to a window whose dark shade had been drawn.

I stepped behind Duane and quietly watched him setting up the lights as Morgan took a seat and read through her notes. I was impressed at how the two prepared—quietly, efficiently, and affably. He would adjust the lights, and she knew instinctively when to look into the camera and then look away when he fidgeted with other adjustments. There wasn't a single word spoken. It was like watching an old Viennese couple dance the waltz.

At precisely 11:45 p.m., the doorbell chimed. Morgan ran her fingers through her hair and tugged at her blouse. Duane went down the short flight of steps to open the door. I retreated even more into the shadows. Seconds later, the guest stood in the makeshift studio. I recognized him immediately—Father Flagger from St. Sebastian, a large Catholic church in the heart of the South Side. Flagger's activism was as famous as his perfectly coiffed sandy-blond hair that had been gelled and styled in the same way for the last thirty years. He was a polarizing man, despised by the wealthy elite of the North Side but practically deified by the African Americans in his congregation and the surrounding neighborhoods. Flagger had always made it clear that his whiteness went no further than his skin color. His heart and soul belonged to the people he ministered to and lived with on the gritty South Side streets.

Morgan stood and reached out her hand. Flagger took it, bent down, and kissed her on the cheek. He nodded in my direction as I stood in the shadows. Duane asked him to take the chair opposite Morgan, then affixed the microphone to his collar. And just like that, the interview began.

"Take me from the beginning," Morgan said. "Who came to you and why?"

Father Flagger cleared his throat, then began speaking in that recognizable crisp voice laced with a southern twang I had heard so many times in TV and radio interviews.

"A young man came to me two weeks after the shooting of Reece Williams," Flagger started. "The young man was very scared and would only meet me at the church in the confessional booth. He was scared because he had seen Reece Williams, in his words, 'get executed' by an undercover Chicago police officer. He wanted me to know the truth because he didn't know who he could safely tell without becoming a target himself."

"What is the name of this witness?" Morgan asked.

"I am not at liberty to reveal that," Father Flagger said. "We made an agreement. He would allow me to disclose the information he shared with me, but I have to keep his identity confidential."

"What exactly did this witness say was happening before the shooting occurred?" Morgan asked.

"A group of them were hanging out on their porches," Flagger said. "They had all been to a basketball game in the park and had come back home. They were just talking, listening to music, and having a good time laughing about the game. Out of nowhere, an unmarked pulls up on the curb. Reece is leaning up against the fence in front of one of the houses talking on his cell phone. The doors to the unmarked fly open, and three guys jump out. Two from the front. One from the back. All three have their guns drawn. Reece throws his hands up in the air and yells for them not to shoot. At that point, his friends nearby start running for cover. The witness was two houses over. He dropped to the ground so he wouldn't be seen. He looked up and saw the muzzle flash and heard two quick pops. The shorter guy who had come from the back had shot Reece at point-blank range. Reece fell to the ground."

"From where he was, could he clearly see Reece?"

"Yes."

"Did he see Reece with a gun or knife or any kind of weapon in his hands?"

"He says emphatically that Reece didn't have a weapon. He'd known Reece since they were little boys. Reece had never been in gangs or any kind of trouble. He was a basketball player growing up. Girls and sports. That's what he did."

"Did he see what happened after Reece was shot?"

"Briefly. All three officers approached his body, their guns still drawn. One of them flipped Reece with his foot. Once the shooting stopped, people started coming out of their houses and looking out their windows to see what happened."

"And the witness?"

"He crawled into his house and closed the door. About five minutes later, he heard lots of sirens, an ambulance, and police. He looked out his living room window. Two officers were standing over Reece while the other one was kneeling next to him. A crowd started forming around them. Other police officers arrived and pushed everyone back."

"The official report was that Reece had an object in his hand, and when they got out the car, he pointed it at them, so one of the officers fired."

"The witness is a hundred percent sure Reece had nothing in his hands, and he's equally certain the officers never verbalized any command. The only thing spoken was Reece screaming for them not to shoot him."

"Just to be clear on what you were told, the officers got out of the car with their guns drawn, and within seconds, the third officer fired his gun twice?"

"Yes."

"What did the witness do next?"

"He went to the back of the house and hid in one of the bedrooms. An hour later, there was a knock on the door. The driver of the unmarked and another plainclothes officer stood outside. They asked to talk to the guy who was on the porch when all this went down. They must've seen him sitting there. The sister goes back and tells her brother they want to talk to him. He comes forward, and when they question him, he assures them he didn't see anything. He just heard gunshots and he went inside to mind his own business."

"Was the shooter the guy who questioned him?"

"No, the shooter was Mankovich. The officer who questioned the witness had been in the front seat. The witness wasn't sure if it was the driver or the passenger, but he just went along and played stupid as if he didn't know anything."

"For the purpose of clarity, it's not that the witness didn't see anything, rather he was simply afraid to tell what he had seen."

"You're damn right he was afraid. Anyone would be after watching a police officer execute an unarmed man. The power that badge wields is almost limitless."

14

So what do you think?" Morgan asked me. I was driving her home from the interview. Duane drove the truck back to the station.

"I think you need to be careful," I said. "You gotta have your ducks in a perfect row before you go live with something like this."

"I'm close," she said. "That was an important interview. I'd have it all if I could get the witness to talk."

"Flagger was a convincing surrogate."

"True, but he's not the eyewitness."

"Have you talked to the cops?"

"I made an official request to speak to the superintendent. The request was denied. Instead, they sent me a pro forma statement that didn't really say anything."

We rode a few minutes in silence.

"You still have any contacts on the inside?" she said.

"Of course I do. Once a cop always a cop."

"Maybe you can ask around. Quietly."

"That's a pretty big ask."

"You weren't afraid to stand up against the Parker shooting."

"I'm never afraid," I said. "Doesn't mean I'm reckless either.

Accusing a cop of executing someone is a big ticket. You get that wrong and there's hell to pay."

"I have it right."

"Why are you so certain?"

Morgan looked out her window for a moment. The streets were deserted as we passed through the shadows.

"I have a source that says it was a hit," she said. "This wasn't random. They were specifically looking for Reece Williams, and they were looking to kill him."

I didn't bother asking about her source because I knew she wouldn't tell. Instead I asked, "Does your source know why they wanted to kill him?"

"No. That's the sixty-four-million-dollar question. And right now I don't have any leads to find the answer."

"How are you gonna run this story on the air without at least offering some motivation for the killing?"

"I can't. Rebecca won't let this air without that in the piece."

"So what are you going to do?"

"What any good journalist should do. Keep digging."

BY THE TIME I PULLED up to my apartment building, it was after one o'clock in the morning. I was hungry and exhausted. It had been a long day. I opened the apartment door but immediately felt like something wasn't right. I stood there for a few seconds. Where was Stryker? He always met me at the door, tail wagging, full of boundless energy. I pulled out my gun. My pulse quickened. Someone had been here. I could feel it.

I walked slowly down the hall past the guest bathroom on my right, then the kitchen on my left. Empty. I walked farther into the apartment, paused a moment, then swung into the living room with my gun raised. Was I hallucinating? Julia sat on my couch with Stryker resting on her lap. I lowered my gun and exhaled.

"What the hell is going on?" I said.

Stryker slipped out of her lap, ran, and jumped on me.

"Ashe," she said. "Good to see you."

"Jules?"

She held up her hand. "I still had my old key."

I hadn't heard her voice in so long. But it was the same—strong with a little rasp.

"What are you doing here?"

"I figured it was time to talk."

Hearing her say those words angered me. "Three years after abandoning me, *you* decide it's time to talk. Priceless."

"I wasn't ready before."

"Well, maybe after all those long days and months full of lonely nights wondering why you left me without any kind of answer, I'm not ready now."

"I understand that you're upset," she said calmly. "And I know it seems selfish. But I needed this time. I needed the space. I'm sorry."

"I'm not upset anymore," I said. "I'm disappointed in myself for letting the hurt you caused get the better of me for so long. And now out of the blue you come back when you decide it's right for you?"

"That's why I sent you the letter last year."

"With no return address or any way to respond to you. That's exactly what I mean. You walked out of my life with no warning or explanation. Nothing. Gone. All this time I've been left trying to make sense of something I could never understand because you didn't have the decency to tell me what happened. And now *you* determine this is the right time. For what? To shred my heart again?"

She stood. She looked as beautiful as I remembered. Her skin was soft, and her eyes sparkled. I had the urge to run over and hug her, run my fingers through her long hair, and press my mouth against hers. But I couldn't move. I felt my heart thumping at the base of my tongue.

"Maybe this was a bad idea," she said. "You're right. I shouldn't've just barged in like this. I just thought . . ."

"Was that you at the restaurant?"

"It was. Was that your girlfriend?"

"You don't have a right to know that."

"She's beautiful."

"Was that you following me in that silver car a couple of days ago?" She nodded.

"Why didn't you say something?"

"I was scared. I wasn't sure how you would react. I knew what I wanted to say, but I didn't know how to say it."

"Which was?"

She walked over to me. I could smell the flowers in her shampoo. "That I love you," she said. Then she moved in and kissed me softly on the lips. I inhaled deeply, then pulled back. She ran her finger around the curve of my lips. I felt like I was lost in a dream again, just like I had been so many nights when I woke up in the middle of my bed only to find myself alone and quivering for the very sensation I now felt as her skin touched mine.

I stepped back from her. "It doesn't work this way," I said. "You can't do this to me."

She stared at me for a moment and smiled softly. "I'll be in town for the next three months," she said. "I'm here working on a project for one of my clients. My girlfriend's letting me use her apartment in the West Loop."

She walked past me and down the hall. Stryker looked at her and then at me as if he didn't know whom he should follow. The door closed behind her. I knew I wasn't ready to tell her to leave the key behind.

15

I barely got any sleep, so I woke up the next morning and went out to the lake for a run to try to clear my mind. I tried everything I could to distract myself from thoughts about Julia, but whatever I tried only lasted for a couple of minutes, then she'd flash back into my mind. The thoughts were so tactile—the touch of her lips, the scent of her shampoo, the light reflected in her eyes. I was so upset at myself, pretending all this time that I was over her and had moved on with my life. Nothing could be further from the truth. I was angry and happy she was there in my apartment. All those nights preparing and practicing what I would say to her if we were ever in the same room again, and I could barely get my words out.

I wanted to grab her, hold her, and undress her. I wanted to make her dinner and fall asleep next to her watching a movie we had already seen a hundred times only to wake up in the morning and make love to her. How could I still feel this way after all she had put me through? I was falling in love with Carolina. At least I thought I was. How could I feel so attracted to Carolina and yet still want to be with Julia? I texted my therapist and asked her to call me when she had time.

I finished my run, took Stryker out for a quick walk, and was just about to fix breakfast when Mechanic called.

"Just a heads-up," he said. "She's in a bitchin' mood today."

"What happened?"

"Something about what some guy wrote in the paper about her. A guy named Robert Leeder in the *Sun-Times*. He writes about the media business."

"What did he say?"

"He predicted she would lose her top ratings spot to some anchorwoman over at WMTQ. He said November would be the changing of the guard."

"Where is Morgan now?"

"Getting some coffee, then going to the station."

"This early?"

"She said she had an important meeting with her executive producer about the article."

"Okay. If you hear anything else, hit me back."

I pulled up the *Sun-Times* site on my phone and found Robert Leeder's column, Don't Bury the Leede. Morgan's picture stared back at me from the top of the page. In two simple paragraphs, he explained how hotly contested the November sweeps would be and how, based on the changes made at WMTQ and the gains they had made in the last two ratings periods, he fully expected Alicia Roscati and her co-anchor Graydon Miles to take the coveted top spot and bragging rights as the most-watched anchor team in the city. Leeder had all but crowned Roscati, and November sweeps were still four weeks away. Seemed a bit premature to me, but I knew nothing about the TV business and how these media watchers calculated their predictions. But I knew enough to know that Morgan Shaw was not going to take this prediction without putting up a fight. As much of a prima donna as she was, it was clear to me she was as tough as she was glamorous.

I had just finished slicing bananas into my bowl of oatmeal when my phone rang. I didn't recognize the number.

"This is Detective Torres," he said. "I was asked to give you a call."

"I appreciate you taking the time," I said. "I'm helping with security detail for Morgan Shaw."

"I know exactly what you're doing," Torres said. "She's made it very clear to me that she felt safer with you and your team taking care of her."

"We're doing our best," I said. "I thought we might get together soon and compare notes."

Torres hesitated, then said, "As you know, this is an active investigation, so there's only so much I can disclose, but someone upstairs signed off on us talking."

We agreed to meet the next day at noon. No sooner had I hung up than Morgan called.

"I really need that favor I asked you about last night," she said. "Maybe you can check with your people inside CPD and see if you can find out anything."

"I can ask, but there's no guarantee," I said. "No one wants to go on the record for something like this."

"I need this story to happen next month," she said. "It's important."

"I heard about the Leeder column."

"He's never liked me," she said. "When I first got here, I gave an exclusive to the *Tribune*, and he's never forgiven me for that. He wants me to lose. But I'm not. I'm the best, and I'm gonna fight like hell to stay the best. Period."

"'Winners never quit, and quitters never win.'"

"Shakespeare?"

"Coach Vince Lombardi, the Shakespeare of football."

"The same guy whose name is on the Super Bowl trophy?"

"That very same guy."

"I need the names of the other two cops who were there that night when Mankovich shot Reece," she said. "If I can get their names, then I can dig around and maybe find a motive."

"You're going from reporter to detective?"

"It's called investigative journalism, and yes, it's like being a detective. And while I don't do it often since I'm stuck behind the anchor desk most of the time, I still get out in the field occasionally, and I'm still damn good at it."

"Have you ever gone after a cop before?"

"In what way?"

"Like you're doing now. Accusing one of doing something bad. And I'm not talking about writing too many parking tickets. Something really bad."

"You should know."

"Exactly. And that's why I'm telling you to be very careful. Going after a shady politician or corrupt businessman is one thing. But going after a Chicago cop is nothing short of declaring war."

16

"Take me through everything that happened," Dr. Khatri said.

She was seated in a modern leather chair with lots of chrome and angles. I sat in a comfortable chair with tufted cushions. She kept the lights off and the blinds open. The wood crackled in the marble fireplace on the other side of the barren room. It had been a while since I had been here, but everything looked the same.

I started with my father secretly meeting with Julia while he was in Paris last year for the French Open, then on to finding her in my apartment with Stryker on her lap. Dr. Khatri made a few notes as I spoke, but her facial expression didn't change.

"How do you feel?" she asked, placing her pen down.

"Like a damn fool."

"Why?"

"Because this woman destroyed my life, hurt me like I had never been hurt before, and not a day goes by that I don't still think about her. And it's been three years."

"There's no shot clock when it comes to grief," she said. "And while others might not agree, it's been my professional experience that there's no such thing as grieving ever being complete or just suddenly disappearing one day. It's a process. For some more gradual than others, but it's a process. People who lost their spouses or grandparents thirty or forty years ago still grieve. They aren't still crying every day or unable to get out of bed, but as they carry on with their lives, they still grieve quietly."

"So I'm never going to get over her?"

"Do you want to?"

"What kind of question is that?"

"A question that you really need to answer, because you haven't done so yet."

She was right. Dr. Khatri was always right and one step ahead of me. It was as if my skull were made of glass. She knew my thoughts sometimes before even I did.

"Are you asking if I still love her?"

"No, I'm not. I know you still love her. What I'm asking is something altogether different. Do you really want her to be out of your life forever?"

"Honestly, I don't know. And it pisses the hell out of me that my answer isn't yes."

We sat there for a moment in silence. I felt like a violent storm had surged in my body and couldn't escape. I felt everything at once and then nothing at all. Dr. Khatri studied me carefully.

"What about Carolina?" she said. "Has anything progressed?"

"We went to Morocco in August."

"How was it?"

"The best trip of my life. I needed the break. My first time in Africa. We had a good time. I could've stayed another two weeks."

"Your first trip together?"

I nodded. "She set everything up."

"You're happy with her. I can tell in your body language when you talk about her."

"She's the total package," I said. "Except for the fact that she likes banana nut muffins and I like blueberry, we're made for each other."

"But?"

"There is no but. I think I love her."

"Have you told her this?"

"How can I when I'm trying to stop feeling the way I do for Julia?"

"And how does Carolina feel about you?"

"She hasn't exactly said, but I know she wants us to be together in a way that it's just us. She's been very patient."

"Have you told her why it's taking you so long?"

"She doesn't bring it up. I know her. She doesn't want to appear like she's pressuring me. She knows I still have this problem with Julia."

"Have you talked about it with her?"

"Of course not," I said. "I can't imagine her being excited about discussing why I can't get over my ex."

"Maybe you're not giving her enough credit," Dr. Khatri said. "Carolina sounds like a mature, thoughtful woman. The conversation could be good for both of you."

"Do you think it's possible to love two people at the same time?"

"Absolutely I do. But I don't recommend it for everyone. It can be very tricky. If you're in relationships with both people, it can be extremely difficult to manage and keep everyone happy and clearly sort through your feelings."

"I'm no longer in a relationship with Julia."

"And that's the other situation. When you're in a relationship with someone—in your case Carolina—but still love another person. That's why I think it's possible to love two people. Because you might not love them in the same way. Different people can fulfill different needs."

I sat there for a minute trying to digest it all. I shook my head.

"What's the problem?" she said.

"It just angers me that I still love someone who would treat me the way she has. It doesn't make sense."

"'Love doesn't need reason,'" Dr. Khatri said. "'It speaks from the irrational wisdom of the heart.'"

"You sound like a poet."

"It's not mine. Deepak Chopra."

Maybe I needed to talk to him.

"What is it that you really want, Ashe?" she said.

"The truth. I want Jules to look me in the eyes and say to my face why she did what she did. I need to know what really happened."

"There's probably no answer she can give you that will make you feel better. The pain she caused can't be erased."

"I know that. But I feel like finally hearing her explain why she did it will take out all the guessing and speculation I've been doing and make it real for me. It will hurt. I know it will. But sometimes you need that kind of damage before the real healing begins."

"You had a chance for that when she was in your apartment the other day," Dr. Khatri said. "It was just the two of you alone. It was a perfect time to ask all your questions and get the answers you've been looking for."

"I wasn't ready," I said.

"Or maybe you were scared."

"Scared of what?"

"That once she said what she had to say and walked out of your apartment, the door would close on your relationship forever."

Frustrated she was so spot on, I stared across the room at her. The fear of closing out our relationship forever was exactly why I hadn't asked Julia to leave her key.

17

I was exhausted after the session with Dr. Khatri, so I decided to do something I rarely took the time to do and went to get a massage at Golden Thai, a boutique spa in Chinatown. I had found this place several years ago while working on a case of a Chinese exchange student who had been kidnapped by one of her father's business rivals. The girl's host family owned the spa.

I had just finished a ninety-minute deep tissue massage and was sitting alone in a steam room that felt more like a sauna. I had a cold bottle of water beside me, and light spa music piped in from ceiling speakers. I closed my eyes and thought about my session with Dr. Khatri. Everything she had said was on the mark. I needed to talk to Carolina, and I needed to talk to Julia. But whom should I speak to first?

My thoughts were interrupted by my phone chirping from the other room. I ignored it and closed my eyes again. Seconds later, it chirped again. I grudgingly got up and fished it out of my coat pocket. It was Mechanic.

"We have a development," he said. "Could be a situation."

"What's going on?"

"Anchor lady has some unexpected company. He's following her in a black jag convertible."

"You got the plate?"

"I'll pretend like you didn't just ask me that."

"Of course. I'm sorry, man. Still in a fog from the massage." I started pulling my clothes out of the locker. "Where are you right now?"

"About two blocks from her apartment building traveling south on Wabash."

"Any idea who he might be?"

"Negative. I spotted him earlier sitting across from her building. He'd been there for about an hour. He never got out the car. Sat there the entire time with his window rolled up. When she pulled out the garage, he slid in behind her."

"Did you get a good look at him?"

"Not too good, but good enough. White guy, early forties, dark hair with sunglasses. Clean cut. Looks big, but it's hard to tell. That jag is so small, a first grader would look big in it."

"Stay on him," I said. "I'm at Golden Thai. I'm getting dressed. I'll be in the car in five minutes. Call me if anything changes."

I was in the car and racing down State Street when Mechanic called back.

"She just pulled into the garage," Mechanic said. "He stopped for a second as if he was about to enter the garage too, then pulled off."

"Where are you now?"

"Michigan and Wacker."

"Can you get close enough to snap a pic of him?"

"Already did. You'll have it soon."

My phone buzzed. I opened up my text messages.

"Well, goddamn," I said.

"What?"

"Didn't see this coming in a million years. It's our man Reinhard Schmidt. Mr. Majority Leader."

"Want me to follow him?"

I thought for a moment. Whomever had first shift was supposed to make the handoff to the station's security team and not leave until she was safely inside.

"Stay with him," I said. "I'll do the handoff. Let me call Morgan."

I hung up and dialed her cell.

"Where's Mechanic?" she said. "The guard is standing outside my car."

"Roll your window down and tell him to wait five minutes. I'm on my way."

I made it into the garage and drove straight to her car. One of the guards dutifully stood a few feet from her car, his hands shoved into his pockets. I jumped out my car and walked to her door. She opened it once she saw me.

"What happened?"

I was about to tell her about Schmidt but thought better of it. I wanted to figure out what was going on before I said anything to her.

"Mechanic had an emergency," I said.

"Is he okay?"

"He's fine. Something just came up."

The three of us walked into the building, and I left them once they were safely inside the station. I ran back to my car and dialed Mechanic's number.

"He just went into a bank on LaSalle and Grand. Should I intercept him when he comes out?"

"I'll be there in a few minutes. If he gets out before I get there, try to slow him down. But gently. He's the Senate majority leader."

"Kid gloves."

By the time I arrived, Schmidt was walking out of the bank toward his car. Mechanic was parked behind him. He opened his door. The three of us converged at Schmidt's car at the same time. He looked at me with surprise.

"What the hell is going on?" he said, his eyes darting quickly between Mechanic and me.

"Just out for a nice drive?" I asked.

"None of your goddamn business what I'm doing."

Mechanic began moving toward him. I jerked my head to back him off.

"How's the wife and kids?" I asked.

"What's this all about?" he said.

"Just checking in. Seeing how everyone's doing."

"Fine."

He started for his door. Mechanic stepped in the way.

Schmidt glared at Mechanic, then at me. "Does this degenerate know he's fucking with the majority leader of the Illinois Senate?"

"He does." I smiled.

"Does he know with one phone call I can have both your asses arrested and hauled off to jail?"

"He does." I smiled. "Problem is, you keep calling him names, and you'll be dialing with your chin because he'll break every one of your fingers and bend them so far back they'll be lying on your wrists."

Schmidt looked at Mechanic, whose face expressed about as much emotion as a piece of dry firewood.

"You followed Morgan Shaw from her apartment building to the station," I said.

Schmidt knew there was no use denying it. "So what?" he said. "I can drive anywhere I damn well please."

"That's true," I said. "But I'm sure your wife wouldn't be too excited to learn her devoted husband was stalking his ex and sending her threatening messages in the mail."

"I'm not stalking anyone, and I'm not threatening anyone. I see either one of you again where I shouldn't be seeing you, and I promise you'll be sorry."

He started for his car, and I nodded toward Mechanic to move to the side and let him pass. We stood and watched as he drove away in a huff.

"Why would a man like him who has so much to lose put it all at risk over good sex?" Mechanic said. "You can find no-hassle sex everywhere."

"'O beware, my lord, of jealousy. It is the green-eyed monster which doth mock the meat it feeds on.'"

Mechanic shot me a look.

"Shakespeare's *Othello*," I said. "Jealousy is a big monster that feeds on your heart. No matter what you do or how hard you try to ignore it, it just keeps gnawing away, never allowing you to have peace."

18

Torres wanted to meet on the South Side bike path that ran along Lake Shore Drive. He had told me to wear sneakers because he wanted to walk and talk. He was waiting for me at the foot of a newly built bridge that carried people across the busy drive and deposited them in a large grassy area running to the banks of the lake. He looked much different than I had expected. He had a head full of dark hair tucked underneath a Sox cap and wore a pair of dark denims with a bomber jacket. He was in great shape and looked like a seasoned cop in his prime, not one on the verge of retirement. He offered a firm handshake when I approached.

"South or north?" he asked. "You have a preference?"

"My default position is always south," I said. "I know it better. I feel more at home."

"Me too," he said as we turned onto the path snaking through the tall grass and wild bushes. "I grew up over in South Shore behind the cultural center. We used to find the lost golf balls in the weeds, clean 'em up, and sell them back to the golfers for a dollar a pop. Bought my first ten-speed bike with that little business."

"Spent my entire life in Bronzeville," I said. "Went to college out East, then came back here."

"Still live over there?" he asked.

"Not anymore. Down in Streeterville now."

Torres smiled. "High rent district. Can't live there on a cop's salary."

A few cyclists drove by and a couple of runners galloped freely through the crisp air. Birds hidden in the thick tree branches chirped loudly to each other.

"You miss it?" Torres said.

I knew he was talking about the work. "Some parts of it," I said. "But I never liked the bureaucracy. Now I still have the action without all the paperwork and court appearances. Are you gonna miss it?"

"Not for a second. I'm almost thirty years in. I've done what I needed to do. Time to start another chapter."

"Which is why I was surprised you took lead on the Morgan Shaw case. I figured that's the last headache somebody would want six months from turning in the shield."

"You think I wanted this shit?" he said. He laughed softly. "Wasn't my choice. Case management assigned it to me. Went to my sergeant to get out of it, and he agreed to take me off. Lieutenant overruled. So here I am."

"None of my business, but that seems strange," I said. "Nobody takes lead six months out. Doesn't make any sense, especially on a major case like this."

"It would make sense to you if you knew my lieutenant. He's just being a hard-ass. We haven't seen eye to eye on some things the last few years. Just his way of sticking it to me on my way out. No problem. I've dealt with lots of shit in my career. Not gonna let this stress me out. I'll stay off the radar and do my job. A hundred and seventeen days until I walk. Three weeks' vacation due, so it's a hundred and two days. Can't come a minute too soon."

We entered a part of the path where the grass rose above our heads and all we could hear was the sound of the waves crashing against the rocks.

"Any idea who might be sending her these messages or why?"

"Not a clue. No prints from the letters. Nothing on the garage cameras at the station, but to be honest, the coverage down there isn't great. Looked at lots of footage from the cameras at her apartment building. Nothing suspicious."

I didn't want to share too much too quickly until I had a better grasp on him and how serious he was about working the case.

"I've met with the station security team and talked to the security guards at her apartment building. Not much came out of it. I have two people with her when she's out and about. If the person is serious and takes a run at her, one of them will be there to intercept."

"Them?" Torres said. "You're not taking a piece of the action?"

"I'm leaving for Arizona in a couple of days. Long-needed golf vacation. Two rounds a day til I can't swing anymore."

"I don't play golf, but I fish. I have a little place on the water down in Louisiana. I'll be out in the boat every day. Rain or shine. I'm leaving these winters for good."

I decided to take a chance. "What do you know about the Reece Williams shooting?" I asked.

Torres stopped and turned toward me for a moment, then turned back around and started walking.

"What are you after?" Torres said.

"Just wondering what went down."

"Wondering? You don't strike me as the kind of man who just twiddles his thumbs and wonders about things like that."

"Fair enough," I said. "I heard there was a lot more behind it. The kid was clean."

"I don't personally know the guys involved, but I've heard things. Can't believe everything you hear. But you already know that."

"Was the kid clean?"

"That's what I heard."

"So what went wrong?"

"That I don't know. Tac team had been working a case in the area. They get a call to that location. They get out, and Mankovich pulls the trigger."

"No reason?"

"There's always a reason, but I have no idea what it was, and nobody's talking—at least nobody who really knows what happened."

"Witnesses?"

"Internal Affairs looked into it. No witnesses who could give them enough to do anything."

I decided not to push too hard. It would appear like I was after something.

"So what's your plan going forward with Morgan?" I asked.

"Still looking into it, but not much to do right now."

"What about tracking down the source of the letter?"

"Better chance of finding a needle in a barn full of hay."

KURTIS LEWIS EASILY STOOD SIX-FIVE with a slight forward hunch in his shoulders. He led me into his small third-floor apartment, which wasn't well decorated, but it was meticulously clean and extremely warm.

I took off my coat and sat in a chair near the window.

"I'll be damned if you don't look like a young Dr. Cayne," he said, reclining on the couch and extending his long legs. "It's been a while since I've seen him. How's he doing?"

"Recuperating," I said. "Too much tennis on his old joints."

"I know the feeling. Arthur finds his way in my joints every morning. Getting old ain't no picnic."

"He says the same thing."

"Well, retirement has been good to me otherwise, so I can't really complain," he said, laughing softly. "How can I help you?"

"I need some help on tracking a letter that was mailed to my client. The letter was sent to her workplace. I want to find out where it was mailed from."

"Was there tracking on it like certified mail or delivery confirmation?"

"No, just a stamp."

"Nothing else?"

"That's it."

He shook his head. "I'm afraid you're on a fool's errand. Unless there was some type of tracking purchased at the time of mailing, you won't be able to track it."

"There's no way to at least figure out the general area where it was mailed from?"

Lewis squeezed his eyes and rubbed his forehead. "Tough to say exactly. Theoretically, you might be able to find out what region it was mailed from, but you'd have to do some serious work and have a little luck to get there."

I took out my phone, pulled up the picture I had taken of the envelope, and handed it to him. He put on his reading glasses, studied the photo for a moment, then handed the phone back to me.

"Well, you caught a break," he said. "The postmark is still legible. You can see the postal facility where it was processed and the date it went through the system. So that's a start."

"What about the barcode at the bottom of the envelope?"

"No help. It contains the address and zip code of the person receiving the envelope. The machine puts it on there so the sorting machines know how to batch the mail and which truck will pick it up. Has nothing to do with the sender."

"What's the journey of a mailed envelope?"

"Depends. If someone drops it off at a free-standing mailbox, for example, then that box is picked up by a mail truck a certain number of times during the day. The driver will take it to a postal branch, and from there it will go to a processing center. See that name on the postmark superimposed over the stamp?"

I looked at the photograph. "Carol Stream," I said.

"So that's the center that processed it. Once it's processed and sorted, then the mail is shipped to a distribution center. Trucks from the distribution center will take the mail to the different branches based on the zip code where the mail is going. Then the individual carriers will pick up the mail for their route and deliver the mail to the final destination."

"But none of this gives any information about where the letter was mailed."

"I'm afraid not."

I needed to think through this more, so I stood to leave. "If you think of anything that might help, let me know."

I left his apartment and was on my way home when my phone rang. I didn't recognize the number, but I picked it up anyway. It was Father Flagger. He wanted to meet with me urgently. I gave him the address to my office, turned around, and headed in that direction.

"ARE YOU WORKING ON THIS story with Morgan?" he asked, sitting across from my desk. The door was closed as his body man waited outside the office.

"Not at all. This is her story."

He nodded. "I know who you are."

"Not sure if that's a good thing or bad thing."

"It's good. You're a hero to a lot of people for what you did with the Payton shooting."

"Says a lot about the times we live in when simply doing what's right makes you a hero. I did what any sworn officer should've done."

"If only it was that easy," Flagger said. "A lot of the people who come to my church and live in the community are constantly overlooked and marginalized. The system oppresses them. Makes them feel inferior and unwanted. Understandably, they don't trust authority."

I nodded.

"Can I trust you, Mr. Cayne?"

"I think you already know the answer to that," I said. "That's why you're sitting in my office."

"Fair enough."

He looked out my window at Buckingham Fountain, which had been shut down for the winter, but people still gathered to take pictures near the large water basin. All of the boats had been lifted out of the lake, leaving nothing but dark blue water stretching out to the edge of the horizon.

"I have new information about Reece Williams," he said, clasping his fingers together under his chin.

"Information you had before or after your interview with Morgan the other night?" I said.

"After. I was just contacted last night."

"Have you talked to Morgan?"

He shook his head.

"Why are you telling me before going to her? It's her story, not mine."

"I need your advice," he said.

"'Give every man thine ear but few thy voice,'" I said.

Flagger smiled. "I was told you quote a lot of Shakespeare."

"Wu-Tang Clan too. Depends on the mood and the audience."

Flagger sang, "'I bomb atomically. Socrates's philosophies and hypotheses can't define how I be droppin' these.'"

"Nice work," I said. "'Triumph.' One of my favorite songs."

"They gave a performance at the church some years back. Some of the best lyricists in the game."

I nodded. I respected anyone who could quote Wu-Tang.

"Another person has come to me in confidence about Reece's shooting," Flagger said. "I had a brief conversation with him over the phone. He's willing to share information, but he's afraid coming forward could get him killed."

"Why is he coming to you?"

"Everyone comes to me." He smiled softly. "They know they can always trust me."

"What does this guy know?"

"I'm not sure. Right now, he won't tell even me. He said he needs to think about it a little more before saying anything. He's scared. He knows how this works. He knows the power of a badge and the evilness of some who wear it."

"You know his name?"

"Nope. I told him I didn't want to know it. I wanted him to get comfortable first and speak only when he was ready."

"You have his number?"

"It was blocked. Our conversation was less than a minute."

"Sounds compelling," I said. "So what advice can I give you?"

"If he were to call me back, I need to know if I should offer him the opportunity to speak with Morgan. Can she be trusted to do the right thing?"

"You trusted her enough to sit down and do your interview."

"No one would dare mess with me. But it's different with these witnesses. I've been around the block many times. I've seen informants get promised the world, then get burned in the end. Once they get informants to talk, and they have the information they need, they throw these guys away like last week's trash."

Sadly, he was right. I'd seen it happen more times than I could count. Gullible, scared witnesses were assured they would be protected, only to find themselves outed and exposed once they had given up the goods.

"Sounds like the first step is finding out what the informant actually has," I said. "It might not be relevant."

"That's exactly why I'm here. I was hoping you might be willing to take that on."

"You're asking for more than just giving advice."

"I am because I know that if anyone can handle this fairly, it's you."

I looked at my watch. "I'm leaving for Arizona in exactly forty-seven hours and twenty minutes."

"Arizona?"

"Several weeks of nothing but sunshine, golf, and chimichangas."

"Phones work in Arizona too."

"Better than the voting machines they damaged because they didn't get the election results they wanted."

Flagger smiled. "Should the informant call me back, will you at least allow me to consult with you remotely?"

"You have my number."

19

I made the decision that I would tell Carolina everything. Dr. Khatri knew a whole lot more about female intuition and sensibility than I did. I needed to trust her recommendation, especially since I would be away in Arizona for several weeks with enough alone time to clear my head. I texted her plans to meet for dinner at seven, and she quickly agreed.

I called Rox, who reported she was currently trailing Morgan in the intimate apparel department of Neiman Marcus. She was looking at lingerie that was more expensive than Rox's monthly car payment and rent combined. She estimated Morgan had already bagged close to two thousand dollars in bras and sheer bodysuits, and they hadn't been there for more than ten minutes.

Next, I called Mechanic, who had been following Schmidt since he left his house that morning. The majority leader had gone to a breakfast meeting with a couple of other suits, then directly to his office where he had been for the last two hours. No sooner had I hung up than Burke called in. Of course, he didn't bother with pleasantries.

"The other two officers were Nettles and Knight," Burke said.

"Sounds like a personal injury law firm," I said.

"Nettles was the driver. Knight was the passenger. About twenty years between the two. Nettles is senior by a little more than a year."

"Have you read their statements?"

"Not personally. IA has them locked behind the wall. But I talked to someone who had seen an early version. Pretty straightforward. No surprises. Call comes with a description of a guy with a couple of warrants out. They arrive at the location, get a visual on the suspect, and approach him. They tell him to stop and show his hands. He reaches for something in his waistband. They think it's a weapon. Mankovich fires two shots. Suspect falls. Three of them had been working together for a little more than a year before this went down."

"Are Nettles and Knight dirty?"

"Not from what I've heard. Nettles had a couple of excessive use complaints a few years back. Knight had just gotten off suspension for a bar fight where he beat up a guy pretty bad. Other than that, they're clean."

"Mankovich?"

"Ten years out of the Sixth District. Worked gangs the last three years. Not a single mark on his record."

"That gun they turned in didn't belong to Williams," I said. "It was dirty. Someone planted it."

"Rumor. No one has backed that up."

"Yet."

"Do you know something?"

"I do, but I can't say."

"Is it bad?"

"Probably."

"Witnesses?"

"At least one for sure. But someone else might wanna talk to Morgan."

"She really better have her shit together before she runs with something like this. HQ won't take this lightly."

"I've told her the same thing. She's determined to deliver this next month."

"Good luck with that."

"Where's Mankovich now?"

"They moved him up to Albany Park. He's sitting on the desk. If I were you, I'd advise her to stay away from him. He has protection."

"How high up?"

"I've heard it's way up close to the top. You know as well as anyone, it's not gonna be easy for an outsider to crack the wall."

"True, but all walls have tiny cracks. It only takes one. You just have to look close enough to find it."

He paused for a moment and said, "We never had this conversation."

"What conversation?"

My answer was a loud disconnection sound.

CAROLINA AND I SAT AT a corner table in the dark dining room of Maple & Ashe. I stared down a ten-ounce filet mignon while she picked around her grilled shrimp and mango salad. She wore a burgundy cashmere turtleneck that perfectly framed her face. The candle in the middle of the table flickered vividly in her eyes.

"Stryker and I are gonna miss you while you're gone," she said.

"It'll go by fast," I said. "I'll be back in no time."

"Morgan's okay with you leaving?"

"She's not thrilled about it, but she doesn't have much of a choice. Mechanic and Rox will take care of her."

"Do you think whoever it is will try something?"

"If they do, I feel sorry for them. Both will shoot first and ask questions later."

"Rox carries a gun?"

"Almost as big as she is."

"She looks so sweet, but I wouldn't want to meet her in a dark alley."

"You wouldn't want to meet her in an alley even in broad daylight. She's an animal. No fear whatsoever."

I took a sip of wine, then pushed my plate away.

"You have that look," she said, nibbling at a piece of shrimp.

"Julia is in Chicago," I said.

Carolina took a hard gulp and placed her fork beside her plate.

"She was in my apartment when I got home a few days ago. She still had her key."

"What's taken you so long to tell me?" Carolina said.

"I wasn't sure how you'd react."

"It's more disturbing that you didn't tell me right away than it is that she was in your apartment. I'm not some fragile flower. You should know that by now."

"I'm sorry. I needed some time to sort this all out."

She took a sip of wine, then said, "So how's the sorting going?"

"Honestly, I've tried not to think about it," I said. "I've been focusing on everything else."

"Not thinking about it won't make it go away or any easier when you do decide to deal with it. Were you happy to see her?"

"I was shocked. I was angry. But I did feel some curiosity about seeing her after all these years."

"Of course you did. Completely natural. How was the conversation?"

"There wasn't much of one. I told her she had some nerve to come and see me out of the blue like that after all these years. She told me she was staying at a friend's house for a few months, then left quickly."

I thought it best to leave out the part about the kiss.

"Have you talked to her since?"

"Nada."

"You still love her."

"Is that a question or a statement?"

"Statement. I know you still love her."

I leaned back from the table. "I feel something, but it's not love."

"I've always known you still felt something," she said. "What she did to you was unthinkable, but she did it so abruptly and without any explanation. You never felt closure. Love is amazing in how much endurance it has. It can withstand a lot of pain and still march on."

"I don't want to be with her," I said. "I will never forgive her for what she did to me. She really messed me up."

"Still, you need to sit down face-to-face and talk to her when you get back from Arizona."

"And say what?"

"The truth." Carolina smiled. "That you're now in love with a hot girl who can finish your sentences and would never leave you standing at the altar."

20

The dry Arizona heat felt good against my skin, thawing the deep Chicago chill buried in my bones. There weren't any distractions or worries other than making sure I chose the correct club to get my approach shot to the middle of the green. My second most important decision was what I'd order for lunch at the turn to the back nine. I had been away for almost five days, and the distance had done me well. The breathtaking views at the Estancia Club not only brought calm but a clearer vision of how I would handle Julia. I knew what I had to do, and I knew how I would do it.

Penny's rambling estate sat nestled at the top of a mountain ridge overlooking the golf course. I had been spoiled with two pools, a tennis court with a pro on standby, a commercially equipped gym, and a full staff to tend to my every need. Sometimes I forgot how incredibly wealthy Penny was until moments like this. I wondered if it could get boring having everything so perfect all the time.

I had comfortably settled into a routine. Each morning started with a sixty-minute massage followed by a full breakfast served on the back veranda with the sun slowly rising in my face. The staff made sure the *Arizona Republic* and the *New York Times* had been laid out for me next to a plate of fruit and a glass of freshly squeezed orange juice.

Penny, paying attention to every little detail, had even left instructions to make sure the pulp had been completely strained from my juice. The day was consumed with golfing, naps, and massages. Evenings were consumed by an episode of a streaming TV show and a wonderful dinner under the stars on the west veranda that overlooked a distant mountain range lit by the dull glow of the moon. I had just finished my crème brûlée when my phone rang. It was Mechanic.

"Everything good?" I said.

"We have a development," he said. "Another message came through a little while ago."

"What was it?"

"A text message. 'I know where you live. I will get you.'"

"Of course this happens while I'm seventeen hundred miles away."

"I got it covered," Mechanic said. "She wants me to spend the night in one of her guest bedrooms. I don't have a change of clothes, but I'll survive."

"Where is she now?"

"Not sure. Somewhere in this gigantic apartment. Did you know she has two kitchens in this place and an entire downstairs? I didn't go down there, but she said there are bedrooms down there also."

"Prima donnas make prima dough," I said. "The good news is with the lobby security and you guys upstairs, you'll be protected. No one can get to you."

"And if they do, I'll have something waiting for them."

"Make sure she knows you carry."

"She knows. I showed it to her."

"What did she say?"

"She felt a lot better when I told her it could take down a bull elephant."

"So macho of you," I said. "Call me if anything happens."

———◇———

THREE DAYS LATER, PENNY HAD arranged for me to play my morning round with the club's golf pro who had taught several players still playing on the PGA Tour. I took my massage that morning half an hour early, changed into my golf pants and shirt, then headed to breakfast. A member of the staff brought out a basket of freshly baked pastries as I settled into my chair. I took a sip of orange juice and picked up the *Arizona Republic*. The big story was the governor threatening to veto a tax bill proposed by the state legislature. Another story covered the campaign of one of the state's US Senators who was a former astronaut and running for reelection. I flipped the paper and immediately felt like someone had swung a battering ram into the middle of my gut. I froze, unable to get beyond the headline: "Beloved Chicago Anchorwoman Found Dead." My phone chirped and bounced on the table. It was Mechanic.

"Have you heard?" he asked.

"I just saw it in the paper. Jesus Christ. What the hell happened?"

"Right now, I only know as much as the news is reporting."

I scrolled down the article and read the name "Alicia Roscati." What? The first paragraph said that the twenty-nine-year-old popular anchorwoman was found unresponsive in her bed by her longtime producer Tyra Martin.

"Wait a minute," I said. "It's not Morgan?"

"No, it's her rival across town. The blond one with the big eyes. They found her in her bed."

The air rushed out of my chest as I settled into the back of my chair, relieved that it wasn't Morgan but shocked that it was Roscati.

"Jesus Christ," I said. "I thought it was Morgan. I just saw the headline but hadn't read the article yet. Where's Morgan?"

"In her bedroom getting dressed. She's going in to the station early."

"Tell me what you know."

"Two days ago, Roscati called out of work. She told her producer that she wasn't feeling well and wouldn't make it. The producer texted her that night but didn't get an answer. When Roscati didn't show up for the afternoon meeting the next day, the producer went to her building and convinced security to let her into the apartment. That's when they found her in bed. She was already cold."

"Was she murdered?"

"Nobody knows. Only thing they're saying is she was found in bed."

"How's Morgan taking it?"

"Upset. Someone called her around midnight with the news. Then she called me and asked me to come back over. I spent the night in one of her guest bedrooms."

None of this made sense. A twenty-nine-year-old anchorwoman suddenly dies in her sleep. It didn't feel right. Sadness accompanied the news of anyone's death, but especially a young person who still had a full life ahead of them. Now it was all gone.

"You and Rox stay close to Morgan all day per usual. Tell her to call me when she gets in the car."

"Copy that."

I sat there in disbelief while reading the rest of the article. It didn't say much more than what Mechanic had told me. I searched several of the local Chicago websites and found a little more information. Roscati had called her boyfriend who lived in LA and had told him how bad she felt. She was nauseous, had vomited twice, and her stomach was in severe pain. She complained of numbness in her legs and weakness. She didn't want to go to the emergency room, instead choosing to lie down to see if rest would make her feel better. That was the last he heard from her. Alicia Roscati was survived by her parents who lived in Iowa City, Iowa, and two older sisters who lived in Florida. She had never been married or had any children. Her job had been her life.

As I ate breakfast, I read several articles that all said mostly the same thing, then I got into the car and drove to the course. As I pulled up to the clubhouse, my phone rang. It was Father Flagger.

"I hope you're not about to hit the ball," he said.

"Nope. Just pulling up to the clubhouse."

"How's the trip?"

"Refreshing. Until this morning, I haven't thought much about Chicago. But I heard about Alicia Roscati."

"Tragic," Father Flagger said. "I've met her several times at events. Sweet girl. The real deal. But God has a bigger plan for all of us. Anyway, I called about what we talked about before you left. He called me back and said he's willing to talk on the phone. He doesn't want to go on camera."

"Morgan can probably do the interview over the phone," I said. "I've seen it done many times. Have you called her?"

"He doesn't want to speak to her. He wants to talk to you."

"With all due respect, Father, this isn't my case or my story. I don't have any skin in the game."

"It's you or no one. He Googled you. He knows who you are. He feels comfortable talking only to you."

I felt myself getting dragged into something I had no desire to get in the middle of. All I wanted to do was play some golf, figure out what I would do with Julia, and keep Morgan from getting hurt on my watch.

"It's just one phone call," Father Flagger said, sensing my hesitancy. "He's very upset about all of this. You really could make a difference."

"Fine," I said, almost regretting it the second I agreed to it. "Text me his number, and I'll call him when my round is over."

"He prefers to call you. Can I give him your number?"

"Sure, but tell him I'll be tied up for the next four hours."

"Hit 'em long," he said. "Isn't that what you're supposed to say before someone starts playing?"

"Long is only good when it's straight," I said.

"Okay. Then long and straight."

"From your mouth to God's ears."

One of the valet boys opened my door when I put the phone down and informed me that my bag had been set up on a cart. I walked into the enormous clubhouse and had just entered the men's locker room when my phone rang again. It was Morgan.

"I hope you're having a great time down there playing golf while the rest of us are trying to survive," she said.

"Golf, daily massages, and a personal chef at the ready. All in balmy eighty-degree weather."

"I'm glad this is all a big joke to you."

"What's the 'all'?"

"My personal safety, my career, poor Alicia found dead in her apartment. None of this seems to faze you."

"I'm fazed. You just can't see it through the phone, and I tee off in about half an hour."

"Well, you go and deal with more important things like pars and birdies. I hope I'm alive when you get back."

"If your news gig doesn't work out, you should try the stage. You have a natural flair for the dramatic."

"Well, things just got even more complicated. Now that Alicia is gone, more people will watch her channel because they want to know what happened and who's going to replace her and all of the uncertainty. Always happens. Someone who people like watching suddenly leaves, and the ratings actually take a bump higher because viewers are curious."

"But that must be an artificial bump. It can't last for long."

"Depends on the circumstances. Knowing the news director over there, every night they'll play it to the max."

"Did she have some medical condition?"

"Not that I've heard. She was very healthy. Worked out every day. Ran the half marathon every year. Mostly a pescatarian. Meditated in her office before every newscast."

"Well, not to sound insensitive, but this means the coast is now clear for you."

"That's very insensitive and very wrong. Now more than ever I will need to be at my best. The scrutiny on me and what I do will be even greater. I need this sweeps story to be a blockbuster. Everything is riding on it."

I considered telling her about Flagger's informant who would be calling me later but thought better of it. I wanted to see what he had to say first, then decide what I would do.

"How's it going with Nettles and Knight?" I asked.

"Slow. I've made official requests through Media Relations. No one has gotten back to me. One of my sources said she might be able to get their cell phones. She's working on it for me. If you were here instead of down there leading the life of luxury, you could help me."

"I am helping you."

"How?"

"By making sure Mechanic and Rox keep you alive so you can keep collecting that million-dollar salary."

PART II

21

I had just gotten out of the sauna in the men's locker room and was about to grab my clothes from my locker when my phone rang. The call came from a restricted number. I picked up. It was a man's voice, deep and steady.

"Padre told you I'd be calling," he said.

"He did," I said. "*El hombre sin nombre.*"

"I don't speak Spanish."

"I just figured, you calling him 'padre' and all."

"You're a funny guy. Padre is his nickname. He said you tended to be a little loose, and I shouldn't be put off by it."

"Are you?"

"Not at all. But I'm calling about something serious."

"I know you are. I'm listening."

"Reece didn't do what they said he did."

"Were you there?"

"No, I hadn't gotten there yet. I was still at Mahalia Jackson Park. All of us were at the game. Men's thirty-five-and-over basketball league. One of our boys stays over that way, so we were heading over there to get something to eat and chill a little bit. I was on my way over there when I got the call they shot Reece."

"They're saying he pulled a gun."

"Man, that's bullshit. You know that's what they always tryna say when they shoot us for no reason. Reece ain't never held a gun in his life. He won't like that. I've been friends with him since first grade. Reece ain't never been in no trouble and didn't want no trouble. He was a ballplayer and ladies' man. That's it. No drugs. No gangs. No nothin'. Ball and pussy. That's all he ever cared about."

"So what do you think happened?"

"I ain't got no idea. They tryna play it off like he looked like some suspect they were looking for. C'mon, man. Reece don't look like nobody but Reece. Handsome. Clean-cut. Always dressed right. Reece won't lookin' like a suspect. They made that shit up."

"He have any beefs with anybody?"

"Nope. I'm tryna tell you. He ain't that dude. He got along with everybody. People liked to talk to him, be around him. He was always positive. Minded his own business. Made good money working streets and sans with the county. Owned his apartment. Had two cars. Reece was clean. We all looked up to him the way he did things right."

"Well, if what you're saying is true, and I believe you, then somebody wanted him bad. A cop doesn't just roll up and shoot an innocent guy, especially when there are witnesses around. There has to be more to it."

"I don't know the motivation," he said. "But I know there's video that shows what happened. And what it shows ain't gonna match what the cops are saying in the press."

"Someone has phone video?"

"No, the old lady across the street has a security camera. Right before I got to the scene, someone said the cops knocked on her door and took the memory stick with the video on it."

"You sure?"

"Was Obama the first Black president?"

"Not if you ask Bill Clinton."

"What the hell that mean?"

"Forget it. You're too young to understand. Will you tell me your name?"

"Not right now. My name don't really matter. The information is what's important."

"How about the name of the lady who they took the video from?"

"Mrs. Cooper. She's the secretary over at Fellowship Baptist Church."

"Thanks for the call. I'll dig around and see what I find."

"One more thing," he said. "I don't know if this means anything, but Reece was messin' around with some lady cop. He was seeing her for about six months."

"You know her name?"

"Nope. But I heard she was fine as hell."

I DROVE BACK TO PENNY'S estate trying to keep my mind off Chicago and focus on my vacation. The staff had prepared a late lunch and set up a table near a large window that overlooked an enormous garden. The cool air felt good as the sun blazed down through the cloudless sky. I had another round of golf planned later that afternoon, but first I would take a quick nap, maybe even get a little massage, then head back to the course. I had just taken the last bite of my grilled salmon when my phone rang. I didn't recognize the number. I almost let it go to voicemail but answered it anyway.

"This is Isaac Johnson," the caller said. "Head of security at WLTV. You have a minute?"

"Sure. What's going on?"

"We have a situation here."

"'Here' meaning?"

"The station. Another message just got delivered about an hour ago. A dozen red roses with a card that said, 'You're next, bitch.'"

The first thought that came to mind was that Alicia Roscati was murdered, and this was a message saying Morgan was next. Why?

"Where's Morgan?" I asked.

"In her office. They just finished their news meeting. She doesn't know about the flowers or the message."

"Okay, take me through the delivery."

"About an hour ago, a messenger shows up at the front desk. He announces himself through the intercom. The security guard on duty buzzes him in. He's carrying a vase of roses. He drops the flowers off and leaves. I opened the card and found the message."

"Who have you told so far?"

"Rebecca knows, and I called Detective Torres."

"What's the name of the floral company?"

"Don's Flowers. It's a small shop over in Bucktown. Torres is following up with them as we speak."

"Morgan usually goes out to dinner," I said. "Don't let her leave the building. I need to call Mechanic. I want him inside with her the entire time she's there."

"We're bringing in two more security guards. We're putting another one up front and another one stationed in the garage."

"Good. That will definitely help."

"When are you coming back?"

"Mechanic will coordinate everything until then. Don't worry. She's in good hands."

22

The next morning, we were seated around a glass table next to a wall of windows overlooking the calm expanse of Lake Michigan. It had been less than twenty-four hours, and the heat and desert of Arizona already felt like it was a universe away. Morgan was dressed in some snazzy bodysuit looking not a dollar short of a million.

"I can't believe it's possible someone killed her," Morgan said, looking out the windows. "They want me next."

"They won't get you," I said.

She turned and looked at me. She wore little if any makeup, yet her skin was still flawless. "If they could get to her, what's to stop them from getting to me?"

"You're looking at him."

She tried to smile. "I'm really glad you're back. Mechanic and Rox have been wonderful, but I didn't feel good with you being so far away. The earlier messages bothered me, but now with Alicia murdered, I'm really scared."

"Understandable. It's a scary situation. But as long as you follow our safety precautions, you'll be fine."

"Someone told me she'd been receiving threats too. Very similar to mine."

"Who's that someone?"

"A friend of her producer. Alicia started receiving threats about the same time I did. The station didn't give her more security or anything. I don't even know if they called the police." Morgan looked out the windows again and shook her head. "Now look at what's happened. They must be sick to their stomachs over there knowing they could've done more to protect her."

"Did you ever talk to Alicia?"

"Sure," Morgan said. "We were rivals, but we weren't enemies. We would see each other out at galas or dinner. We always spoke, chatted for a few minutes, took pictures together. She was a sweet enough girl. Very likeable. But I still wasn't going to let her beat me. I've worked too hard to get where I am."

"I talked to Johnson," I said. "He's doubling up security. Rox and Mechanic will remain in the station with you the entire time. I will alternate into the shifts also. You'll be fully covered."

She sighed and shook her head. "As if I didn't have enough stress trying to get this story together. Now this."

"How's the story going?"

"Rebecca wants to kill the piece."

"Why?"

"She says with all that's going on, now is not the time."

"Maybe she's right."

"Not at all. This is absolutely the time. Alicia's death or murder, whatever it is, will dominate the news cycle for months. This story has enough heat to break through the chatter."

I told her about my call with Reece's friend.

"Why were you keeping something like this from me? This could be critical."

"I wanted to check it out first. See if there was anything to it."

"And?"

"I haven't had a chance to follow up."

"Can I talk to this man?"

"I don't have his name or number."

"So how will you find him?"

"I won't have to. He'll find me when he's ready to talk again."

DON'S FLOWERS OCCUPIED A SLIVER of space a few doors down from one of my favorite Japanese restaurants, Kamahachi. Its narrow window had been crammed with an assortment of colorful flowers that gave the otherwise drab building a feel of vibrancy. An old Asian man with an easy smile greeted me as I entered the shop.

"Are you Don?" I asked.

He smiled. "I'm Hiro. The owner. Don owned the business many years ago. How can I help you?"

"My name is Ashe Cayne," I said, handing him one of my cards. "I wanted to ask you about a delivery you made yesterday."

"Was this the dozen roses that went to the TV station?"

I nodded. "How did you know?"

"The police already came here yesterday and talked to me about it. Two detectives. Do you work with them?"

"Something like that," I said. "But I'm really working for the woman who was sent the flowers."

"I'm sorry for such a mean message," he said, shaking his head. "I only print out the message that is sent in the order. That is what they sent me."

"Who's 'they'?"

"The internet company."

"Internet?"

"Half our business is online. People don't come to see the

flowers or smell them like they used to. Everything is faster on the computer."

"So it's through your website?"

"We have a website, but we don't take the orders through it. We just show the flowers we have available."

"So how do you get orders?"

"Someone goes online and finds a company they want to order flowers from. But these places aren't floral shops. They're brokers. Hundreds if not thousands of them. They handle the transaction, then they email us the order information and what the message is supposed to be on the card. Sometimes there's no message, just a name. This time there was no name but a message."

"Can you track who made the order with the broker?"

"Not really. The broker gives us the delivery address of the recipient. They don't give us the name or any information about the person who placed the order. I guess we could always ask them for that information, but we've never had to."

"What's the name of the broker for this order?"

Hiro scribbled something on a small card and handed it to me. *Flowers of Joy.*

"Have you done a lot of business with them?" I asked.

"One of my best customers," he said. "We've had a relationship for several years. They send me business almost every day. Unfortunately, without the brokers, we couldn't stay in business."

"Does the person who delivered the flowers work for you, one of your employees?"

"No. He works for the courier service we use. They have many drivers and messengers. They come to pick up the flowers and then go make the delivery."

"Is there a contact person at the company you talk to?"

"No, we only talk through email."

"Can I get their address?"

"It's easy. Info-at-Flowers-for-Joy-dot-com."

I didn't have great expectations of getting much from a company that existed only online. Some guy in his boxers living in a one-bedroom apartment over a hardware store in Montana was probably the brains behind the operation. I called Rox since she was in the flower business and explained the situation to her. She confirmed my suspicions and assured me I wouldn't get any kind of response from the online company. And that I was probably wrong about it being based in Montana. It was probably run out of some obscure bare-walled office in Southeast Asia.

I had just gotten into the car when my phone rang. It was Burke.

"How was your desert vacation?" he asked.

"Warm, relaxing, and too short."

"And your prima donna?"

I updated him on the roses, the message, and the increased security. I then told him about the conversation I had with the anonymous caller.

"So where's the video card now?" Burke asked.

"If I had to guess, probably at the bottom of Lake Michigan or buried under a mountain of trash at the city dump."

"I spoke with someone who saw the case report," Burke said.

"And?"

"Straightforward stuff. No smoking gun."

"How close is your source?"

"Right there in the office. Nettles and Knight have been partners for seven years. Mankovich works out of the Sixth District with them, but his partner was on furlough that week, so he rode along with those two. They were working third shift. That night, they were out trying to bag sacks and heads. They got a call about a low-level dealer that had been under surveillance for several months. Their lieutenant had given marching orders to the entire department. They needed more heads in custody. HQ was turning up pressure because they felt the numbers around the city were too low. Usual shit during an election year. Call comes out over the radio. These three responded. They were given an address. They were only a few blocks away. They arrived at the location and found Williams. He fit the description. They told him to put his hands up. He reached for something in his waistband. They saw a gun. Mankovich fired at him twice."

"And the other guys never fired their service weapons?"

"Nope. Just Mankovich."

"Doesn't sound right," I said. "If Reece had a gun, and they all saw the gun, and they all had their weapons pointed at him, why was Mankovich the only one who fired?"

"Maybe he saw the gun first, so he fired first."

"I'm not buying it. You've got three guys. All veterans. They're on a hunt. Juice is flowing. They have a target about to pull a gun on them. The threat is imminent and deadly. Maybe all three of them might not have fired, but you have to think given the circumstances at least two of them would. And let's say the two don't fire at the same time. Mankovich is the first to see and process the gun, so he fires first. At least one of the other guys would've fired right after, if not because they saw the gun then because they heard the pop of another gun. But with all that, Mankovich is the only guy who fired? Nope. Doesn't register for me."

Burke remained silent.

"Then you have two people with information," I continued. "Both insist Reece never owned or carried a gun, and he definitely didn't have one that night. Somebody swipes the security camera footage from the old lady across the street. Who knows where the hell that is? Was there any bodycam footage?"

"Nothing to corroborate what you or the witnesses are saying," Burke said. "They all had bodycams, but they didn't turn them on until the target was already on the ground, and they were trying to stop the bleeding."

"Convenient. Which is why they took the old lady's footage. Probably showed every second from the time they pulled up to the time they bagged the kid. There's gotta be more in the report. Let me read it."

"I haven't even read it myself. I can't go near it. I'd leave fingerprints. And I definitely can't get near the IA report. They have it locked away behind the wall."

"Can you find out the IA lead on it?"

"I can ask around."

"What about the Roscati case?"

"There is no case. She's still on the slab."

"There will be."

"What do you know?"

"Morgan Shaw got another threat. This time sent with a dozen roses. The message was simple. She's next."

"Jesus Christ. This is gonna be a shit show."

"That's the eloquent way of putting it."

"Your client is not only being stalked and harassed by some psycho, but she's also sniffing around the Williams case that could set off a bomb in this city. You really know how to pick 'em."

"She's tenacious and determined to get this story. At first I had my doubts there was anything to this story, but things aren't adding up for me either. I don't know exactly what it is, but there's something wrong, and what they're feeding to the press is bullshit. This was no case of mistaken identity or the belief that Reece had a gun. I think Mankovich answered that call and went there with one specific purpose, and that was to kill Reece Williams."

"Gonna be damn near impossible to prove that."

"Impossible never stopped me before. I like my odds."

23

I'm trying to forgive you for coming back home and not seeing me until the twenty-third hour," Carolina said. We were sitting at a high-top table at Pops for Champagne, sipping from a five-hundred-dollar bottle of Jacques Selosse. "This is one way to start the process." She tapped her glass against mine and took a shallow sip.

Champagne was not my first choice of drink, but there was something uniquely celebratory watching the fizzy bubbles work their way to the top of the glass. I knew how much she liked it, so I tolerated it more than I enjoyed it.

"I haven't stopped running since I got back," I said.

"I didn't expect you back for another several weeks."

"I'll get to that in a minute," I said. "But first, I want you to know I made a decision about Julia."

"Do I need to pull out my package of tissues?"

"Only if you cry when you're happy."

She gave me a huge, delicious smile.

"I'm going to meet with Julia," I said.

"That's a good place to start."

"And so are you."

Her eyes widened.

"You meeting Julia and her knowing that you exist is important," I said. "I want her to see you so she knows you're real. That what I feel for you is real."

"I don't know what else to say other than this is an unconventional approach."

I slid my hand across the table and rested it on hers.

"You can say that I'm an out-of-the-box thinker and determined and smart and the sexiest man you know."

"Then you would never be able to walk out of here tonight."

"Why's that?"

"Because your ego wouldn't fit through the door."

She leaned in to me, ran her hand slowly down the back of my neck, and kissed me softly on the lips. I opened my mouth and accepted her.

When we had explored the limits of what was acceptable given our proximity to other diners, I said, "Now the reason why I'm back so early." I told her about the flowers sent to Morgan, the message, and the trip to Don's. I told her how Morgan insisted on being able to finish this piece about Reece in time for the November sweeps. I also filled her in on the caller who was Reece's friend.

"Is she doing this to help bring justice to him and his family, or is she doing it for ratings?" Carolina asked.

"I think it's both. She definitely thinks this story is important for her career, but she's also disgusted that this unarmed guy was shot and killed by the police for reasons that have yet to be explained."

"What are you going to do?"

"What I always do."

"It was stupid of me to even ask."

I smiled. "I need your help."

"Hence the expensive champagne and soft lighting. You're trying to ply me with drink so you can take advantage of me."

"There could be worse things."

She smiled and took another sip of champagne.

I said, "It would be nice . . ."

"To get the case file from the Reece Williams shooting," she said.

"Only you can finish my sentences."

"And only you can get me to consider doing things that could get me arrested five times over."

"I tried Burke, but it's too hot for him to get near it. You can work your magic without raising any alarms."

She looked pensive. "I've never said no to you before," she said.

"But?"

"This is gonna be tricky, even for me."

"I need that file. Something has to be in there, but I won't know unless I read it myself."

She sighed softly. "I have a friend who owes me a favor. She's an admin. Give me a little time to figure this out."

WHEN I GOT HOME THAT night, Stryker was at the door waiting to go out. I dropped the mail on the kitchen counter and took him out into the crisp night air. I decided to take him to a newly renovated dog park a couple blocks away. Two other dogs were chasing each other and tumbling. As I released Stryker's leash, my phone buzzed. It was a number I didn't recognize.

"This is Kurtis Lewis," the man said. "Hope I'm not catching you at a bad time."

"It's a perfect time," I said. "I'm just sitting here watching my dog run wild."

"Well, I think I might have something for you," he said. "I can't tell you which specific mailbox that letter was mailed from, but with a little luck and a little research, I can probably get you in the general area."

"How long will it take?"

"Probably a few days. We know the center where the envelope was processed. I can find out which drivers' routes get directed to that center. We also know the time the envelope was processed, so if we get lucky, we might be able to find out which trucks delivered into the center close to that time. Once we figure out the trucks, then we can find out their routes and what area they pick up from. That's probably the best we can do."

"If we find the general area, can we then find out how many mailboxes are in that vicinity?"

"It'll take a little work, but I'm up for the challenge."

"Anything I can do to help you get started?"

"No, just sit tight. One of my friends still works at the Elk Grove Village facility. He might know someone out at Carol Stream where your letter was processed. That will get the ball rolling."

There was something about the certainty in his voice that made me feel confident this would get me a step closer to identifying this psycho. My adrenaline suddenly surged thinking about dismantling him one broken limb at a time.

I THOUGHT THE RING WAS in my dream. It kept ringing and wouldn't stop. I turned over, but it wouldn't go away. Finally, my eyes opened in the still of the darkness. The ringing continued. My phone. I reached over and picked it up. Stryker stirred at my feet.

"I want to meet with you," the caller said. I knew right away it was Reece's friend. He sounded anxious, unsettled.

"It's three o'clock in the morning," I said.

"I'm sorry, man, but I can't sleep. I can't stop thinking about Reece and what happened. It's killing me. I gotta talk to somebody."

"When do you wanna meet?"

"Ten o'clock at the church?"

"Which church?"

"Padre's. He said it was okay if we meet there."

24

St. Sebastian Church was a typical Catholic colossus—a Gothic soaring pile of old limestone, spires, and ornately fenestrated towers spanning an entire square city block in the hardscrabble Auburn Gresham neighborhood. Started as a storefront church serving Irish immigrants in the early 1900s, it became the church of African Americans during the Civil Rights Era and the tumultuous sixties. Like most of the South Side, white residential flight created a vacuum filled by the Black families who had arrived from the Deep South during the Great Migration.

I found an unlocked door and entered an enormous vaulted nave that transported me from the gritty Chicago streets outside to what the great Roman basilicas looked like thousands of miles away. Stained glass windows, expansive arcades, elevated niches with marble sculptures—it was impossible not to feel small and ordinarily human amid the architectural splendor. The lights were off, but the morning sun beamed in through a long, uninterrupted line of arched windows. A lone figure sat on the aisle in a middle pew. I walked toward him. After several steps in, I heard the clatter of a heavy lock behind me and turned to find a small, hunched-over woman in the shadows walking away after dead-bolting the door shut.

I slid into the pew behind the man, bowed my head toward the altar, and closed my eyes the way my mother always did every time she entered a church. The man didn't turn toward me. He wore a white baseball cap with long braids sticking out from underneath. His thick gray hoodie bunched around his shoulders.

"Quite a church," I said once I had finished praying. "First time I've ever been here."

"Padre always does it right," the man said. "I've been sitting in this sanctuary since I was a little boy. Got baptized here. Padre looks out for all of us. He doesn't care where we come from or what we look like. He's always here for us."

"Did Reece come here?"

"No, he went to Fellowship. His grandmother was a Baptist. My grandmother was Catholic. But they were best friends from way back."

"What's stopping you from sleeping?"

"I just can't take this anymore," he said. "I'm angry and frustrated, and I feel guilty about what they did to Reece. I'm about to lose my shit."

"Guilty?"

"I should've been there with him."

"You didn't know this was going to happen."

"I didn't, but I should've been there. Reece asked me to ride over with him after the game. But I was trying to holler at this little shorty. I ain't seen her for a while since we messed around back in the day. She was looking good as hell that night. So I wanted to see what was up. We talked a little, then I left to meet Reece. They said I got there five minutes after they killed him. He was already on the ground. They wouldn't let me get near him. I could see the blood spilling out of him onto the sidewalk." He lowered his head and closed his eyes. "I missed saving my friend's life by five fuckin' minutes. I can't stop thinking about how little time that is. Now Reece's gone for good."

"You can't beat yourself up about this," I said. "There's no guarantee you could've stopped it. They might've shot you too."

He shook his head. "Nah, if I had been there, nobody would've gotten shot. Cowards like that only flex when they got lopsided numbers. They cornered him alone like a damn animal hunt. Unarmed. Minding his own business. They just ran up on him like that."

"Any talk out there?"

"Ain't none really. Nobody can figure it out. Nobody knows what Reece could've done to make them do that. Some people talking about killin' that muthafucka. They moved his ass up north to protect him."

"Maybe Reece had something going on with Mankovich and nobody knew about it."

"Like I said before, Reece wasn't that type. He didn't beef with nobody. Never. He just wasn't that kind of guy."

"Anyone in the neighborhood ever see those officers before?"

"Couple of guys said they knew the first two. They come around now and again tryna get people to snitch. But ain't nobody got nothin' to say to 'em. Still, they was all right as far as cops go. For the most part, they didn't do much. They left people alone."

"What about Mankovich?"

"Nobody ever saw him before."

"How many people were there that night?"

"When they shot him?"

"Yes."

"Four people were actually there. Outside."

"Did they all see the shooting?"

He nodded. "Yup, all of 'em. Car just rolled up out of nowhere, ran over the curb, and Reece backed up against the fence."

"What else did they say?"

"Same thing I already told you. They got out with their guns and just shot 'em without saying a word."

"How many shot their weapons?"

"Just the guy from the back seat."

"Nobody got anything on their cell phones?"

He shook his head. "Not the shooting. Soon as they heard the shooting, everybody started running. They didn't know what the hell was going on. When it stopped, that's when a couple of people came out the houses and took out their phones."

"Have you seen the footage?"

"Yeah, but it doesn't show much."

"Can you get it for me?"

"Yeah. One guy shot it from his house, and a girl shot it from across the street."

"Does Reece have family?"

"He's got an older brother, but they ain't close. Larry's been on drugs since he was fifteen. Reece ain't seen him for probably ten years or more. He got a younger sister—Gina. She stays over in Englewood with her two kids."

"Parents?"

"Father got killed when he was in high school. His mother's still around, but they always had a jacked-up relationship. She abandoned him. His grandmother raised him. He didn't hate his moms or anything. He just didn't feel no kind a way about her. They talked every once in a while but nothing serious. His grandmother was his mother. She died from cancer a couple years ago."

"Tell me about this cop he was dating."

"Ain't much I can tell you. He met her at the gym. He asked her for her number, and she gave it to him. I told him to be careful messin' around with a cop. She might look good and shit, but she still police with a gun and a badge."

"Anybody know her name?"

"I don't, but I can ask around."

"Where did Reece live?"

"Over on Prairie and Fiftieth."

"Can you get me the sister's and mother's phone numbers?"

"Done."

"Who has access to his apartment?"

He turned toward me for the first time. His skin was dark and shiny. His eyes were tired and bloodshot as if he had been crying for weeks.

"My name is Earl," he said, reaching his hand out and shaking mine firmly. "Anything you need to help bring Reece justice, I can get for you."

GINA WILLIAMS LIVED IN THE garden apartment of a six-flat building deep in the heart of Englewood. Her youngest was home from school with an upset stomach. She reluctantly agreed to meet me but had invited me in when I arrived. It was too cold to stand outside and talk. I followed her into a tiny living room. She was dressed in a comfortable black sweatsuit, her maroon-streaked hair pulled back from her face and tied into a ponytail. She was an attractive woman with big brown eyes like her brother. I couldn't help but notice her perfectly manicured blue nails painted with geometric designs.

The sound of cartoons filtered in from a room down the hall. I heard the rumble of a dryer somewhere in the distance. The apartment was comfortably warm.

"I'm sorry about what happened," I said, taking a seat at a small table with a vase of plastic flowers at its center. "I know this isn't easy."

"When is this gonna stop?" she said, shaking her head. "The police can't keep doing this to our Black men and boys. Reece was a good person. Always an upstanding person. Wasn't in any gangs, never arrested before, no trouble ever. He liked basketball and girls. That's it. He worked every day. Paid child support on time for his children. The police gotta stop killing our people for no reason."

"Is it possible, and I'm only playing devil's advocate here, that he got mixed up in the wrong crowd? Maybe got caught up in drugs or something?"

Gina shook her head emphatically. "No way. Reece was never into that stuff. He was always on the straight. He had a good job with the county. Made good money. Whatever they're saying is nothing but lies. They got some nerve. First, they kill him for no reason, then they try to kill his character."

"They said he pulled a gun out of his waistband."

"Another lie. Reece didn't own a gun and probably never shot a gun his entire life. They always think we're stupid. Making up shit to cover their asses."

"Have you talked to the police?"

"I tried, but what they're saying doesn't make sense. Reece matched the description of someone they were looking for. He pulled a gun, so they shot him before he could shoot them. I've been over there twenty times. Asked to talk to a supervisor, someone in charge. They keep saying no one is available, but someone will get in touch with me. I haven't heard from anybody. The NAACP is helping me find a lawyer to fight this, but they said this could take years depending on what the police do."

"And your mother? Is she helping you?"

Gina lowered her eyes. "My mother is different," she said. "She didn't raise us. Granny did. My mother doesn't believe what they said either, but she ain't trying to fight it. She's angry too, but she's just accepting it."

"Do you know any of the women Reece might've been close to?"

"I know he was popular with women, but I never met any. Reece always had someone. He was really handsome. Had his own money. Not like a lot of these men out here still living with their mother and don't own anything. He was a good catch."

"Did you know he was seeing a cop?"

"Who told you that?"

"Earl."

She smiled softly. "Well, if Earl said it, then it's true. He would know. They've been friends forever."

"Who's in charge of all your brother's possessions?"

"We're still trying to figure all that out. We don't think Reece had a will. So I guess his kids get everything, but his son is only thirteen, and his daughter is sixteen. Hopefully the lawyer can help us with all that stuff too."

"Earl said he owned an apartment."

"He did and paid it off in five years. His car too. Reece had good credit. He didn't like debt."

"What's going on with the apartment?"

"Nothing right now. It's just sitting there."

"Have you been to it?"

"Only to pick out a suit so we could bury him. That was months ago. Nobody's been there since."

"Would you be able to take me there?"

"What are you looking for?"

"I want to see if he had any security cameras."

"I know he did," she said. "I saw one when I walked up the front steps."

If I was lucky, the unidentified girlfriend cop would no longer be a mystery.

25

Robert Leeder's column appeared as a front-page story in the *Sun-Times*. "Roscati Threatened before Death." The article quoted her producer as saying the anchorwoman had received three letters—two sent to her Gold Coast apartment and one to the station. They had been received over the last couple of months. The medical examiner was waiting on the results of bloodwork to determine cause of death, but so far it appeared there was no foul play involved.

I picked up my phone and called Torres. His phone went to voicemail, so I left a message. I then tried the main number to WMTQ and asked to speak to Tyra Martin. After a couple of transfers, a woman answered the phone. I was surprised I had gotten her so easily. I told her my name.

"Ashe Cayne from the Parker case?" she said.

"The one and only," I said. "I was hoping I could talk to you about Alicia."

"What did you want to talk about?"

"Those letters she received."

"This is a police investigation now," she said.

"Were they investigating the letters before she died?"

Martin paused for a moment then said, "I really can't talk right now."

"Can you talk later?"

"Not while I'm here. After work. I'll be done after the five o'clock show."

"Where can we meet?"

"Moneygun over on Lake Street. Six o'clock. It's dark in there. The booths are very private."

"How will I be able to tell it's you?"

"Don't worry. I know very well what you look like. Everyone in the business does."

I CHANGED INTO MY RUNNING gear and made my way outside. The air was cold and heavy, the sky a dyspeptic gray. It had been almost two weeks since I had gone for a run, something my body impolitely reminded me of within the first quarter mile. The path around the lake was unusually quiet, which I welcomed because fewer distractions meant I would be able to get into a rhythm and stay there. A good cadence had a way of numbing the mind and making the run appear faster.

I allowed myself to get lost in the ambient sounds, rubber tires speeding by on the cold asphalt of Lake Shore Drive. Over my other shoulder, the loud clap of waves crashed relentlessly against the unprotected shoreline. My breathing grew rhythmic, my stride stretching at a familiar pace. The air felt good rushing into my lungs, a little burn at the end of each inhalation. By the time I looked down at my watch, I was already two and a half miles out. I made a loop and headed back. My breathing and heart rate had settled, and now it was easy, like putting a car on cruise control. As I completed the five miles, my legs felt alive, my head a little tight from the cold. I left the path feeling reinvigorated and headed toward my building. My phone rang. It was Detective Torres.

"Things got a little interesting while you were away," he said.

"That's one way of putting it," I said.

"We're not taking any chances," he said. "For the next couple of days we're putting an unmarked outside of her building and one outside of the station."

I couldn't help but think of the irony. Morgan was working her hardest to air a story that aimed to expose police malfeasance. Meanwhile, they were doubling their efforts to keep her safe.

"I assume your team is on high alert," Torres said.

"All hands on deck," I said. "Are you hearing anything about the Roscati case?"

"ME hasn't come back with anything official, but word is they haven't found anything yet. The letters she received are a new development."

"Anyone know about the letters before she died?"

"Not sure. They're working it out of the Nineteenth."

"Who's lead?"

"Guy named Vreeland. Twenty-year vet. He's as solid as they come. He's coming to see me later this afternoon."

"I'm curious about the letters," I said.

"They're at the top of my list."

"Let me know if they have the same Carol Stream postmark."

"You're all in my head."

MONEYGUN WAS DOING BRISK BUSINESS by the time I walked in a few minutes before six. Tupac's "California Love" piped over the din of the bar. I wasn't able to find a photograph of Tyra Martin online, so I wasn't sure what she looked like. I scanned the expanse of the semicircular bar but didn't see any single women nursing a drink. I walked along the perimeter and a row of banquets, but everyone seated was already in pairs. I walked toward the back and found a woman sitting by herself in a large booth with a drink in front of her typing on a phone. She looked up and smiled as I approached. She had short, straightened hair that had been curled at the ends and rich chocolate skin set off by her black rectangular glasses. She looked serious and much more attractive than I expected for someone who did her work behind the camera.

She offered her hand and a smile as I took a seat.

"What are you drinking?" I asked.

"Sazerac," she said.

"Whiskey or cognac?"

"I'm a cognac girl," she said. "Whiskey is for those who've never tried cognac."

I liked her already. My father would like her too.

The waitress came to take my drink. I looked at Tyra.

"He'll take a sidecar," she said. "Make it with Remy."

"Come here often?"

"More often this time of year. Our ratings period starts soon. The stress in the newsroom goes up by at least a thousand percent."

"Sweeps," I said.

"Look at you knowing the lingo." She smiled. "You've been hanging around Morgan too much. You must have your hands full with her." She rolled her eyes.

"How did you know I was working with her?"

"Because I work in news where there are no secrets. Word travels faster than that eighty-six Porsche you drive."

I smiled and nodded. Tyra was definitely not a rookie.

"Do you think Morgan knew about the letters Alicia received?"

"No, only three of us in our newsroom knew, but we didn't make a big deal about it. It wasn't the first time she'd received letters like that. The others in the past were even worse."

"I didn't know the news business was so dangerous."

"It's gotten worse over the last few years. The perverts and psychos are more emboldened than ever because they can hide behind social media. They say and do whatever they want because no one will go after them. We cover a story they don't like or interview someone they disagree with politically, and our social media is scorched with all kinds of nastiness. People have lost their minds these days. If we followed up on every threat or crazy post, we'd have to dedicate our entire news team to chasing down all the madness, and that still wouldn't be enough to stop it."

The waitress returned with my drink. Tyra and I tapped glasses and took a sip. The last time I'd had one of these was at the Ritz in Paris with my father. The hotel claimed they created the drink, but this version was just as good as theirs, if not better.

"I know it was common for your on-air talent to get harassed by the crazies, but did your station provide Alicia with any kind of protection?" I asked.

"The station isn't gonna protect someone around the clock," Tyra said. "News people aren't presidents or heads of state. Security is tight around the station. She never went out on stories alone. But if you're asking whether she had someone traveling with her every second she wasn't working, the answer is she did not. No one does."

"The newspaper said you found the body. What happened?"

Tyra closed her eyes and exhaled slowly. "I got a call from Alicia late morning. She does the ten o'clock broadcast, so she doesn't get into the office til early afternoon. She didn't sound like herself. She said she wasn't feeling well. She was nauseous, her stomach hurt, and she had numbness and tingling in her legs. She said she was too weak to get up, so she was going to stay in bed and get some rest. I asked her if she had called her doctor or needed to go to the emergency room. She said it wasn't a big deal. She was just tired, and her body was telling her she needed a break. I told her to call me later that day if she was up to it, but otherwise, I would check on her in the morning. I didn't hear from her all night. I sent her a text message before I went to bed just to check on her. Next morning, I got up and still didn't have a response from her. I waited a few hours and called her. She didn't pick up. I went to work and started answering emails and looking through the wires for stories I could put into the show that night. She's usually at work at the latest one or one thirty. By two o'clock I didn't hear from her. Then the three o'clock meeting came, and she still hadn't come in. She never misses that meeting. Once the meeting was over, I jumped in the car and went to her building. The doorman said he hadn't seen her leave that day, and he called the overnight doorman who said she hadn't left the night before either. We went upstairs. They let me in. I found her in her bed. She was under the covers. Her body was cold. Her arms were stiff. She had been dead for a while."

"Everything looked normal in her apartment?"

"I didn't walk around the apartment, but nothing looked strange from what I remember. But it's all such a blur. I wasn't really paying attention to anything but her body."

"Do you think she was killed by the person sending her those letters?"

"Why do you think she was killed?"

"Because Morgan received similar letters."

I could tell in her eyes that what I had just said genuinely took her by surprise. "When did that happen?"

"Last few months or so."

"I remember she had a stalker who actually got sent away. Didn't he just get out of prison a few months ago?"

"Can we go off the record?" I said.

Tyra smiled. "We're sitting in the back of a dark bar after work drinking cognac with Notorious singing 'One More Chance,' and you want to know if we can go off the record. News flash, Ashe Cayne. This entire conversation has been off the record."

"Fair enough," I said. "Morgan started receiving similar letters about a couple of weeks after he got out. But it was more than the letters. Her car was vandalized, and she was sent a box of floggers."

"Floggers as in sex floggers?"

"Presumably."

"Not surprising."

"Why do you say that?"

"Because Morgan has always been, let's just say, active."

"She's that indiscreet?"

"Morgan is a master at crafting an image for her legion of fans. But the rest of us are real journalists. The very essence of our jobs is to be nosy, ask questions, share information. Don't get me wrong. Morgan is the best at what she does, and she's worked very hard to get where she is. But she's human just like the rest of us, and she's not without faults or needs. Morgan likes to fuck. That's not a crime."

"Does she know that you all know?"

"Of course she does. Rivals or not, we all talk. You can't fool the very same people who've helped you get to the top. She's never tried to hide it from us. Before Morgan got her first big contract, she was propping her image up just like anyone else. I'll never forget shopping with Alicia once over at Neiman's. She had to host the Discovery Ball and needed a new gown. One of the saleswomen and I were just chatting while Alicia tried on dresses. She told me they all would avoid helping Morgan because once she wore a dress to an event, she'd return it the next day with the tags still hanging as if she hadn't worn it, stains on the armpits. Morgan's a sucker for men who are either rich or powerful or both."

"Do you know any of her latest conquests?"

"I've heard names floated, but personally I can't confirm them. You never know what's true or the product of someone's overactive imagination. Being in the news business, I like to see the evidence before passing judgment."

"Do you think Alicia was on the verge of unseating Morgan?"

"Had Alicia not died, there's no doubt we were going to snatch the crown away from Morgan."

"But how are you so sure you were going to win?"

"Simple math. Alicia has been gaining ground every quarter for the last three years. The last big sweeps was May. We lost by less than a tenth of a point. Given the way we were trending, we were on course to win this November. Everyone gets the overnights. Everyone knew it was going to happen."

This confirmed that Morgan's fears of losing the ratings war were substantiated.

"What have the ratings been since Alicia died?" I asked.

"Through the roof," Tyra said. "Highest numbers ever. They moved our popular morning anchor, Art Normen, to the evenings. He won't be her permanent replacement, but he's a Chicago legend, and the viewers love him. We've won every night since he's been in the chair."

Morgan had predicted there would be a bump in their numbers. The real question was how long it would last.

"What's going to happen come November?" I asked.

"We're going to win."

"Even without Alicia?"

"Our bosses are distraught that Alicia died, and they're more determined than ever to win. The difference between being number one and two in our business is the difference between millions of ad dollars. They're hatching a plan as we speak to do something for November that has never been done before in the history of local television."

"Care to share?"

"You're very charming and very nice to look at." She smiled. "But that's something I can't tell even you."

26

She sounds like a complicated person," my father said. We sat in a pair of leather low-sitting chairs that straddled the ornate fireplace in his study. He always sat in the chair facing the wall of books. Many of them were rare, signed first editions, something he always found a way to remind me of at least once in the conversation.

"She's very driven," I said. "I still don't have her figured out. Everything is one big competition to her."

"Ambition by all accounts is admirable, but left unchecked it can bring a great amount of loneliness."

"Her work is her life. It's her true oxygen." I told him about the Reece Williams shooting, her determination to get the big scoop, and the ratings war.

"That Roscati death is really tragic," my father said. "I really enjoyed her. She was beautiful, but she had a folksiness about her, like someone who didn't always have to appear perfect."

"Very different from Morgan," I said. "Nothing folksy about her at all. She needs to own the room, and she wants you to know she does."

"I dated a reporter once," my father said. "Many years ago before your mother and I got serious. She was so beautiful she would stop traffic on Michigan Ave. But her ego. My God. The pure embodiment of narcissism. It only lasted about six months."

"What happened?"

"Well, I wasn't in short supply of confidence either. I had just finished my training and had become a junior attending at the university hospital. That was a big deal back then. Only three Black doctors on staff at the time. Both of our egos simply couldn't fit in the same room. I also felt like she was using me a little. I was good for her image. Young Black doctor with a good education and a tennis player to boot. I was good company at her fancy dinner parties."

I took a sip of cold root beer while my father took a long swallow of vintage cognac he had purchased a couple of years ago in the French countryside.

"You seem to be getting heavily invested in this Williams shooting," he said.

"You think so?"

"Seems that way. You were hired to protect Shaw from some creep sending her threatening letters, and now you're charging full speed into an investigation that's plenty her business but not yours."

"The fact that an unarmed man was shot point-blank without any legal justification makes it my business."

"You can't solve all the world's problems."

"True, but I can try to put a small dent in the ones I know about."

My father looked up at the wall of books. "You know, I have several signed first editions of Raymond Chandler up there," he said.

I knew this for sure. He had told me at least a hundred times.

"You should read *The Long Goodbye*," he said. "Some said it wasn't as good as the others, but Chandler himself said it was his best. It's been a long time since I read the book, but the plot from what I remember was a long zigzag, the way good mysteries are supposed to be written.

Makes me think of you and this anchorwoman. In the book, a drunk guy befriends Detective Marlowe and asks him for help. The detective agrees but insists he wants limited knowledge of the motivation behind the guy's request for help. Marlowe helps the guy get across the border to Tijuana, Mexico, only to find out upon his return to LA that the guy's wife was found dead in the guest house and had died before the guy fled. Marlowe now finds himself sucked into a murder case that he had no intention of being part of when he first agreed to help. Maybe Morgan Shaw's intentions weren't as transparent as they could've been. Maybe she hired you less because she needed protection and more because she needed your help in cracking this case."

What he said made complete sense, and it bothered me like hell to admit it, because he was always so damn smart.

EARLY IN THE MORNING, MECHANIC, Rox, and I sat in a coffee shop across the street from Morgan's building. Rox was taking first shift that day, while Mechanic and I planned on meeting Gina Williams at Reece's apartment. We were exchanging ideas about Morgan's harassment case and its parallels to Alicia Roscati. I told them about my meeting with Tyra Martin.

"Smile in your face, daggers in your back," Rox said. "Not surprised at all. That's par for the course for these TV personalities."

"Thanks for the golf metaphor," I said. "But what makes you say that?"

"I have a friend who's one of the hosts over at *Windy City Life*. He tells me all about the rivalries, the fighting, and the double crossing. At least with boxing, your opponent is standing right there in front of you and you can see the punches they throw. These guys are vicious. Smile in your face and plunge a dagger right between your shoulder blades when you turn around."

Windy City Life was a popular afternoon local TV program that mixed local news with entertainment. It was co-hosted by a handsome former sportscaster named Bryan Sheverini and a beautiful former traffic reporter named Valencia Werner. They had local and national guests and amusing segments, but I imagined most viewers were glued to their screens every afternoon to admire the incredibly attractive duo.

"Which host do you know?" I said.

"Bryan," Rox said. "I know every time he has a new model girlfriend because he comes into the shop to buy a couple dozen roses. People always say that women like to gossip. Men are just as bad. Bryan can talk you under a table."

"Has he ever said anything about Morgan or Alicia?"

"Nothing I specifically remember."

"Maybe Valencia and other anchorwomen around town received letters too but haven't talked about it," Mechanic said.

"I never thought about that," Rox said. "But I can ask Bryan. If anyone would know, I'd put my money on him."

GINA WAS JUST GETTING OUT of her car in front of Reece's apartment building as we pulled up. I had looked up information on the property. There were six apartments in total, two on each floor. The building was a typical Chicago affair—weathered brick, sparse in design, small patch of grass out front that looked like it hadn't been cut in over a month. Reece owned one of the apartments on the second floor. Mechanic and I joined her at the front gate. I made the requisite introductions, then we followed her up a couple of steps to the walkway that led to the front door. Gina opened the front door to a small foyer with a row of mailbox slits and plaster walls that were flaking and badly in need of fresh paint. She opened a second door, and we scaled the narrow, carpeted stairwell. The second we hit the mezzanine landing, I saw the camera.

"Does that camera belong to Reece?" I asked.

"I'm not sure," Gina said.

We continued walking up the next flight of steps.

"Camera two," Mechanic said.

A similar camera to the first was positioned in the corner of the ceiling facing the steps and landing. Gina opened the door marked 2A, and we followed her in. The apartment was dark and cold. My breath hung in the still air. Gina pulled up the curtains in the living room, which gave us enough light to see. The apartment was meticulously arranged and much bigger than I expected.

"Do you know where the recording box might be?" I asked.

"I have no idea," Gina said. "I only came in that one time to get his clothes and haven't been back since."

We walked down the hallway. A bedroom was situated to the right. It had a queen bed in it and a dresser with a small TV perched on top. We continued farther down the hall, which opened up to a kitchen on the left. A small table of laminated wood and four matching chairs had been set off near one wall, the stove and other appliances against another. Three windows looked out to the back of the property. I couldn't help but notice the curtains were very feminine and floral. I wondered if he had picked them out or if one of his girlfriends had marked her territory.

Past the kitchen there were two more bedrooms, one obviously the master with a king-size bed, posters of basketball players, and a framed Derrick Rose Chicago Bulls jersey. In the other bedroom sat a twin bed and a large barber chair.

"Reece used to cut hair on the side," Gina said as if reading my mind. "He was a barber before he got his job with the county."

I turned to Mechanic and said, "I'll start in the master bedroom, you start in the front bedroom. The DVR box has to be somewhere."

Mechanic turned and walked back down the hall. Gina stood behind me. I started in his closet, which was full of sneakers, some still in their boxes with the tags on them. The shirts and pants had all been color coordinated and neatly hung. I carefully moved things around, making sure I put everything back in order. The closet was empty. It was unlikely I would find anything in the drawers or under the bed, but I checked anyway. Once his room was cleared, I walked across the hall to the other bedroom. I started in the closet. It was full of winter coats and boots. I searched the shelves, but there was nothing but some folded T-shirts and sheets. I was just about to open the drawers when Mechanic appeared.

"Bingo," he said.

I turned to find him holding a memory card.

"Where did you find it?"

"With the mechanicals in a small closet on the other side of the kitchen."

"Was there a monitor with it?"

"A small one."

"Show me."

We walked to the small closet just big enough for me to squeeze in sideways. With no electricity in the apartment, the monitor was dark, as was the instrument panel on the DVR. I checked the memory slot and confirmed there was only room for one card. I backed out of the closet and closed the door.

"We have company," Mechanic said, peeping through the blinds of the living room window. Gina and I joined him. There was an unmarked parked behind my car. Its windows were tinted. A steady stream of exhaust flowed from the tailpipe.

"Someone called us in," I said. "Or they followed us. Either way, it's no coincidence they're here at exactly the same time we are."

"Maybe one of the neighbors heard us in here and got scared and called 911," Gina said. "Nobody's been in here for months."

"Possible," I said. "But we'll find out soon enough."

We waited five long minutes. No one got out of the car. It just sat there. Waiting. No movement at all.

"This wasn't a response to a breaking and entering call," I said. "They would've been in here by now."

"So why are they here?" Gina asked.

"We're about to find out."

"I'll take the back steps," Mechanic said. "You guys go out the front."

Mechanic opened the back door and headed down the porch. We locked the door behind him. Gina and I headed out the front. Her hand tightened as she locked the door. When we reached the foyer on the first floor, I said, "Stay inside until I come back and get you."

I saw the car through one of the small windowpanes flanking the front door. A couple of minutes later, I saw Mechanic making the turn around the corner at the end of the block. He started heading directly toward the car. He walked slowly. When he was two cars behind them, I opened the front door and walked out. I got halfway down the walkway when the car jerked off the curb and burned rubber. Mechanic walked into the middle of the road, his gun drawn tight against his right leg. He turned to me and nodded. He had gotten the license plate. I turned to Gina and motioned for her to come out.

"Who was that?" she asked when she reached me.

"Cops," I said.

"What do you think they wanted?"

"To send me a message."

"What's the message?"

"Watch your back. We know what you're doing."

27

Mechanic and I jumped into my car and headed back to the office to look at the video. I called Burke and gave him the license plate number. He said he'd have an answer within the hour. Carolina called in to let me know she had gotten a copy of the general case file which included the police shooting team's supplementary report. She would drop it off at the apartment later that night.

We got back to my office and plugged the memory card into an adapter, then into my computer. The first couple of attempts to open the files failed, but then I downloaded free software that was able to read the video format. The video popped up on my screen. The images were black and white, but they were clear. The video from the different cameras had been separated into two different strips. The monitor showed a slot for a third video strip, but it was blank.

"How many cameras did you see when we were at the apartment?" I asked.

"Two," Mechanic said. "One on the mezzanine and the second above his door."

"Did you see a third camera in the apartment?"

"Negative."

I shrugged it off. Maybe the system was set up for three cameras, but since he only had two, the third recording slot remained empty. I pushed the play button for the camera-one strip. According to the date stamp and time code, this went back a little more than two months before Reece was killed. This was the camera positioned on the mezzanine landing. I increased the playback speed, then froze the video frame when someone came into view. I printed the frozen images as still photos. The tape suddenly stopped, which made me think that was when the electricity had been turned off. I had been able to isolate and print forty-three different faces. Many of them had shown up multiple times, so I wrote on their photos how many times they had appeared in the video.

I pushed back from the computer, and Mechanic fell back into his chair. We looked out my window facing east overlooking Buckingham Fountain and across the lake. We sat there quietly for a few minutes until Mechanic said, "Needle in a haystack."

I kept thinking. There had to be a way to streamline the targets. Not everyone caught by the cameras had been going to Reece's apartment.

"The second camera will probably help us cut the numbers down," I said. "We should be able to see only those who stopped at his door and presumably went in."

I was just about to click the camera-two video strip when my phone rang. It was Burke.

"With two minutes to spare," I said, answering the phone.

"Just remember the information flows both ways," he said. "Are you sure you got the tag number correct?"

I covered the mouthpiece on my phone and said to Mechanic, "He's asking if you got the right tag number."

Mechanic responded exactly as I had expected. He continued looking at the lake without interruption.

"That's the tag for sure," I said.

"Well, that car is registered to a unit in the Sixth District," Burke said.

I wasn't surprised. That's what I expected. Mankovich, Nettles, and Knight were out of the Sixth District where Reece was killed. Reece's apartment, however, was in the Second District, so their visit was definitely intentional.

"A Sixth District car out on a field trip to the Second District," I said.

"I'm a step ahead of you," Burke said. "I already have a call in to find out which team was assigned to that car today. I should have the answer soon."

Were they watching Reece's apartment or were they tailing me? Either way, it was clear someone wasn't happy.

"This doesn't look good for the blue team," I said.

"No clue, Sherlock," Burke said, then hung up the phone.

"Camera two," I said, clicking the playback button.

Mechanic and I watched carefully. This view showed everyone who actually stopped at Reece's door. It also showed others who walked by and went up to the third floor or who were passing by on their way down from the third floor. By the time we had finished, we had printed twenty-three photographs. I kept track of how many times they appeared just as I had done with the previous photographs. Mechanic and I spread them out across my table.

"Reece was a busy man," Mechanic said.

"Basketball and girls," I said. "Both Earl and his sister said that's what he did."

I closely examined the photographs. Reece was an equal opportunity romancer. All races, all different ages, all very beautiful.

"Now you have your lineup," Mechanic said. "What next?"

"Tricky part," I said. "Figuring out which one of these women has her badge in her purse."

BY THE TIME I GOT back to my apartment building, Carolina was sitting in the lobby looking like she had just walked off the cover of a glossy fashion magazine. Her hair had been curled at the ends, and she wore makeup—something she rarely did. She looked delectable.

"Perfection personified," I said, walking up to her and giving her a soft kiss. "Are you coming up with me?"

"I wish I could." She smiled. "The girls and I are going out for drinks."

"Sure you don't need a chauffeur?"

"Maybe later tonight." She winked. She reached into her purse and pulled out an envelope. "In the meantime, reading this should keep you busy."

"Did you take a look at it?"

"I did."

"And?"

"I can't make much of it, but that doesn't mean anything. I don't read these often. Your eyes are much better than mine."

I smiled at her.

"Why are you looking at me like that?" she said.

"I really like what my eyes are seeing right now," I said. "I'm trying to figure out if I kidnap you right now and get caught, what's the chance of me just getting off with probation?"

"You wouldn't have to worry about that. In order to be charged with kidnapping, I'd have to be abducted against my will."

She pressed her lips softly against mine, then left me standing there in the lobby like a lost child looking for his parents.

I went up to my apartment, took Stryker out for a quick walk, then went to my computer and popped in Reece's memory card. I watched the video strips again, matching the faces with the photos I had printed, double-checking to make sure I hadn't missed anyone. This time, however, I made sure to record the date of the person's appearances and the time of day. I noticed Reece was not shy about having two different women in the same day—one in the morning and another that night. How did he have the energy to do that and still hold down a full-time job with the county?

I sat at my desk looking at the photographs. Nineteen were women and four were men. I called Earl, and he agreed to meet me tomorrow afternoon once he was off work. He said he knew some of Reece's girls but not all of them. He would do his best. I then called Gina. She said she didn't know any of Reece's girlfriends, but she would take a look to see if she recognized anyone. She told me to come by tomorrow night before dinner.

Looking at those photographs of nineteen beautiful women, I couldn't help but wonder why the one who was a police officer hadn't come forward in his defense.

28

I ordered a cheese pizza, set myself up in the living room, and turned on the TV. Morgan would be coming on in about forty minutes. I opened the envelope Carolina had brought me and began reading the supplementary report.

Officers Nettles, Knight, and Mankovich were out on watch in the Sixth District. They had been scouting activity near the Mahalia Jackson Park on South Birkhoff Avenue. Late that afternoon, they had received a tip that a suspected drug dealer who had an outstanding warrant would be at the basketball game watching his younger brother play. They parked their car on the street within view of the court and the surrounding area. They watched the entirety of the game. They were able to identify the target's brother, but there was no sighting of the target. They waited for the game to end and the crowd to disperse to see if he might show up, but nothing happened.

The officers decided to go and grab a bite to eat at Italian Fiesta on South Halsted. They were turning onto South Eggleston when they heard the dispatch call about a person of interest in the vicinity of South Eggleston and Normal Avenue. They radioed back to dispatch and drove to the location. They arrived at 8517 South Eggleston and visualized a person who matched the description. Once they approached, the target appeared like he was going to run. They drove the car up on the curb to discourage him from running. All three officers immediately got out of the car. Officer Nettles was the driver, Officer Knight the passenger, and Officer Mankovich in the back seat. Once they got out of the car, Officer Knight yelled for the target to get on the ground. The target turned back toward the house as if he were going to run, stopped, then turned back toward the officers. As soon as he turned, Officer Mankovich yelled, "Gun!" All three officers pulled their guns and aimed them at the target. The target reached for his waistband. Officer Mankovich fired two shots, both hitting the target. Officers Nettles and Knight did not discharge their weapons. All three officers confirm they saw the target reach for his waistband. All three officers saw the gun. Once the target was incapacitated, the officers approached and tended to his wounds until EMS arrived.

The rest of the report contained perfunctory information about how they secured the scene and assisted EMS and conferred with Assistant Deputy Powell, who arrived approximately thirty minutes after the shooting.

I heard Morgan's voice enter my apartment and looked up to find her on the screen. She was a perfect combination of refinement and beauty. I admired how composed she appeared given all that was going on behind the scenes. Someone once told me that news people were the best actors in the world. I now understood what they meant. They could turn it on and off like a light switch. Right now, Morgan Shaw was all the way on, and over a million people in the Chicago area were glued to their television sets watching her at the top of her game. What would Alicia's fans do now?

I read through the report again, half listening to Morgan and her co-anchor, when I heard him read a story about a woman's packages being stolen by a neighbor's dog and how it all had been caught on camera. This reminded me of what Earl had said about the old woman who lived across the street from the shooting. She had been questioned by the police that night, who then took her video and presumably returned it. I called Mechanic and told him I would meet him and Morgan at her apartment building after the newscast was over.

THE TWO OF US SAT in yet another room in Morgan's apartment. It was situated at the end of the hall and stuffed with large comfortable furniture. The biggest TV I had ever seen took over one wall while two of the walls were floor-to-ceiling windows with sweeping city views facing south and east. I could see the lights of Soldier Field burning in the distance. The Bears game was just letting out.

"You were very good tonight," I said. "It's the first time I've watched an entire broadcast."

"It was a slow news day, but we always try to find a way to make it interesting."

"Your co-anchor didn't look right sitting next to you. Watching him was like watching paint dry."

"Bob is very safe. His Q score with the suburban housewife demographic is through the roof. He's everything they wish their husbands could be. I own the rest of the demos. I know he's not the most exciting, but this is a numbers game, and numerically speaking, he's a perfect partner."

"He read a story near the end of the show about the woman who caught her neighbor's dog on camera stealing her Amazon packages from her front porch."

"It was buried way down in the D block of the show. I don't remember much about it."

"After the third package went missing, she angled her front door security camera so she could see who was taking the packages. She was at work when she got a notification there was movement at her house, and that's when she spotted the neighbor's dog walking away with a package in its mouth."

"Okay," Morgan said, shrugging. "A small, throwaway human-interest story. Our producers like to put them near the end of the show."

"But that got me thinking about the old woman across the street whose video they confiscated and never returned. What if her camera also had remote access and the video was stored in the cloud like our cell phones do with photos and videos?"

Morgan's eyes widened. "Holy shit," she said. "If I could get my hands on that video and the video clearly shows Reece didn't have a gun and wasn't reaching for his waistband, then game over."

"My thoughts exactly. Someone should talk to her and find out if the camera was backed up to the cloud."

"Would you be willing to do it?"

"I would, but you should take the lead. Old educated Black woman living on the South Side. You own that demographic."

29

Gaynell Cooper lived in a small, well-appointed brick townhouse across from 8517 South Eggleston Avenue where Reece Williams had been shot. A weathered black Nissan sat in the driveway, its rear bumper held up on the car frame with the help of heavy black rope. Her small patch of grass had been cut low and even. The hedges flanking the front stoop had also been well attended. I let Morgan step forward and ring the bell. Seconds later, a series of locks clanked back, and the door opened slightly at first. The old woman tilted her head to get a better view, then the door fully opened. She was a tall, broad-shouldered woman with silver-white hair and a pair of tortoise-shell eyeglass frames. She stood there with her hand covering her mouth.

Morgan smiled, and in that pitch-perfect anchorwoman voice said, "Sorry to bother you, but I'm Morgan Shaw."

"I know very well who you are," Ms. Cooper said. "I can't for the life of me believe I'm staring at you *in person* on *my* porch."

"It's me," Morgan said. "And this is Ashe Cayne who's working with me. Would you mind if we came in and talked to you? It's a little chilly out here."

"Lord Jesus, where are my manners?" she said, unlocking the screen door. "Of course, come in."

She closed the door behind us after we had entered and then re-attached the cadre of locks. We followed her up a short flight of stairs and into a spacious living room. Everything was neat, the furniture wasn't fussy, and a large, framed black-and-white print of Martin Luther King Jr. at the March on Washington hung over a gas fireplace. She directed us to the couch as she settled into a larger recliner.

"Can I get you something to drink?" she said.

We declined.

"Is it Ms. or Mrs. Cooper?" Morgan said.

"My husband died ten years ago, but I will always be Mrs. Cooper," she said, smiling softly. "Thank you for asking."

Morgan nodded. It was interesting watching her work in such humble surroundings far away from her nine-room apartment down on the Gold Coast. She knew exactly what it took to make others feel comfortable talking to her. It was a similar approach detectives took when trying to get a witness or suspect to open up and give information. People responded more openly when you stood with them and not above them.

"We don't want to take up too much of your time," Morgan said. "We just wanted to ask you a few questions about the shooting that occurred across the street several months ago."

Mrs. Cooper's expression quickly turned to disdain as she shook her head. "Good Lord, what is this world coming to?" she said. "Literally right across the street from me. When is this going to stop? They can't keep killing our young men like this. I pray every night that he'll help us find a way that's better than this. Something has got to change."

"Do you remember what happened that day?" Morgan said.

"Like it was yesterday. How could I ever forget it?"

"Would you share that with us?"

Mrs. Cooper leaned forward in her chair. "Let me tell you something," she said. "I've lived on this block for thirty years. Gerald and I bought this house a year after I got hired over at Simeon to work as a secretary in the principal's office. There have been fights now and again and parties over the summer that got a little out of control, but nothing like what happened that night. We work hard to keep this block safe and peaceful. What they said happened didn't make any sense to me at all."

Morgan opened her purse and pulled out a recorder. "Mrs. Cooper, would you mind if I recorded our conversation?"

"Not at all," Mrs. Cooper said. She smiled, then said, "I trust you."

Morgan pushed the record button and set the recorder on a small coffee table covered with old editions of *Ebony* and *JET* magazines. "Take me from the beginning if you would," Morgan said.

I sat back and watched her work. She was so smooth.

"It was a Saturday night," Mrs. Cooper began. "I remember that because I was baking a couple of sweet potato pies for our church bake sale the next morning. I was back in the kitchen watching *Black Voices*, that program on WTTW with that lovely young woman Brandis. I forget her last name right off. Anyway, I'm in the kitchen making the pies when all of a sudden I hear a big commotion outside. Sounded like a car had hit something. The noise stopped, then not a minute later, I heard gunshots."

"How many?" Morgan asked.

"Two."

"Are you sure?"

"Absolutely. Two. Pop. Pop. When you've been living on the South Side as long as I have, you know what gunfire sounds like, and you know how to count it. I heard the shots. I was just putting the pies in the oven. I closed the oven door, then went to the front door as fast as I could. I got bad arthritis in my right hip, so I can't move too fast, but I did the best I could. When I got down to the door, I didn't open it, but

I went to the window and pulled back the curtain. That's when I saw the police officers and the car up on the curb."

"How many officers did you see?" Morgan asked.

"At the time, there were only three. Two white guys and a Black guy. They were kneeling on the ground. I saw two legs coming out from where they were kneeling. I remember looking at the sneakers. They were bright yellow, almost like they were fluorescent. The legs were splayed to the side like this." She took her hands and opened them into a *V*. "The officers were doing something with their hands, but I couldn't tell from where I was."

Morgan cut her eyes at me, then back at Mrs. Cooper.

Mrs. Cooper continued. "The Black officer got up and started looking around and talking into a walkie-talkie pinned to his shoulder."

"And what did the other officers do?" Morgan asked.

"They stayed down on the ground. Then a couple of people started coming out their houses and onto the porches. One girl walked over there, and the Black officer pushed her back. She was yelling and crying." Mrs. Cooper closed her eyes and grimaced. "That poor child was hollering to the top of her lungs. 'You killed him. You killed him.' That's all she kept saying. 'You killed him.' She fell to the ground, and another woman went over to hold her. A few minutes later, the sirens started coming, and cars suddenly appeared from all directions. More people started coming down the street to see what happened. It was just pandemonium. I couldn't stop looking at his sneakers. They never moved. They just flopped over and sat still. He was just lying there. I knew he was gone. I got so nauseous. I'm seventy-five years old, and I've been living on the South Side since I was five. It was the first time in all my life I had seen a dead body in the street. I'll never forget it." She pulled a tissue from her pocket and dabbed underneath her glasses.

"I know it's tough to go back to that night," Morgan said. "But we're doing our best to piece together what exactly happened so we get a cleaner picture."

"I don't understand why no one downtown is talking about the shooting," Mrs. Cooper said. "They killed that boy for no good reason, and nobody got punished. No disrespect, Ms. Shaw, but nobody in the media is talking about it either. It's almost like these killings are so common people have become desensitized to them. Even you media folk."

"I understand what you're saying," Morgan said. "But that's why I'm here. I'm still sensitive to it, and I want the truth to be heard. Every life matters. I want to ask you a few more questions if I could."

Mrs. Cooper nodded.

"Did you see the officers when they got out of the car?" Morgan asked.

"No, they were already on the ground by the time I got to the window."

"Did you hear them yell anything prior to the shots?"

"I did not."

"Did you see Reece with a gun?"

"Like I said, he was already on the ground by the time I saw anything."

"Did you speak to the police officers?"

"I did. I spoke to them about forty-five minutes after the shooting. I had gone to take the pies out of the oven before I overcooked them. My doorbell rang. I went to answer it. Two police officers were there. They asked if they could come in and talk to me. I told them they couldn't come in, but they could talk to me through the screen. They asked if I had seen anything. I told them everything I just told you. The shorter officer was taking notes of what I said. They said they noticed my security cameras outside on the house. They asked me if they worked.

I told them, of course they did. It would be stupid to have cameras that don't work. They said it was important for them to see if my cameras had any video that might help them sort out what happened. It was important for the young man's family. I agreed with them. They asked if they could look at it. I told them I didn't know much about this technology stuff, but I could show them where my son set everything up. I let them in and took them to the basement closet where my son had stored the recording box. They fiddled around with it, pushed a button, and pulled out a memory card. The taller officer put it in his front pocket. They went back upstairs and told me they would be in touch with me. Should've known they were telling a lie then. I ain't heard a word from anybody."

"Do you remember the officers' names?" Morgan asked.

"They didn't tell me, and I was so upset I didn't think to ask."

"Did they show you their badges or any identification?"

"No. But I knew they were cops. They were in jeans and T-shirts with black vests on."

"Have you talked to anyone about what you saw and the video card they took?" Morgan asked.

"The only people who asked me about what happened were those two police officers that night. I called over to the Sixth District several times to ask about it, and they kept transferring me to what they said was the area detective office. I left several messages there, and about three weeks ago, someone called me back. He said he would look into the card and find out what happened to it. His name was Officer Hakeem Jefferson."

"Has he called you back?"

"Not a word," Mrs. Cooper said. "And that was over a month ago. I know everyone's busy, but this seems like a very poor effort in my opinion. If this is how they handle case evidence, God help us all."

I made a mental note of Jefferson's name. I would address that later.

Right now I wanted to learn more about her security system. "Do you mind if I ask you about your cameras?" I said.

"Sure, but I don't know much about them. My son set them up for me."

"Where does he live?" I asked.

"He and his family live in Philadelphia. He set them up a couple of years ago after my husband died so he could keep an eye on the house. If you had told me computers and electronics could be so sophisticated that someone could watch your camera on their cell phone hundreds of miles away, I would've thought you were crazy."

"Your son monitors your cameras?" I asked.

"All the time," she answered. "He knows when I leave the house and when I return. He can see the postman dropping off the mail. He sees everything, and I feel very safe that he can."

This could be the break we needed. If her son was monitoring everything remotely, it was possible he had some type of external storage device that kept a copy of the recordings. Mrs. Cooper gave us his name and number, then took me down to the DVR box in her basement. I wrote down the make, model, and serial number and asked Mrs. Cooper to do one more thing before we left. I had her and Morgan go upstairs to the kitchen where Mrs. Cooper had been when she heard the commotion outside. I told her to turn on the television at about the same volume she normally listened to it when watching the news. I went outside and closed the door behind me. I walked across the street toward the makeshift shrine of melted candles, dried flowers, and a deflated balloon that had been erected in Reece's memory. I stood on the sidewalk where the officers would've been when they got out of the car and yelled, "Get your hands in the air!" I yelled it twice. Then I walked back and entered Mrs. Cooper's house. She and Morgan were still in the kitchen. Morgan nodded as soon as I walked in.

"I heard you clear as day," Mrs. Cooper said. "Both times."

We thanked Mrs. Cooper, then at her request, I used her phone to take a picture of her and Morgan. Sometimes in a case, regardless of how hard you work, you don't find the critical answers you need by skill or ingenuity. Sometimes by pure luck alone you stumble upon a source or small piece of information that can crack a case wide open. I had that feeling walking away from Mrs. Cooper's small house.

30

I drove Morgan directly to the station and handed off watch to Rox, who was already sitting inside the garage awaiting our arrival. I then turned right around and drove over to St. Sebastian to meet with Earl. Father Flagger had given us permission to meet quietly in his office. As I drove, I called Mrs. Cooper's son. He didn't answer, so I left him a voice message.

I finally made my way through morning traffic to St. Sebastian, and once I arrived, a young dark-haired priest with a heavy, course beard and long ponytail directed me down a maze of connecting hallways until we reached a suite of plush carpeted offices. Large, framed baroque paintings of graphic religious scenes adorned the mahogany walls. All of the furnishings and decorations looked like they had been saved from ancient Rome. We walked past a young woman sitting at a desk and into a long conference room whose walls were covered with paintings of popes going back to the first, St. Peter. Earl was seated at a circular table. The priest closed the door behind me and left us to our business.

I took out the nineteen photographs and spread them across the table. Earl stood and studied each one carefully. I could tell those he recognized because his face would soften into a smile, and he'd push them forward. For some of them, he would say their names aloud. One was the mother of Reece's children. Earl was surprised she had been to Reece's apartment. He said the two of them weren't on the best terms after their divorce. Forty minutes later, Earl leaned back from the table. Ten of the photographs remained unidentified.

"That's the best I can do," he said. "I don't know what to tell you about the others."

"Gina is going to take a look at them later tonight," I said. "Maybe she'll be able to pick out a few. Is there anyone else you know who might recognize some of these women?"

"Only one other guy I can think of," Earl said. "Reece used to be tight with a guy he played ball with over at Morgan Park. Spider Dawson. I haven't seen him in a couple of years, but he's still around somewhere."

"You know his real name?"

"Nope. Everybody just called him Spider 'cause of his long arms and legs."

"How can I find him?"

"He used to play ball over at the Cole Park courts in Chatham, but it's too cold to be outside now. He's probably in a game over at Marquette Fieldhouse. I think they play Thursday nights and Saturday mornings. Somebody over there would know. But if you go over there, you better bring backup. They don't like fuckin' around with people they don't know."

As I got on the expressway to go back north to meet Mechanic for a workout at Hammer's, Torres called.

"I got a chance to look at the letters sent to Roscati," he said. "Same postmark as the letter sent to Morgan. Carol Stream."

<hr />

GINA WILLIAMS WAS STILL IN her blue CTA uniform when she opened the door. Her smallest son peered around a wall at the end of the hall, then disappeared when I walked into the house. The sweet smell of barbecue wafted from the kitchen. Gina was pleasant but looked tired. I followed her into the same room we had sat in during my last visit.

"You think she knows why they killed him?" she said as I handed her the ten unidentified photographs.

"I don't know," I said. "It's just odd to me that he was seeing a cop, he gets shot by a cop, dies, and no one hears from her. Might not amount to anything, but it's worth some effort to see if she knows anything or has an opinion about what happened."

The doorbell rang.

"That's my friend Felicia," Gina said. "I asked her to come over. She and Reece hung out at some of the same places. I figured she might recognize someone."

Gina went to the front door and returned with a tall, shapely Latino girl with long black hair and bright fancy nails that looked like small pieces of art. She wore a white leather jacket trimmed in fur around the collar and cuffs. Gina introduced the two of us and then they sat down beside each other and looked at the photographs.

"That's Damitra from Simeon," Gina said. "I didn't even know Reece was still talking to her."

"That's a damn good weave," Felicia said.

"Girl, she always had her shit together even back in the day," Gina said. She handed me the photograph.

"He was messin' around with *her*?" Felicia said, picking up the next photograph.

"Who is she?" Gina asked.

"I forget her name, but she used to host a party over at Thirty-First Street Beach in the summer. Used to be packed. Then the park district

gave the permit to somebody else and messed her flow all the way up."
Felicia handed me the photograph.

The next photograph was one of two white girls. Gina and Felicia looked at each other, shook their heads, then handed the photograph to me. They did the same with the next photograph.

"That's Tiffany," Gina said. "She used to live down the block from my grandmother's house. She used to fool around with a guy who moved here from Detroit and sold a lot of weed. He bought her one of those small Mercedes sports cars. Then they caught him, and he went to jail. She lost that car too. I'll never forget it. She had her name painted inside the door." She handed me the photograph.

This is how it went for the next twenty minutes—reminiscing, sharing notes, and checking Facebook and Instagram to confirm their hunches. When they were finished, they had positively identified seven of the ten women. Only one white woman and two Black women remained.

"What will you do now?" Gina asked.

"There's one more guy he played basketball with I need to find," I said. "Hopefully, he might recognize them."

"Who is it?"

"Some guy they call Spider."

AS I PULLED INTO MY garage that night, Rox called me.

"How did things go today?" I asked.

"Nothing unusual except for her shopping," Rox said.

"What happened?"

"She said she needed to pick up a few items at Gucci. First of all, who goes to Gucci to pick up a *few* items? Most people can't even afford to walk through the door. All of the salespeople know her as soon as she walks in. The manager comes from the back to help her. She sees a purse she likes on a wall in the center of the store. She doesn't even ask for the price. She asks the manager what colors they come in. The manager tells her four. Without missing a beat, she tells him she'll take all four of them, wrap them all up, and send them to the station tomorrow. When she turned to look at a coat, I peeked inside the bag to look at the price tag."

"How much?"

"Five thousand. By the time we left, she had racked up twenty thousand dollars in charges and never flinched. Bryan said that she's the only evening anchor in the city who still has a wardrobe clause in her contract. Fifty thousand dollars a year. Bryan said he's willing to meet with you. He prefers to do it in person rather than talking on the phone."

"When can he meet?"

"First thing in the morning after he works out. He suggested Kanela Breakfast Club at nine."

"Perfect. It's only two blocks from my apartment building."

"I assured him that everything would be off the record."

"Good by me."

I was happy to finally be in my apartment. It had been a long day, and I was exhausted. I heated up some leftover teriyaki steak, rice, and vegetables, then settled on the couch. I turned on the Golf Channel and watched a re-airing of the British Open. How badly I wanted and needed to get back out on the fairways again. I was just dozing off when my phone rang. It was Mechanic.

"A little action over here at her apartment building," he said.

That woke me up quickly.

"What's going on?" I asked.

"She pulled into her garage, and I was driving away to go home. I noticed our friend again. The majority leader clown."

"Schmidt?"

"Yup. He's sitting in a different car this time. A black two-door BMW."

"What's he doing?"

"Just sitting there looking down at his phone."

"Was he alone?"

"Yup."

"Did he see you?"

"I don't think so. He's still sitting there. What do you want me to do?"

"Can you position your car so that you get a clear view of both him and the entrance?"

"Already done."

"Good. Then don't do anything else. Don't approach him. Don't let him know you're watching him. Just observe."

"Man, I was hoping to have a little fun."

"Mechanic, this guy is the second most powerful politician in the state."

"That makes it even better."

"Just stay there until he leaves. And keep your distance."

"Copy that."

I went back to watching the British Open. I had never played golf overseas, but I had decided that my first experience would be playing the Old Course at St. Andrews in Scotland. I watched as the golfers walked across the famous Swilcan Bridge on their way up to the eighteenth green, the most famous and revered walk in golf. My phone buzzed.

"He's out of the car and walking toward the front door," Mechanic said. "He has his phone out."

"What the hell?" I said. "He's out in the open, walking into her building?"

"Just like he had a golden invitation."

I tried to quickly run through the possibilities but couldn't get past the idea that Schmidt could be so brazen as to just walk into her apartment and try to harm her. It didn't make sense. He knew there were security cameras everywhere.

I was in the middle of deciding if I should tell Mechanic to intercept him or just stay back and wait. I thought about calling Morgan and warning her that he was about to enter her building when Mechanic said, "Hold on. He's turning back to his car."

"What do you mean?"

"He was halfway to the front door, stopped, just turned around, and now he's walking back to his car."

"Is he leaving?"

"He just started the car. I can see the exhaust from the pipes."

"Don't leave until he leaves."

"Okay. Wait. What? Well, here comes the prize."

"What?"

"Morgan is walking out of the building with a baseball cap on, and she's heading right to his car."

"What the hell is going on?"

"I have no idea, but she just opened the passenger door and got in."

"Now what?"

"Headlights just turned on," Mechanic said. "He's pulling off the curb. What do you want me to do?"

"Follow them but from a distance," I said. "See where they go."

"Call you in a few."

The golfers had worked their way up the eighteenth fairway and were sizing up their putts on the green. The wind and slight drizzle blew sideways as the hardy fans stood their ground in the gallery bleachers and cheered on the golfers. I had read so many stories about the weather in Scotland and how it was so unpredictable, helping at times and hurting at others, sometimes the single variable that could decide the entire championship.

Mechanic called back minutes later.

"They're pulling up to a row of single-family townhouses on Goethe Street."

"It's not Goth Street," I said. "Gur-tuh. It's German."

"Well, I'm not, so it's Goth to me. And while you're giving me language lessons, your client is walking up the stairs of this townhouse on her own willpower with the same man she told you she had broken up with a while ago."

There was very little that shocked me, but at that moment I was stunned. Both of them had played me in a way, and that made me a bit angry. Why couldn't they just tell the truth? Why all the pretense about an acrimonious split? I didn't give a shit if they were still sleeping together. What two consenting adults do in the bedroom is their own business. No judgment from me.

"What do you want me to do?" Mechanic said.

"Text me the address, then leave."

"I could go knock on the door and ruin the party."

"Leave 'em alone," I said. "None of our business."

"Why didn't she just come clean with you?" Mechanic said.

"Maybe that would be too easy."

31

Bryan Sheverini walked into Kanela one minute before nine and didn't disappoint. Everything about him was as flawless as he looked on the screen. Perfect teeth. Perfect hair. Perfect fingernails. He wore a chocolate leather puff jacket with a fur-lined hood and matching gloves. His regular exercise routine had paid many dividends. He had an unmistakable confidence in his swagger.

He sat down with a ready smile and shook my hand. I couldn't stop looking at his face. I couldn't tell because of the lighting, but it definitely looked like he was wearing eyeliner.

"Getting chilly out," he said, immediately adjusting the plate and silverware and lining up the edges of the placemat in front of him. Rox had warned me that he suffered from a mild case of OCD. "Our weather team says we might even get a little snow next week. Doesn't matter how long I've lived here. I'm never ready for this shit."

"Tell me about it," I said. "I was in Arizona last week. Eighty degrees before the sun was even up. Makes you wonder why we subject ourselves to this every year."

"Where in Arizona?"

"Scottsdale. Near the Estancia Club."

"That course is beautiful," he said. "I played it several years ago when I was anchoring sports. Gotta love the eleventh hole par three with that elevated tee shot staring down at the green nestled in the rocks."

The man knew his golf, which was my first sign we'd be getting along. The waiter came and took our order, then disappeared.

"So Rox tells me you're working with Morgan," he said, lining up the sugar packets in the small dish in the center of the table. "She's a handful. One thing I like about Morgan is you always know where you stand with her."

"How long have you known her?" I asked.

"Since she first came to town," Bryan said. "A small group of us took her out to dinner to introduce her to the city. I was doing sports over there at WLTV then. I've been in this business awhile. Worked all over the country with all kinds of talent. Morgan Shaw is the most naturally beautiful woman I've ever seen, and her delivery on camera is smoother than two pieces of silk blowing in the wind."

"You haven't met Carolina Espinoza," I said.

"Who's she?" he leaned forward and whispered as if we were trading secrets.

"The woman who puts Morgan in second place."

"What station is she with? I don't recognize her name."

"She doesn't work for a TV station. She works for a police station. CPD."

Bryan nodded, still flashing that trillion-dollar smile. "Maybe I need to meet her," he said. "Unless she's already hooked up."

"Not sure how she'd feel about the whole celebrity thing. She's a down-to-earth kinda girl, but by all means, you can take your shot."

Bryan nodded as if evaluating his odds. The waiter delivered our drinks. Bryan took the straw out of his glass and replaced it with a new one he pulled out of his pocket.

"Did you know Morgan received a letter similar to the ones sent to Alicia Roscati?" I asked.

"Val told me about it," Bryan said. "She knows everyone and everything. Crazy shit. Alicia was the best. Beautiful, salt of the earth, fun to work with. I can't believe she just died in her bed like that."

"I don't believe it either."

Surprise quickly registered on his face. "Do you know something?"

"Not as much as I need to know."

"Wait a minute. You really think she was killed by that fan who was sending her those letters the last few months? Seriously?"

I raised my eyebrows.

"I doubt it," he said. "We all have these over-the-top fans who get obsessive and occasionally cross the line or get a little too close. But to actually kill one of us? That doesn't make sense."

"It did some years ago in Waco and Little Rock," I said. "Two anchorwomen. It's been a while but doesn't mean it couldn't happen again. All threats should be considered serious threats until proven otherwise. Have you had fans cross the line?"

"Plenty of times. Women sending me flowers and showing up at the station saying they're my girlfriend. Guys sending me naked photos and asking me out for drinks. Val gets hit on everywhere she goes. Guys walking up to her car and knocking on her window. It comes with the territory."

"But these were threats, not love letters. Val ever get threatened?"

"She gets tons of letters from fans, but she's never said anything about receiving death threats. That's what I found strange about Alicia's letters. Everyone really loved her. Also, she wasn't one of those opinion journalists. She stayed neutral. Fought for the underdog. Was always hosting charity galas and volunteering with kids and the homeless. I don't know why anyone would want to hurt her."

"The leading contenders are pretty reliable—money, sex, or jealousy."

"Or just plain derangement."

"That's always in the mix," I said.

We both took long sips of our drinks.

"Love her or hate her, Morgan is a fierce competitor," Bryan said. "When she wants something, she goes all out."

"You have a fifty-thousand-dollar wardrobe budget too?" I asked.

"You gotta be kidding," he said, laughing. "Morgan's the only talent in town, man or woman, who has a wardrobe budget. She's also the last anchor to have her own staff makeup artist. The rest of us in the afternoons and evenings have to use freelancers, and all the morning anchors around town have to do their own makeup. That's one thing I respect about her. She makes her management respect her power. Since the day she's gotten to this market, she's never been afraid to stand up to those bean counters and fight for what she wanted."

"Why didn't Alicia have the same clauses in her contract?"

"Because she wasn't Morgan. Yet."

I understood.

"Alicia was definitely on her way to beating Morgan," Bryan said. "It was probably gonna happen during next month's sweeps."

"Who knew that?" I asked.

"Everyone. It wasn't a secret. We all get the overnights. The numbers were there." Bryan leaned over and said, "Quietly, we were all rooting for Alicia."

"What will happen now that Alicia's gone?"

"The same thing that always happens when a big name dies or retires or gets fired. The fight for ratings always rages on no matter whose ass is sitting in the chair. People think our business is just about the story or the big scoop. Hell no. This ain't the world of Edward R. Murrow anymore where journalism was spelled with a capital *J*. There's only one thing that matters to those suits in the big corner offices—numbers. Pure and simple. Those numbers equal advertising dollars, and that equals profits. The more money the station makes, the bigger the bonus they get at the end of the year."

"So with Alicia gone, Morgan will maintain her number-one spot."

"That's the conventional wisdom, but I wouldn't put my money on it just yet."

"What could stop her now?"

"When it comes to sweeps, stations pull out every trick in the book and then some. I'm hearing from some of my old friends over at MTQ about some master plan management has put together that's gonna send shockwaves through the industry."

"Care to share?"

Bryan lowered his voice and said, "They're temporarily relocating one of their weekend morning anchors to Chicago from their national morning show. She'll take over for Alicia until sweeps are over, then they'll name Alicia's permanent replacement. The whole city will be talking about this."

"Why?"

"Because she's a really hot blond and one of their rising stars at the network. It will be the first time in history the network has essentially loaned national talent to one of its local stations to help out in a ratings war. It's like taking a major league pitcher and sending him down to the minor leagues temporarily because you want to win a few games. It just doesn't work that way. But MTQ hasn't won since Morgan got the chair at LTV. They'll do whatever they can to break her streak."

"What makes them so sure this network anchor will beat the hometown hero?"

"Because not only does she have a gazillion fans across the country, but she's also married to this actor hunk who used to be a soap opera star. Women drool over him, and even straight guys can't help but stare at him. Trust me, when they announce the two of them are coming to Chicago for the month, it's gonna set the city on fire. Lots of viewers that don't even watch that channel are gonna turn to see her."

"I wonder if Morgan knows this."

"If she doesn't, she will soon. They're making the announcement at the top of next week. The promos are already shot. They'll run those bad boys around the clock."

"Jesus Christ," I said. "The soil over Alicia's coffin is still fresh."

Bryan shook his head. "You think the pinheads give a shit about that? This business is like a clock caught in the middle of a storm. Doesn't matter how bad things get—it just keeps on ticking."

32

I sat on my couch reading the police shooting team's report. Something about it just didn't feel right. I couldn't say exactly what it was, but it had my gut tingling. Maybe something wasn't adding up with the officers' stories or the sequence of events didn't mesh. I circled the time Reece had been shot: 7:15 p.m. It was mid-June, so there still would've been some daylight, but dusk was quickly approaching. I looked outside my window. The light was probably similar. I picked up my phone and called Mechanic.

"How about a little field trip?" I said when he answered.

"When?" he said.

"Now?"

"Where to?"

"Auburn Gresham."

"Been a while since I rode those streets."

"Well, strap up and let's go."

MECHANIC AND I JUMPED ON the expressway and turned south. I had read somewhere that if a visitor to Chicago wanted to understand the demographics of the different neighborhoods, all they had to do was watch the changing cityscape. Starting from the luxury high-rises and shiny new developments crowding downtown, then traveling through the trendy South Loop before passing into the working-class neighborhood of Bronzeville, the towering skyline of downtown progressively shrunk with every passing block as the named skyscrapers gave way to squat mixed-income apartment complexes and scattered vacant lots. Sprawling shopping centers filled with discount stores and old row houses with carpet-size patches of grass as front lawns told a story of hardship and stark disconnection to the more affluent neighborhoods farther north.

We exited at Eighty-Third Street. Street vendors crowded the road, selling everything from caramelized walnuts to knockoff Bears and Bulls sweatshirts to motorists waiting at the traffic light. Tinted-window cars and trucks drove by, the bass of their music so loud it shook cars standing at the intersection. We drove west and passed a couple of enormous shopping centers with big-box retail and home improvement stores. We finally reached a forked intersection with Vincennes Avenue, a long diagonal road that predominantly ran north and south.

"There's Simeon down there to the right," I said. The gigantic orange brick building perched gloriously on an enormous plot of land, completely incongruous with its squalid surroundings.

"Never heard of it," Mechanic said.

"Some of the greatest basketball players never to make it to the NBA played there. Had a guy named Benji Wilson back in the early eighties. Better even than Derrick Rose and some of the other Chicago greats."

I took a left and drove in the direction opposite of Simeon. About a hundred yards down, I turned onto the Eighty-Third Street extension that ran on the other side of Vincennes. As soon I took a right, the park was in full view. I pulled off on a crumbling road adjacent to the park and kept the motor running. The basketball backboards were the old kind—clamshell shaped and made of old metal. There were no nets hanging from the rims, and most of them were rusty and tilted slightly from too many players dunking the ball and hanging on too long afterward. The park was completely empty.

We just sat there, the motor rumbling in the falling darkness, the reliably calm voice of WGN's Bob Skirott flowing out of the radio delivering the day's news.

After several minutes, Mechanic said, "So what happened to that kid Benji Wilson?"

"Sad story," I said. "I was a little kid, but I remember it like it happened yesterday. Upset the entire city. While he was in high school, his girlfriend had a baby. They were having relationship problems, being young parents and all. One afternoon, Benji and his girlfriend left school during their lunch period. Lots of kids liked to go to a small store nearby. He and his girlfriend were talking, and Benji wasn't paying attention and accidentally bumped into two kids who were standing on the sidewalk waiting for a friend to come out of the store. They went to Calumet High School. Words between Benji and the other boys were exchanged. Then one of the boys pulled out a twenty-two and fired twice. One bullet split open Benji's liver. The other one nicked his aorta. Took paramedics forty-five minutes to arrive and take him to the hospital where he waited even longer to go into surgery. He lost so much blood while waiting, he died before they even got him back into surgery. Chicago's greatest basketball star gone just like that."

Mechanic and I sat there in silence for several minutes, the wind blowing across the park, punishing tree branches, and carrying leaves across the entire expanse of the cracked asphalt courts. Other than a large construction site with heavy machinery and piles of dirt sitting to the west of the park, there was nothing else nearby. Total isolation.

I imagined what the park might've looked like full of spectators enjoying the basketball game on that hot summer night, Reece hanging out with his friends watching a game he loved so much. Within an hour of the game coming to an end, so would his life.

"What are you thinking about?" Mechanic said, breaking the silence.

"What I always do in these situations," I said. "How we all just have one life, and for so many people it just ends so unexpectedly. Think about it. Here you are living your normal life, going on about your business, death not even a trace of a thought. Then in an instant, you're dead. No second chance. No do over. Gone. It makes me so goddamn angry. What right does a person have to just take away another person's ability to live? Injuring someone or making them uncomfortable is one thing, but to just kill someone recklessly like that? Makes my blood boil."

Mechanic stared straight ahead, his hand caressing the barrel of his .500 Magnum resting on his lap. I pulled out the report and read it again.

"Okay, let's trace the steps," I said. I pulled up a map of the area on my phone. "They were heading to get something to eat at Italian Fiesta over on Halsted and Eighty-First Street. So from here, they had to travel north on South Birkhoff, a left on Eighty-Third Street, then a quick right on Halsted until they got to Eighty-First Street. Let's do a dry run and time it."

Mechanic tapped the stopwatch button on his phone, and I joined the moving stream of cars heading north. I followed the directions. We drove through a couple of lights, turned left onto Eighty-First Street, then arrived in the parking lot of Italian Fiesta.

"Seven minutes and forty-three seconds," Mechanic said.

"Okay. Now let's go over to 8517 South Eggleston where Reece was shot."

I pulled up the address on Google Maps and settled on the fastest route. We drove back along the same roads we had just taken, and then once we got back to the park, I turned south on Vincennes, then to Parnell, and onto Eggleston.

"Nine minutes and twenty-five seconds," Mechanic said.

We sat there parked across the street from where Mankovich shot Reece. Mrs. Cooper's house was behind us. The one eyewitness who had spoken to Father Flagger lived a couple of doors down at 8521. I could see his porch. He would have been able to see everything from his vantage point.

I thought about what the scene must've looked like that night. A bunch of guys hanging out, laughing, talking a little trash. Maybe somebody was going inside to get some brews or there was a barbecue smoking in someone's backyard. The sun was starting to set, but there was still enough light where visibility was good. The tac team rolls up on the curb and basically hems Reece against the fence. It happens so fast, he's totally caught off guard. People start yelling and running. Seconds later, the gunshots ring out. Reece Williams is dead.

Looking across the street, I could see his makeshift memorial. Someone had placed a new batch of roses since I was last here with Morgan talking to Mrs. Cooper. I turned on the light in the car and read the report again. That's when I finally caught the sentence that was bothering me.

The officers decided to go and grab a bite to eat at Italian Fiesta on South Halsted. They were turning onto South Eggleston when they heard the dispatch call about a person of interest in the vicinity of South Eggleston and Normal Avenue.

"Sonuvabitch," I said.

"Whatchya got?" Mechanic said.

I read him the sentence carefully.

Mechanic thought for a moment. "Doesn't match the geography," he said. "How could they *just* be turning onto South Eggleston when they were heading to Italian Fiesta, which is completely in the opposite direction?"

"Bingo. Italian Fiesta is at least a seven-minute drive north of the park. If they were heading to Italian Fiesta, there's no way they could *just* be turning onto South Eggleston when they heard the call from dispatch. They weren't going to Italian Fiesta. They were already in the vicinity of South Eggleston."

"So it's just a coincidence they were near South Eggleston?"

"Not at all. They lied about their location because they were going after Reece the entire time. They were never going to Italian Fiesta. They followed him the moment he left the park til he arrived on Eggleston. They were after him, and it had nothing to do with some drug deal or him being a suspected criminal. But what had he done that was so bad they wanted him dead?"

AS WE PULLED UP TO my office building, I could see Mechanic's Viper under the streetlights and a large man leaning against it. He noticed it just after I did. His eyes tightened.

"Looks like we have company," I said.

We drew closer. One guy was leaning against the driver's door, and there was a second guy almost twice the size of the first standing in the shadows next to the front bumper. They both wore dark coats that were open and fell just above their knees.

"Friends of yours?" Mechanic asked.

"Never seen them before."

"Good to know. That removes all consideration for what I'm about to do."

I stopped my car a few feet from Mechanic's Viper. The second guy stepped out of the shadows and joined the first guy, who had now stepped between our cars. Mechanic eased his Magnum into his holster. We exited the car at the same time. The two guys stood tall.

"You guys lost?" I asked. We were about six feet apart. I didn't want to get any closer. Big guys always had the advantage in tight proximity.

"Exactly where we intend to be," the big one said. Even his ears looked muscular.

"I don't think you mean to be resting on that car," I said. "It's not yours. Let's just make this easy for everyone. Just scurry along, and we'll pretend like this never happened."

The shorter guy grunted, made a strange sound in his throat, and blew a mouthful all over the hood of the Viper.

"Jesus Christ," I said. "You just had to do something even more stupid. Up until that point, you only had an ass whoopin'. Now you're spending a few nights in the hospital."

"Fuck you," the big guy said. "Keep away from Reinhardt Schmidt, or they'll be looking for you at the bottom of Lake Michigan."

"Now I get it. The majority leader wants to flex his rented muscle. Any other message you're supposed to deliver? You might as well get it out now, 'cause you won't be talking for the next couple of weeks."

"Wiseass," the smaller guy said.

No sooner than he said that, Mechanic lunged forward. I knew he was going for the big one first. The most basic rule in a multi-person fight—neutralize the biggest threat. Hercules braced himself for the impact, but he did what amateurs did by tightening his fists and keeping his hands too low. Still charging forward, Mechanic jumped, did a half turn, and scissor kicked his right foot so that it landed squarely on the side of the guy's head, causing him to stumble backward. Just as soon as both of his feet hit the ground, Mechanic delivered a monstrous uppercut to the guy's chin. The sound of his jaw splintering was loud enough to hear all the way at the other end of the block.

The smaller guy was about my height but a little wider and heavier in the chest. He charged at me full speed. I was ready. I relaxed my body, then as he launched his right fist toward my face, I quickly jerked my head, ducked underneath it, and punched him as hard as I could on his left flank, hitting my target perfectly—that soft spot between the upper rim of his pelvis and just beneath his last rib. The next time he went to the bathroom, he would be peeing blood. He took the punch well and quickly turned with a left jab that caught me in the shoulder. Luckily, I was still somewhat crouched and didn't take the punch full on, but what I did take hurt like hell. I gained my footing and thrust upward with my right forearm, hitting him square in his face, a squirt of his blood catching me on the side of the neck. I wasted no time getting him to the ground, making sure we didn't fall on the Viper.

As I went to work on my guy, I could hear the impact of Mechanic's blows as Hercules let out several loud grunts before falling silent. I delivered several quick jabs to my guy, splitting his nose wide open. His eyes had already ballooned to the size of golf balls, and when I delivered one more blow, he didn't have any fight left in him. I rolled him over on his stomach so he wouldn't drown in his own blood. I looked up to find Mechanic hoisting Hercules off the ground. He grabbed him by his hair and rubbed his face in the spit on the hood of the Viper until the big man started choking. Mechanic then pulled him back up, kneed him in the other jaw that hadn't been broken yet, then opened up his car door, started his engine, and simply drove away. It wasn't until his taillights had disappeared down the street that I realized he hadn't said one word the entire time.

33

The next morning, I went to Hammer's for an ice bath to help my bruised hands and shoulder, then I eased into the sauna to relax my muscles. If I was feeling this sore, I could only imagine how sore the two of them must've felt once the anesthesia wore off from their surgery. I was almost dressed when my phone rang. I knew it was a Philadelphia number by the 215 area code. One of my first girlfriends in college lived in a neighborhood called Germantown and had the same area code.

"This is Rodney Cooper," the caller said when I answered. "Sorry it took so long to get back to you."

"Not a problem," I said, sitting down on a bench in front of my locker. "I wanted to talk to you about your mother's surveillance system."

"How are you involved in all this?" Cooper said. His voice was suddenly suspicious.

"I used to be a detective with CPD, but now I'm a private investigator. One of my clients is investigating the shooting of Reece Williams."

"Listen, Mr. Cayne, I want to be honest with you," he said. "My mother is seventy-five years old. She lives alone. She doesn't bother anybody. She's lived in that house for over forty years, never had any trouble, and she doesn't need any right now. With all due respect to your investigation, I don't want my mother to get into any kind of situation because she says or does something the police don't like. I live all the way over here in Philly. I'm not there to help or protect her, and I'm an only child, so it's just me."

"I completely understand your concern," I said. "I don't want to put her in harm's way either. I was part of CPD, but I also grew up all my life here in Chicago, so I understand both sides. I'll treat and protect your mother as if she were my own."

There was a slight pause on the other end of the line, then Cooper said, "I looked you up. I read about you. I believe you're a man of your word. How can I help you?"

"You mother says two officers came and took the memory card from her DVR that stored the video files."

"They did. She called me after they left. I wish she would've called me before she let them in. I would've told her not to let anyone in without a search warrant. I also grew up in Chicago, and I know the kind of shit the police have pulled over the years. I wouldn't let them into her house without someone being there with her. But she let them in thinking she was doing the right thing, and they took the card. Now they're acting like they never took it."

"Have you called anyone?"

"We both have. I talked to several people, but they kept transferring me around. No one knows anything. Some detective called my mother back and said he'd look into it. Haven't heard a word. Like I told my mother, better to leave it alone and stay out of it. This is a bad situation."

"I took down the make and model number of the DVR and looked it up," I said. "The manufacturer says there's an option to store the video not just to the card but also in the cloud."

"There is."

"So you have the files backed up?"

"They should be."

"Why don't you know?"

"Because I didn't want to see the video."

"Wait, I'm confused. You have the video, but you won't look at it?"

"I don't have it yet," he said. "But I could probably download it from the cloud. I purposely haven't looked at it. If the video matches what I heard happened out there, I don't want it on my conscience and not say anything. Sometimes it's best not to know. It's also safer for my mother if they think she doesn't know anything. That way they'll leave her alone."

I had to handle this delicately. I completely understood where he was coming from and his concerns, but at the same time, that video could be the linchpin in a case against Mankovich. I needed to see that video.

"What if there's a way to do this without you seeing the video or getting your mother involved?" I asked.

"I'm listening."

"What if you don't look at the video, but I do? You'll be none the wiser about the video contents and can't be accused of knowing something you don't know."

"I might be able to go along with that," he said. "Just give me a little time to think this through. Like I said before, I don't want any trouble for my mother or me. We live a quiet life, and I want to keep it that way."

"I respect that completely," I said. "When you're ready, you have my phone number."

No sooner had I hung up the phone than Burke called in.

"I got the info on that car you asked about parked outside Williams's apartment building," he said. "It was signed out to the team Garrity and Francetti. The strange thing about it was that it wasn't their normal car. Maybe it means something, maybe it doesn't."

A pool of tac cars sat in a parking lot behind all the police stations. No team owned a particular car, but teams used the same cars all the time, so everyone respected each other's preferences. The teams would report to work, sign out a car, then head out into the streets. There were occasions when teams had to use another car. Either their car was in the garage for service or another team for whatever reason took their car. However, this rarely happened.

"I know what you're thinking," Burke said. "And I already asked. No one remembers the specific reason why they used a different car that day."

"Just seems strange," I said. "Not only were they at Reece's out of their district, but they also weren't in their usual car."

"I wouldn't make a federal case out of it," Burke said. "Sometimes these things happen for completely benign reasons."

There had been nothing benign in the case of Reece Williams. In fact, there had been all kinds of irregularities. I felt completely justified in my suspicions. Garrity and Francetti didn't just so happen to take a lunch break parked outside Reece's apartment building while we were inside. They had clear intentions, and I was determined to find out what they were.

34

Thursday night, Mechanic and I jumped in his Prius and headed south. We decided it might not be the best idea to show up at Marquette Park in his Viper. A Black and white guy showing up together would raise enough suspicions, let alone arriving in a car that screamed for attention. This was not a part of town that opened its arms to strangers. The color of my skin meant nothing there. Even I was considered an outsider in this part of the city.

Marquette Park occupied an enormous three hundred and twenty-three acres in the rough Chicago Lawn neighborhood, making it the largest park on the city's southwest side. It boasted an eighteen-hole golf course, lagoons, pool, tennis courts, and a colossal fieldhouse that featured two gymnasiums. The current condition of the park gave little acknowledgment of its historical significance, one I vividly remember reading about in my history class in elementary school. Marquette Park and the surrounding neighborhood had been built for the exclusive pleasure of the white community, one that turned violent in 1966 when Dr. Martin Luther King Jr. and others of the Chicago Freedom Movement marched to a nearby Realtor's office to demand that properties be sold to everyone regardless of race or creed. Shortly after arriving, King was met with a hostile mob of hundreds of white protesters who hurled bricks, rocks, bottles, and almost any-thing that wasn't tied down. King was struck in the head with a rock and knocked down but minutes later got back to his feet and finished the now-famous march.

In later years, as more Blacks moved into the neighborhood, whites fled in large numbers. The city no longer invested in the upkeep of the park, and its beautiful offerings deteriorated and withered in the face of an increasing Black patronage. It was too familiar of a story in Chicago's deeply segregated past that gave birth to the economic, health, and social disparities that still plagued the city today.

The battered Marquette Park Fieldhouse was a shining example of this purposeful neglect from City Hall. Mechanic parked at the end of a small cluster of cars. As we walked through the massive, heavily fortified doors, we could hear the sound of sneakers squealing on hard-wood and the rapid beat of a bouncing ball. Two guys, both looking like former athletes past their prime, met us in the lobby. They were carried away in conversation until we approached.

"We're looking for Spider," I said.

The short guy with salt-and-pepper hair and a large silver necklace hanging over his sweater said, "Are you cops?"

"Not at all," I said.

"Spider know you're coming?" the taller one said.

"He will once we talk to him," I said.

The two quickly looked at each other.

"Ain't no reason to get smart," the short guy said. "This is Marquette Park, brutha. You can't just roll up here any ole kinda way."

"It's still a public fieldhouse, so we can enter, right?"

"It is," the tall one said, stepping forward. "But we need to pat you down."

I spread my legs and raised my hands. He patted me down front and back, then signaled for Mechanic.

"I'm carrying," Mechanic said. He pulled out his .500 Magnum and showed it.

"Sweet Mother of God," the short one said. "Damn thing almost as big as me."

"You can't bring that in here," the tall one said. He pointed to a no-gun sign posted on a column several feet away.

Mechanic thought for a moment. I nodded, then he turned and headed outside. They patted him down when he returned, then let us pass through into the gymnasium.

There was one main full court with about eighteen guys total including the ten currently on the floor. A tall, lanky guy ran down court, dribbled between his legs, spun around a defender, then sliced his way in the air shooting the ball off the backboard and in. I knew right away it was Spider. His smoothness was effortless. Mechanic and I took a seat on the empty bleachers under the suspicious stares of the guys waiting to play the next game. Chicago had always boasted some of the best street players in the country, and what we were now watching did little to disprove that notion.

For the next fifteen minutes, Spider put on a clinic with all of his slicing, dicing, dribbling, shooting, and dunking. It wasn't that the other players weren't good—it was that he was just so much better than everyone else. He finally ended the game when the point guard on his team raced down the court on a fast break and passed the ball to Spider, who was so far behind the three-point line he was almost falling out of bounds when he caught it. Spider squared his shoulders and shot. The ball never touched the rim. Nothing but net. His teammates ran over and tapped hands as the losing squad headed for a seat on the bleachers. Spider walked over to his gym bag and grabbed a bottle of Gatorade. He gulped down half of it without stopping.

"What's up?" Spider said as Mechanic and I approached. His name was well deserved. He stood at least six foot six, all arms and legs, low-cut hair graying at the temples, not an ounce of fat on him.

"Earl told us we could find you here," I said.

"Earl Bannon?"

I nodded.

Spider sized up Mechanic, then looked back at me. "How do you know Earl?"

"I've been looking into what happened to Reece Williams. Earl told me the two of you used to hang out. He said you still played ball here."

Spider took another long swallow, then said, "All true. So what's up?"

"I have a few photographs of some women who went to Reece's apartment. I was hoping you could take a look and see if you recognize any of them."

A guy called out to Spider and asked him if he was ready to start the next game as the opposing teams were assembling on the court. Spider raised his finger at the guy.

"Which side are you on?" Spider said.

"The good side," I said. "I didn't know Reece, but I know something happened that night that shouldn't've happened. I want him and his family to have some justice."

"Justice? Sheeit. Ain't nothing gonna bring RJ back. He was my man. Good dude all the way around. Muthafuckas killed him for no reason. Only real justice is putting one of them in the ground just like they did RJ."

"I can't promise that, but I can promise I'll get to the bottom of what happened and hold whoever was responsible accountable. But to do that, I could use your help."

I pulled the folded photographs out of my inside jacket pocket.

Spider grabbed his gym bag and said, "Let's go out in the hall." He turned to the court and said, "Boom Boom, take my spot for a minute. Be right back." A guy as wide as a delivery truck jumped off the bleachers and walked onto the court.

We followed Spider into the lobby and away from the two guys at the front door who looked at us suspiciously until Spider nodded that everything was all right. Once we were alone in a side hallway, Spider opened up his bag and pulled out a pair of reading glasses.

"I don't want nobody seeing me wear these things," he said, laughing. "They'd give me shit every time I missed a shot saying I can't see the rim."

"From the damage I just saw you do out there, I don't know who could give you shit," I said. "You made five of the last six shots."

"And today's an off day for me," he said matter-of-factly. "I've lost half a step the last couple of years. But the stroke is still there." He made a shooting motion with his right hand.

"What's the word on the street about all this?" I asked.

"He ever talk?" Spider said, jerking his head at Mechanic.

"Only when necessary."

Mechanic stood there not paying us any attention. I knew he was thinking about his piece locked in his trunk. He didn't like being naked.

"It was a hit," Spider said. "Pure and simple. That's what they're saying."

I didn't have to ask who he meant by "they." These never-to-be identified people operated in the shadows of the streets.

"They was comin' for RJ," Spider said. "No other explanation. He was never mixed up in anything. Was always put together. That's bullshit about him matching some description of somebody they were looking for. Git the fuck outta here. They was looking for RJ and only RJ."

"Any guesses why they were after him?"

Spider shook his head. "Not a damn clue. That's what's got us all messed up. Bad enough they killed him, but we don't even know why. We've gone through the channels. Can't get no answers."

"Did you know Reece was seeing a cop?"

"I knew," Spider said. "Wasn't nothing serious. RJ always had plenty of women. Since we was kids, girls always just took to him. We'd be at a game or walk into a party, and they'd just come and start talking to him, giving up their numbers. He had it like that. He had some of the finest ass in all of Chicago."

Seeing the photos, I had no disagreement.

"Did you ever meet his girls?" I asked.

"Of course. We hung out. Sometimes he brought a little piece with him. I didn't know all of 'em, but I met plenty."

I handed the three photographs to Spider. He put on his glasses, then quickly moved through the three photos. He handed them back to me when he was done.

"None of them girls is a cop," he said, quickly folding his glasses and stashing them back in his bag.

"Are you sure?"

"Hundred percent."

"You know all of them?"

He nodded. "First girl is named Nina. She's a teacher somewhere on the West Side. The second girl is Rashawna. She runs a youth center over in Englewood. And the white girl works at Stroger in the pharmacy department. Ain't none of them girls cops."

"Did you ever see the cop?"

"He never brought her around. Said she liked to keep a low profile. She mostly went to his apartment after her shift was over, and they did what they had to do. Sometimes she'd stop by during her shift, but he said the whole public stuff wasn't her thing."

This was not what I had expected. All nineteen women had been positively identified and none of them was the cop. How the hell was this possible? I had made a mistake somewhere. I needed to retrace my steps and figure out how it was possible all of these women had been captured by his camera except for the lady cop.

35

I was starting to get a complex," Carolina said. "You've been spending more time with Morgan than you have with me. I started thinking I had lost you to Hollywood."

We were seated at a small window table at Prosecco, one of my favorite Italian restaurants. I was hastily working my way through a plate of norcina with its spicy sausage and homemade rigatoni noodles. Carolina had opted for the pesce bianco, a sautéed white fish with lemon, white wine, capers, and a bed of spinach. The lighting was low, and the restaurant hadn't gotten full yet.

"Hollywood?" I said. "Me? Never. I'd have to be a fool to trade down like that."

Carolina winked. "Who's on duty tonight?" she asked.

"Both Mechanic and Rox drew the short straws," I said.

"Both of them at once?"

"I won the draw, so I get to be here with you and pretend like we're at La Terrazza in Rome."

"Is that a real restaurant?"

"Of course it is."

"Have you been there?"

"Several years ago."

"Did you like it?"

"No, I loved it. Besides the great food, it has some of the best views of any restaurant in the city. Overlooks one of my favorite landmarks—this gigantic marble structure called the National Monument of Victor Emmanuel II in the center of the city in the middle of this really busy roundabout called Piazza Venezia."

"It sounds so romantic."

I smiled. "You'd look gorgeous sitting at one of those window tables."

"Well, just in case you're wondering, my passport is still valid and has a lot of empty pages that still need to be stamped."

I reached across the table and kissed her softly. "I have a secret to tell you," I said.

"I tend to like your secrets."

"My plan is to fill every available space in every single one of those passport pages and leave you with no choice but to get a new one."

She ran her hand over the back of mine and said, "I have a lot of vacation time in late spring."

"We can go right before high season starts over there," I said. "After this case, I'm gonna need a break."

"You think it'll last until the spring?"

"Nope. I think it'll be over by the end of November."

"What makes you say that?"

"Because I think Morgan will have no use for me after that."

"You think you'll catch the pervert who's been threatening her?"

"If there really is a pervert."

Carolina dropped her fork. "Excuse me?"

"I don't know if Morgan is really in danger," I said. "I had a talk with my father last week, and he made a good point."

"What did he say?"

"Maybe Morgan hired me less because she needed protection and more because she needed help in solving the Reece Williams case."

Carolina took a sip of her white wine and said, "I didn't want to say anything, but you really have been working that case like it's yours."

"I can't help myself. The more I learn about what happened to Reece, the angrier and more determined I get."

"And like your father said, that's maybe what Morgan was counting on. But let me play devil's advocate. Let's say her real intentions were not for you to protect her but to get you involved in the Williams case. How do you explain the letters and her car getting vandalized and the floggers?"

"That's the problem," I said. "I can't."

"Or looking at it another way, maybe both things are possible. Someone's really out there trying to get to her, and on top of that, she wants you to help her crack this case so she can get the big story and win the overnights."

"That seems the most plausible explanation to me."

"She's using you," Carolina said matter-of-factly. "And I think you know that. I'm surprised you haven't called her out about it."

"Not yet."

"What are you waiting for?"

"'Patience is bitter, but its fruit is sweet.'"

"Poet or rapper?"

"Aristotle. In some ways he was both."

"So what's next?"

"Me asking you for help."

"I have no problems confronting Morgan," Carolina said. "Women like to mark their territory just like men do."

I smiled and wondered how I could get so lucky. Carolina was the most beautiful when she got feisty.

"What I need help with is some background on a detective," I said. "His name is Hakeem Jefferson. He works out of the Sixth."

I explained to her Mrs. Cooper's video and the missing memory card and the promised callback from Detective Jefferson that never came.

"What do you need to know?" Carolina asked.

"The basics. Start with his record, where he worked before the Sixth, partners, anything that would give me an idea of who he is and where he comes from."

"You think he's not on the up and up?"

"Not sure, but I think he knows what's on that memory card and why it hasn't resurfaced."

STRYKER AND I HAD JUST gotten back from our evening walk, and I felt like I had at least burned off half the calories of my dinner when my phone rang. It was Morgan. She had just gotten off air. She was driving home with Mechanic trailing behind her. There was excitement brimming in her voice.

"Did I wake you?" she said.

"Not at all," I said. "Just got back in from a walk. About to call it a night."

"You're not gonna believe what I'm gonna tell you."

"The Bears finally won a game."

"I'm not talking miracles." She laughed. "You would've seen the fireworks over at Navy Pier if that happened. It's about Reece Williams. I actually got the witness to agree to an interview."

"The witness that told his story to Father Flagger?"

"Yes. Can you believe it?"

"When did all this happen?"

"I just got off the phone with him. He called and said that he's watched me for many years, and he trusts me and is ready to talk on camera. I agreed to blur his face and disguise his voice. He agreed to give me the entire story."

"When is this gonna happen?"

"Tomorrow night at the safe house."

"Does your news director know?"

"She was my first call. She said if it's compelling enough, we might be able to make the piece work for sweeps."

"Who else knows?"

"Just my EP and Duane, the photog you met when I interviewed Father Flagger."

"What about CPD? I thought your news director wanted a response from them before she would run the story."

"She does. I had Father Flagger's interview transcribed and typed up. We sent the parts where he describes what the witness told him to the media relations team at CPD to give them an opportunity to respond. Ideally, we'd want them to go on camera with a response, but a written statement will work too."

"And if you don't get any response at all?"

"There's still a good chance we can run it. We'd have to button it up by saying they never responded to our request for an interview. We do it all the time. Sweeps start next week. The ball is in their court."

36

I woke up early the next morning after a dream that Julia was lying in my bed waiting for me when I got home from work. I stood there paralyzed, uncertain what I should do. She woke up and found me staring at her, then motioned for me to join her. I took a step forward, then heard my name. I turned and saw Carolina standing in the doorway. She too was dressed in black lingerie. She motioned for me to join her. I stood there frozen, looking back and forth between the two. I turned and took a step toward Carolina. She tilted her head slightly and smiled. Then I stopped and looked at Julia who had gotten out of bed and stood there smiling at me too. That's when the dream ended.

The first thing I did when I got up was send Julia a text telling her that I wanted to meet with her tomorrow. I could no longer put off the conversation, and I knew exactly how I wanted it to go down.

My phone rang. It was Rox.

"Front page of the *Sun-Times*," she said. "Bryan was right."

I hung up the phone and clicked on the *Sun-Times* app on my home screen. There was the headline: "Giselle Burgos Comes to Chicago."

Robert Leeder's article had stated everything Bryan had told me almost to the word. The network honchos had done what had never been done before and called in one of their network stars to battle it out in a local ratings war. The photograph of Burgos and her husband looked more like a Hollywood power couple rather than some hard-nosed journalist. Handsome, expensively well-dressed, and the air of being untouchable, they were everything that Midwesterners were not. This was a clear signal from WMTQ that while Roscati was resting in a small cemetery in Iowa, the station was still willing to fight at all costs to capture that top spot. Game still on.

My phone suddenly vibrated in my hands, and I almost dropped it.

"I was just thinking about you," I said.

"You read the article," Morgan said.

"And saw the photo."

"They're coming at me with all guns blazing."

"She sounds like a pretty big gun. And she's very easy to look at."

"I'm not afraid of her," Morgan said. "We started out together in Bowling Green, Ohio. It was market 181 out of 210. She had hair as dark as yours and a chest as flat as a countertop. Now look at her. You wouldn't even know it was the same person."

"So I take it you won't be inviting her to a welcome-to-Chicago dinner."

"She's coming to *my* city, not the other way around. She wants to talk to me, she knows how to reach me."

"You're no shrinking violet."

"I hate losing more than I like winning," Morgan said. "And I would be physically ill losing to a big phony like her."

"I'll meet you and Duane in the garage tonight right after your show," I said. "Then I'll follow you to the safe house."

"I haven't been this excited for an interview in a long time," she said. "Any update on Mrs. Cooper's video?"

"I haven't heard back from her son. He has my number. I don't want to pressure him. It's better he reaches a decision on his own."

"Sweeps start next week. I really need that video."

"When was the last time you prayed to God?"

"I believe in God, but I make it a point not to pray for specific outcomes."

"Well, now might be a good time to start."

I DROPPED OFF MY EIGHTY-SIX Porsche at a garage on the South Side that stored it for me for the winter. The salt and snow wreaked havoc on old cars, and my Porsche, in pristine condition, only had thirty-seven thousand miles on it. My garage guy would give it a service, disconnect the battery, and cover it for the winter. I would pick her back up when temperatures broke into the fifties sometime in the first or second week of April. In the meantime, I pulled out my silver-and-black customized eighty-five Land Rover Defender. The V8 engine was a beast in the snow, and its new set of tires handled even the harshest of Chicago's roads with a dismissive smirk.

As I pulled out of the garage, Carolina called from her cell phone.

"Aren't you at work?" I asked.

"I am," she replied.

"Why are you calling me from your cell phone?"

"I wanted to step out of the office to have this conversation."

"This isn't a good start."

"There's a problem with your Detective Jefferson," she said. "First of all, he's not a detective, and second, he doesn't work out of the Sixth."

"He's been transferred?"

"No, he was never a detective, and he never worked the Sixth. He's a sergeant who works at HQ in the Street Operations Unit."

"He's a paper pusher."

"Basically. He assists the street deputies working in the field."

Whenever there were shots fired at or by police personnel, the street deputy on call would respond to the scene and take charge. Street deputies rotated duty, but there was always one available around the clock ready to be dispatched should the need arise. Running a scene was the exciting part of the job. Dealing with the reams of paperwork and reports that had to be filed was their dread. They had a team of administrative officers who helped them sort through it all while following a myriad of departmental policies and procedures.

"This doesn't make sense," I said. "First of all, why would a sergeant in street ops respond to calls left for district detectives? He has nothing to do with processing a scene or collecting evidence. That memory card was evidence. He's way out of the chain of command getting involved in this."

"That's not all," Carolina said. "He's accessed the case report seven times, and that was just in the last two weeks."

"I don't have the org chart in front of me, but who do the street deputies report to?"

"The deputy chief in the Office of Operations."

I tried to put the pieces together but couldn't make them fit. There were still too many missing.

"You have any biographical info on Jefferson?" I asked.

"I'm gonna work on that next. I just wanted to call you when I found out he wasn't a detective and wasn't even in the field when the shooting happened."

Jefferson was definitely not the one who should've been responding to the calls from the Coopers. If the detectives themselves weren't going to respond, at least their supervising sergeant or lieutenant should've been doing the follow-up. Who was Sergeant Hakeem Jefferson, and why was he even involved?

"Try to find out where Jefferson worked before street ops and who he worked with," I said. "He has to have some kind of connection, or the order for him to get involved must've come from above."

I hung up the phone and called Burke right away.

"I'm just about to get into the barber's chair," he grumbled. "This better be good."

"A pig with the most expensive lipstick is still a pig."

"You've been reading through your jokes book again. What the hell do you want?"

"A quick refresher on chain of command."

"Jesus Christ, now I'm a damn tutor. What do you wanna know?"

"When would a request for the return of collected evidence ever be answered by a sergeant in street ops?"

"Is this some sort of trick question?"

"Not at all."

"Then it's a stupid question. That would never happen. At least not in any chain-of-command scenario I can think of. Why would some pinhead at HQ have anything to do with evidence gathered at a crime scene? They live on a computer all day long. They have nothing to do with field work."

"That's what I thought."

"Are you gonna tell me what this is all about?"

I told him what I knew about the Cooper video and Hakeem Jefferson.

"I'm a commander in the Chicago Police Department," Burke said. "I have no official comment on what you just said."

"Understood," I said. "Now tell me your unofficial opinion."

"You and your prima donna better go buy some long waders fishermen wear when they walk out into the water, 'cause you're about to step in some serious shit, and it might be much deeper than you think."

"Opinion and fashion advice duly noted."

37

I walked into my office, kept the lights off, and reclined behind my desk. I couldn't get Hakeem Jefferson out of my head. I turned on my computer and Googled his name. The search returned several pages, but none of them were relevant. There were lots of articles and links to a smiling political science professor by the same name at Stanford University who was well published and worked in the Center for Comparative Study of Race and Ethnicity. He was definitely not a police officer. Ironically, a lot of his research dealt with police reform and the debate regarding wholesale change to the foundational policies of law enforcement.

Looking at the Stanford crest on his page made me think of Julia. She did her undergrad at Stanford. I wondered if she knew this professor. I opened my desk drawer and found the note she had left with her phone number on it. I wanted to confirm I had the right number since she hadn't responded to my text. I called. Her voicemail picked up after several rings. I didn't leave a message. Instead, I sent her another text message telling her that I wanted to meet with her as soon as possible. She had created enough turmoil and confusion in my life. I needed clarity and certainty. I was more ready than I had ever been to deal with this. I needed the truth—both hers and mine.

I went back to my computer and played around with various word combinations hoping to get something on Sergeant Jefferson. I was several minutes into the new search when my phone rang. My heart raced thinking it was Julia calling me back. It was Father Flagger.

"They killed him," Father Flagger shouted. "Dear God, merciful and almighty. Most despicable and inhumane murderers. They killed him in broad daylight."

"Slow down, Father," I said. "Who's been killed?"

"Slim Henderson."

I racked my mind, but the name didn't register.

"Who is that?" I asked.

"The eyewitness," he said. "The one I told you about who saw everything from his porch. They tracked him down and killed him. I know they did. I won't believe any other explanation for what's happened. He had agreed to go on camera with Morgan. They were supposed to talk tonight."

"Calm down, Father," I said. "Where's the body right now?"

"About thirty feet away from where I'm standing. They're trying to cut him out of the car as we speak. The car is split almost completely in half. It's a mess down here. Glass and blood and metal everywhere."

"Where are you?"

"Eighty-Third and State at the southbound ramp to the Dan Ryan. Five minutes from his house. He was a good kid. Never in any trouble. His grandparents got married in my church."

"I don't understand. First you said they killed him. Now you're saying he was in a car accident."

"He crashed his car because they were chasing him, and he was scared to death. They made him crash."

"How do you know this?"

"Because his cousin was on the phone with him the entire time, and she's standing right next to me."

"Don't go anywhere. I'm on my way."

IT TOOK ME TWENTY MINUTES to reach the scene, and they still hadn't been able to extract Henderson's body from the wreckage. I had worked many accidents before, but this was one of the worst I had ever seen. Not only was the car almost totally split in half, but the front bumper and hood had been smashed so far back, there no longer was a front seat. The only blessing in all this mess was there was no doubt he died on impact. A small crowd of civilians had gathered with their cell phones out, the brisk cold keeping most people away. One of the news stations' helicopters frantically buzzed above us. Marked and unmarked police cars parked in every direction circled what remained of the mangled car. Several firemen and police officers, feverishly working on the crushed frame, huddled around the driver's door. One group manipulated the jaws of life as they attempted to cut through the twisted metal while the other group worked in concert using a hydraulic spreader. A large pool of blood had collected underneath the car. I spotted Father Flagger standing behind the tape talking on his cell phone. He stood next to a short girl whose hair hadn't been completely combed. She wore what looked like pajama pants underneath a long coat as if she had just run out of the house. Tears streamed down her face.

"Jesus, Mary, and Joseph, this has got to stop," Father Flagger said as I approached, and he disconnected his phone call. "They're barbarians, and they're getting more brazen. Talk about gangsters running the streets. They're gangsters in uniform."

"Take me through what happened," I said.

Father Flagger put his arm around the girl. "This is the man I told you about, LaShawnda," he said to her calmly. "He used to be a detective. He's on our side. Can you tell him what you told me?"

She nodded, her stare not leaving the activity surrounding the battered car. Another chopper arrived above us and added to the noise.

"Let's walk over here," I said.

We stepped back from the tape and walked about fifteen yards up the bridge that crossed the expressway. Once I had turned her around so that she wasn't facing the wreckage, I said, "I know this is tough, but tell me everything that happened from beginning to end."

She closed her eyes and nodded her head softly as she exhaled slowly. "I was at the house when Slim called me," she said between sobs. "He didn't sound like himself. He was scared. He told me he had just been at J&J on Sixty-Third, and the cops came out of nowhere and pulled him over."

"Was this J&J the restaurant?" I asked.

"No, the rim shop. They sell tires and lots of car stuff. He was heading back home when he noticed a cop car come up behind him and turn on the lights. He pulled over right away because he didn't want any trouble. That's when he called me to let me know he was being stopped. He told me he was pulling out his insurance paper and his license right away so when they walked up to his car, he'd already have them out. He didn't want to reach for them when they was at the car 'cause he was worried they would be suspicious and think he was reaching for a gun or something. While he was waiting for them to come up to the car, we kept talking. I told him to stay calm and don't worry about it. He didn't do anything. All his papers were in order. It was gonna be all right."

"So you were on the phone with him the entire time this was going on?" I said.

"Yes. I told him I wanted to stay on the phone so I could hear what happened. Then all of a sudden, he just started screaming. He said one of them had his gun out and was walking to the car. He panicked and said he was gonna take off. The way they were acting didn't feel right. So he put the car in gear and just took off. I told him don't stop until he got some place that would have a lot of people around. I told him to go to the big shopping center over off Eighty-Seventh and the Dan Ryan. There's a big Jewel-Osco over there, and lots of people are always shopping. They wouldn't do anything to him while people were looking."

She closed her eyes and shook her head, her lips quivering. I gave her time.

She took a deep breath, then continued. "We stayed on the phone while he was driving. He said they were chasing him. Then they hit him from behind, and he started yelling. I told him to go faster. He said he was going as fast as he could, but his car was too old. It could only go so fast. He said they were right on him. Then I heard him yell, 'Oh shit!' And then a loud bang like an explosion. I ain't never heard anything like that my whole life. I kept calling his name, but he didn't answer me. I looked at my phone, and the line had disconnected. I called him back, but his phone just kept ringing. It went to voicemail. Over and over I called him, but he didn't answer. I knew something bad happened. Now look. They killed him. They hit him from behind and made him crash. Sorry-ass muthafuckas killed him."

"Was he alone in the car?" I asked.

"Yes," she said. "It was just him."

"Were you there the night Reece was shot?" I asked.

"I wasn't outside. I was in the house. I didn't see it, but I heard the gunshots. What does this have to do with Reece?"

I wanted to avoid answering that question for now. "Do you know if anyone ever came back to the house looking for witnesses to the shooting?"

"You mean after the night it happened?"

"Yes. Maybe a couple of detectives came by asking questions."

"Nobody. After that night we didn't hear nothing. And we didn't want to. We don't trust them. And this is why."

She turned and looked at the wreckage. It looked like they were almost done cutting an opening big enough to pull Henderson through. I noticed one of the officers standing near the caution tape. Pam Rigby. We worked out of the Tenth District together when we were both in patrol. She was always a bright spot in what were some long, dark days. Funny, generous, always with a positive outlook. The dreariness of the job never dimmed her light. She looked exactly the same except her hair was a little shorter. I walked over and called her name when I approached. She turned, paused for a moment, then when I smiled, she reached out and gave me a tight hug.

"Ashe Cayne," she said. "How the hell are ya?"

"By the looks of that car, feeling really happy to be on this side of the tape."

"That wasn't a happy ending," she said, shaking her head. "Not the way I'd wanna go. I heard you moved to Florida or California—some place warm. They said all you did was play golf."

"'Can the Ethiopian change his skin or the leopard his spots?'" I said.

"You're still quoting all that stuff." She smiled. "I missed that."

"Those sergeant chevrons are looking really good against that crisp white shirt."

"Got the promotion two years ago," she said. "Finally. A little more responsibility. A little extra in the paycheck. A white shirt that I have to keep taking to the cleaners, which eats up the little extra in the paycheck. Otherwise, not much is different. What's the latest with you? Married? Kids?"

I held up and waved my naked ring finger. "Still a work in progress." I smiled. "But there's always hope."

She tapped me playfully on the shoulder. "Yeah, right," she said. "I bet the ladies are still coming after you left and right."

"What about you?" I said. "Life good?"

"Married, then divorced. No kids. Still not giving up. Life marches on." She laughed, then said, "What the hell are you doing here anyway?"

"I saw all the commotion. Figured I'd take a look. What the hell happened?"

She looked back at the other officers working on the car, grabbed my arm, and pulled me to the perimeter. When we were far out of earshot she said, "This is a real shit show. Supposedly, the guy had a busted taillight. They ran the tag. Some violations. They went to pull him over, he stops, then he just takes off. They chase him, he loses control of the car, and here we are."

"Where's the team?" I asked.

"Over there talking to the deputy," she said, pointing to three men huddled tightly.

Two plainclothes officers talked to a tall man with a thick blond mustache. All three officers were white. The deputy listened intently, nodding his head, while the officers made their case.

"I know it's been a while for me, but since when does a deputy show up at a car crash?" I said. "Procedures have changed that much?"

"No idea what he's doing here," Rigby said. "Tell you the truth, I thought the same thing when he rolled up. Maybe he was nearby and heard the call. I have no idea. He's been talking to them for the last twenty minutes or so."

"You know the two officers?"

"One of 'em," she said. "The bigger one with the red beard. Garrity. He's been working out of the Sixth for a few years. The other guy is his partner. They just teamed up about five months ago."

"Did you just say Garrity?" I said. Burke had given me that name when I asked him about the two guys parked outside of Reece's building. He had said Garrity and Francetti. Could this be the same Garrity?

"Yup, Keenan Garrity," Rigby said. "A bit of a cowboy. Too loose for my taste. Shoot first, ask questions later."

"You know his partner's name?"

"I don't. He's pretty new in the district. They teamed up after Garrity's old partner got shipped far away up north." Rigby lowered her voice. "Mankovich," she said, raising her eyebrows. "The guy who shot Reece Williams."

I stood there calmly, trying to appear unfazed by what she had just said, but the adrenaline had definitely kicked into high gear. Sometimes when working a tough case and hitting a lot of dead ends, the universe takes pity and sends you a gift.

"Just to be clear," I said. "Garrity and Mankovich were partners?"

"Copy that," Rigby said. "For six or seven years. Still would be partners if that shooting hadn't happened. Garrity went on a scheduled furlough. Mankovich ends up riding with another team and shooting Williams. By the time Garrity gets off furlough, Mankovich has already been transferred."

"Was it a good shooting?"

She shrugged. "I don't know," she said. "Tough call. I haven't heard all the details or seen the report, but from what most people are saying, I heard it was one of those situations. All three stories matched up. They saw a gun. The guy reached for his waistband. Mankovich hits him twice. Problem comes from the neighbors' accounts. They insist he didn't have a gun. Who's telling the truth? I can't make the call. Last I heard, IAD is looking into it."

Now a known witness to the shooting had been chased to his death by the former partner of the same police officer who had killed Reece Williams. You'd have to believe there were three purple moons in the sky every night to believe this was just a coincidence. For my money, they were covering their tracks and closing the circle. I took one last look as they finally pulled Henderson's lifeless body out of the carnage, his limbs dangling as if held together by string, his face so disfigured the family was going to have no choice but to make it a closed casket. I had seen enough. I turned and walked away.

38

I figured it best to break the news in person, so I jumped in my car and drove to WLTV. Morgan was seated in her office looking at her computer screen when I entered the newsroom. She quickly read the expression on my face as I walked in and closed the door behind me.

"Something happened," she said, pushing back from her desk. "You have that look."

"Slim Henderson died about an hour ago over on Eighty-Third Street and the Dan Ryan."

She stiffened in her chair and tightened her eyes. "What the hell are you talking about? I'm interviewing him tonight."

"Not unless you have a psychic who can help you communicate with the dead. I just left the scene. He crashed head-on into a concrete barrier. Split his car in half. His body is on the way to the morgue as we speak. Father Flagger was the one who called me. He was at the scene with the guy's cousin."

Morgan slumped in her seat, her head dropping into her hands. A woman carrying a stack of papers tapped on her door, and Morgan looked up and waved her away. "Unfuckinbelievable," she said. "It's like this story is cursed. Every time I get close to what I need, something snatches it away."

"This wasn't some freak accident," I said. "They killed him." I walked her through what I had learned from Henderson's cousin and Rigby. I carefully explained to her Garrity and his connection to Mankovich.

"This is really out of control," she said. "They can't just keep getting away with this shit. How could this happen?"

"It probably started with that request you submitted to the media relations team at CPD."

"What do you mean?"

"You tipped your hand. You told them you had a witness to the shooting, and you wanted them to go on record with a response. Word already travels fast over there, but something like this moved up and down the chain at warp speed. Their response was pretty straight-forward. Eliminate all witnesses, destroy the case against them."

She buried her face in her hands and said, "So now what do I do? I needed that interview. Without him on record or any video from the scene, my news director will never let me air this story." She picked up a paper on her desk and waved it at me. "All of this and these damn overnights are getting worse by the day. We're now losing to MTQ outside the margin of error. They got that bump from Giselle, and she hasn't even hit the air yet. Imagine what'll happen when she finally sits in the chair."

I empathized with her, but I really didn't know how to help. I was already working every angle I could, but nothing was coming together. My working theory was this had all been part of a bigger scheme, but I didn't have the evidence to make the case. Most importantly, we still didn't have the motivation for Reece's murder.

"Have you found the cop he was sleeping with?" Morgan asked.

"No luck," I said. "All nineteen women in the photographs are spoken for, and none of them is a cop."

"How's that possible? Didn't his friends tell you she came over to his apartment? How could she not be on camera, yet the other women were?"

"Been asking myself the same question," I said. "Earl and Spider both said Reece and the cop never met out in public. It was always at his apartment."

"And with two cameras, there's no video of her coming or going? So she just magically teleported inside his apartment?"

"I've been over the video five times. I downloaded all of the people who entered the apartment. The cop was never caught by the cameras."

"Jesus Christ. I can't catch a break."

The woman who had come to her door a few minutes ago returned with a greater sense of urgency. She tapped on the door, then tapped her wrist.

Morgan nodded and stood. "I need to go shoot promos," she said. "Give me fifteen minutes."

She walked out the door, and the woman handed her what I assumed were her scripts. Morgan lifted her earpiece that was hanging off the back of her collar and slid it into her right ear as the woman talked to her.

I got up to go to the bathroom and headed down the long hall leading from the newsroom. The bathroom was located near the front lobby. I walked by the security office and took a passing glance at the array of monitors against the wall. Something caught my eye. I stopped, turned around, and walked into the office. One of the security guards was seated behind a desk filling out paperwork. I looked more closely at the monitors. There were nine in total—three rows of three.

"Can I help you?" the security guard asked.

"I'm working with Morgan Shaw," I replied.

I gave him my card. He looked it over, then said, "I thought that was you. Isaac mentioned your name. Is there something you need?"

"That camera right there," I said, pointing to the second monitor on the top row. It showed an empty, poorly lit stairwell with several steps and a door with a fire extinguisher next to it. "Where is that?"

"Rear stairwell on the northeast side of the building," he said.

"How do you get there?"

"Back hallway on the other side of the studio."

"Can anyone use it?"

"Only employees. You need a key card to get in and out."

I looked at the other monitors. Most of them were interior cameras, including the one located over the reception desk. Several people walked in and out of the frame. I looked back at the stairwell. Still empty.

"Does anyone use that entrance?"

"Only the smokers."

"What do you mean?"

"There's a no-smoking policy inside the building. A few people in the newsroom are smokers. They use those stairs to leave the building and go out back where they can smoke. They don't want anyone else to see them, so they can hide better back there. There's really no other reason to use that door. Everyone pretty much uses the front or side entrances."

I looked at the adjacent monitor, the last on the top row. Its POV was the exterior of the rear door and a small area surrounding it. There weren't any smokers. In the corner of the screen, I could barely see the windshields of several cars.

"Where are those cars parked?" I asked, pointing to the last monitor.

"In one of the lots that belongs to the building next to ours."

I walked closer to the monitors. I looked at the stairwell again and then the exterior shot. I shook my head. I could hear Morgan's words: "So she just magically teleported inside his apartment?" I cursed myself for not thinking of this earlier.

———◇———

I LEFT THE STATION BEFORE Morgan got back to her office and called Gina Williams as soon as I got into my car. She was picking up her kids from school but agreed to meet me at Reece's as soon as she could get there. I sent a text message to Morgan letting her know I would call her soon. It took about twenty minutes with all the rush hour traffic to get to his apartment building. This time, I turned the corner and drove directly to the back. A small, gated parking lot ran from the rear to an alley shared by the neighboring apartment buildings. The gate was open, and it looked like the closing mechanism no longer worked, so I pulled in. Reece's apartment was on the north side of the building. When I looked up at the second floor, I got immediate confirmation that the first half of my hunch was correct.

I got out of the car and walked up the same steps Mechanic had gone down when we were last there and the unmarked was parked out front. As soon as I arrived on the second-floor landing, I stared into the lens of a camera anchored a couple of feet to the right of Reece's door. How did I not think of this before? The lady cop wasn't one of the nineteen women in the photographs because they were all taken from the cameras in the front of the building, and she never used the front door. She only arrived and exited through the back, hidden from others just like the smokers using that rear stairwell at the station.

I returned to my car and waited for Gina. I turned on the radio and caught Steve Cochrane eviscerating the mayor and his allies who had quietly signed a contract with a private company comprised of investors all the way from Abu Dhabi. For a little over a billion dollars, Bailey sold off the city's entire parking meter system for seventy-five years. Only eleven years into the deal, and the company had already recouped their investment and raked in more than half a billion dollars in profits. Cochrane had the perfect voice for the city's ire over the absurd deal.

Morgan called just as Cochrane took his first caller.

"Where did you go?" she said.

"Reece's apartment," I said. "I needed to check something out."

"What is it?"

"The magical teleporting you mentioned."

"I don't follow."

"There's a reason why we didn't see the cop on the video footage. She used the back stairs. And finally some good news. There's also a camera back here just like the cameras up front."

"There is a God," she said. "Can you get in to see if there's any video?"

My phone buzzed. It was Gina.

"That's his sister calling me on the other line," I said. "I'll call you when I figure out what's going on."

I clicked over, and Gina told me she was out front with the key. I drove around, got the key, and went inside while she waited in the car. The apartment was cold and lifeless, but in the same condition it had been the last time we had been inside. It didn't look like anyone else had been there. I walked to the small closet and picked up the DVR. I flashed my phone light on it and pushed the button that opened the front cartridge door. I tilted the DVR slightly so I could better see what was going on. The second half of my hunch was confirmed. There had been two slots in the DVR. Last time we had only retrieved the memory card from the first slot. That card was for the two cameras in the front of the building. But for some reason, we missed this second slot that held the memory card for the rear camera. That slot, as I expected, was empty. Someone had beat me to it.

I put the DVR back, locked up the apartment, then returned the key to Gina. When she pulled away, I jumped into my car and circled back to the rear of the building. I went up and down the alley several times until I spotted a newer building on the other side of the alley. I drove closer. It had two cameras facing the back of Reece's building.

If I was lucky, they might've picked up a piece of Reece's parking lot and hopefully the cop getting in and out of her car.

I left the alley and drove around the corner to the front of the building. The entrance was protected by a tall gate with a panel of intercom buttons labeled only by the apartment numbers. I started at the bottom only because it was instinctive to start at the top. When I got to the third button, someone finally answered.

"I'm looking for the superintendent," I said.

"There is no superintendent here," an older woman's voice replied.

"Is this a rental building?" I asked.

"No solicitations allowed," she said. The intercom disconnected.

I buzzed it again a couple of times, but she didn't answer. I hit the button above hers and someone answered.

"I'm trying to get ahold of the management company," I said.

"They don't have an office in the building," a man replied. "You have to call Hewitt Brothers for more information."

I got back in my car and Googled Hewitt Brothers on my phone. Their website sat atop the search results. They had an address in West Town. I dialed their phone number and after being put on hold for a couple of minutes got one of the managers on the phone.

"I'm calling about your building over at 4417 South Indiana," I said. "I was wondering if the cameras in the back of the building are active and who monitors the recordings."

"Are you a tenant?" the man said.

"I'm not. Something happened in the back alley, and I was wondering if I could take a look at the footage to see if the cameras caught anything."

"Is this a police investigation?"

"I'm not a police officer," I said. "I'm a private investigator."

"Sir, with all due respect, I'm not at liberty to release any information related to the security systems at any of our locations. And that address isn't one of the buildings I manage. That manager is out of the office and won't bc back for a couple of days."

"Can I get his name and contact information?"

"It's better if you leave your contact information, and I can pass it on to him."

I gave him my name and number and stressed how urgent it was that I hear back from someone. However, I wasn't convinced that my expression of urgency created any within him. I would need to find another way to apply pressure.

I dialed Burke. He didn't answer, so I sent him a text message to get back to me. As I started to drive back to my office, I had the first real surge of hope. Sometimes it only takes one domino for the rest of them to fall.

39

That night, I turned on the heat lamp on my balcony, poured myself a cup of hot chocolate, and bundled up against the evening chill. Stryker had come out for a few minutes, then decided it was too cold and went back inside where he currently sat looking at me through the sliding glass door. I looked over the lake, black and endless. A deserted Navy Pier jutted out into the empty darkness like a lone index finger cut away from the rest of the hand. The faint sound of sirens floated ominously in the thin air, a reminder that danger and urgency were impervious to the hour on the clock.

So many disorganized thoughts bounced freely in my head, from the plush fairways of the Estancia Club to what the scene must have looked like when Reece was shot to Julia and why she still hadn't responded to my text. The answers were always out there, but sometimes, regardless of how hard you pursued them, they never materialized. I had come to learn that like almost anything in life, hard work alone was often not enough. Sometimes you needed a little luck as an accelerant. That's exactly what happened that night as I surveyed the cold Chicago landscape, my insides warming from the sweet hot chocolate. I had just taken out my phone to see if I could capture a photograph of a distant red light blinking on the lake when it buzzed with an email notification. The subject header simply read, *Video*. I opened it.

> This is very bad. I don't know if there's anything you can do at this point, but I hope you find justice for this man and his family.
>
> Please honor your promise not to involve me or my mother. We don't want any problems.
>
> Rodney Cooper

I tried to play the video, but my phone didn't have the right software files to match the video's format, so I quickly went inside and got on my desktop. I downloaded the file and hit play. For the next ten minutes, I remained glued to my screen.

The time code started at 7:10 p.m. The camera caught the entire length of Mrs. Cooper's driveway all the way across the street and into the front lawn of 8517 South Eggleston where Reece had been shot. The picture was in color and extremely clear. Two minutes into the tape, several people walked by 8517. They were on the screen for less than a couple of seconds. The first person was a woman with long braids who was drinking from a can. A few seconds later, two guys walked by in the opposite direction of the woman. One was talking on the phone while the other waved at someone out of frame. Thirty-three seconds went by and a white car sped by, then a man walked into frame, then quickly out. Five seconds later, the same man walked back into frame and stopped. He wore a pair of light-colored creased shorts, sandals, and a matching shirt open at the collar. His small afro had been meticulously trimmed. I froze the video. It was Reece Williams. He was very handsome, leaning against the fence, looking down at his phone smiling. I took a moment to study him as my mind played back the words others had used to describe him. *Reece never got into any trouble . . . Basketball and girls. That's all he did . . . He worked every day . . . Never missed a child support payment for his children and was never late.*

7:13:09. A little more than a minute after Reece stopped at the fence, a guy in an LA Lakers cap and LeBron James jersey walked over, shook Reece's hand, and talked to him for twenty seconds before walking out of frame. Reece went back to looking at his phone.

7:15:16. Reece suddenly jerks his head up and looks to the right. He freezes, then he starts backing up until he's pressing against the fence.

7:15:23. A dark gray unmarked lurches into frame from the left of the screen and stops when its front bumper is only feet away from Reece's legs. Reece turns as if he's going to jump the fence, but then he turns back around.

7:15:27. Three doors of the car fly open—the driver's and the front and rear passenger doors. And that's when I saw it. I froze the screen. All three officers did not have their guns drawn. Mankovich was the only one who exited the car with his gun unholstered and pointed directly at Reece. The other two drew their guns a couple of seconds later after Mankovich ran in front of them, taking the lead position. Reece's hands flew in the air the second the car doors flung open.

7:15:37. Two quick muzzle flashes exploded from Mankovich's gun. Reece fell to the ground instantly.

7:15:49. The three officers walked toward Reece's body with their guns still drawn. Mankovich holsters his gun and rushes to Reece while the other two stay back.

7:15:52. Mankovich knelt down next to Reece and started doing something with his hands. He is there by himself for eight seconds.

7:16:00. Nettles and Knight approached Mankovich and Reece. They both looked down, then Knight turned back toward the street and spoke into his radio. A woman ran into frame from the right side, and Nettles stood up and quickly intercepted her before she could reach Reece.

7:16:17. The tape ends.

I sat back for a minute and took a breath. I stood, went outside to the balcony without my coat, and tried processing what I had just seen. There was so much about the video that bothered me, from Mankovich exiting his car with his gun already drawn to the eight seconds he spent on the ground alone with Reece while the other two stayed back.

I walked back inside and sat down at my desk with pen and paper then went back to the tape. This time, I really took my time, stopping and starting, rewinding and freezing the frames, carefully making de-tailed notes while logging them against the running time code. It was all so fast. Fourteen seconds from the time the unmarked arrives to the time Reece is on the ground. The tape made two things extremely clear and indisputable. All three officers did not exit the car with their guns drawn. Only Mankovich had his gun unholstered. Second, Reece had a cell phone in his hand, and once he raised his hands, he never lowered them before he was shot. This meant the video so far had contradicted at least two important points of the officers' stories.

I rewound the tape to the point where Mankovich knelt next to Reece's body. He was down there for eight seconds before Nettles and Knight approached. The camera was too far away to see exactly what he was doing, but he was definitely doing something. I looked carefully at Nettles and Knight to see what they were doing during those eight seconds. Neither of them looked at Mankovich. Instead, they looked around as if scanning to see who was watching them. Why weren't they looking at Mankovich and Reece, especially since they had a target that had just been shot twice? Why did they wait eight seconds before going to assist?

It was just after midnight when I finished, but I was so charged with what the tape revealed, I couldn't stop. I texted Rayshawn Jackson. He was a computer and video whiz I had met a couple of years ago when I worked the case of a missing wealthy North Shore girl. He was a college student then, and he helped me analyze a critical piece of video that was instrumental in cracking the case. He now was in graduate school studying for his masters, but he ran a little video business on the side.

I had just turned my computer off when my phone rang. It was Rayshawn.

"It's been a while," he said. "Whatchya got?"

"A seven-minute piece of surveillance video," I said. "But I have to warn you—it's graphic. Police shooting from about four months ago."

"Man, when is this shit gonna stop? Every week there's another shooting, another one of us dead."

"This was a shooting over by Marquette Park. A guy named Reece Williams. Did you hear about it?"

"The name sounds familiar," he said. "I think Father Flagger held a press conference with a couple of aldermen. I like that dude. He was giving the cops the business. What do you want me to do with the video?"

"It's in pretty good shape already as far as the resolution, but the camera was across the street from the action, so some of the details aren't totally clear. I need to be able to work with it better, zoom in and not lose the resolution so I can grab some still images. I think I'm seeing what I need to see, but it needs to be clear beyond a doubt."

"Do you have the native video, or did someone copy and send it to you?"

"It's a copy. Is that a problem?"

"Maybe not. But each time you copy video files they lose a little quality. How far away was the camera from the shooting location?"

"Probably fifteen or twenty yards."

"Most decent cameras can handle that distance pretty well. I'll take a look at it and see how much I can do with it. A lot will depend on how good the camera lens is. Send it over to me now, and I'll render it tonight and start working on it tomorrow morning before I go to class. I should have something for you to look at in the afternoon. I'll shoot you a text."

"My man," I said. "And this time I don't care what you say, I'm paying you."

"I'll accept it," he said. "Grad school is putting a hurting on me. Talk tomorrow."

Before turning in that night, I read the case report again, then watched the video on slower speed. I was certain the tape was inconsistent with the officers' report. There was so much about what they did and didn't do that raised questions. Why was Mankovich the only one who fired if all three said they saw Reece reach for a gun in his waistband? And what was Mankovich doing for those eight seconds?

40

The next morning, I woke to my phone vibrating on my nightstand. Light was just starting to slide through the windows. I picked it up but didn't recognize the number. I answered it anyway.

"This is Tyra Martin," the caller said. "Alicia's producer at WMTQ. Sorry to call you so early."

I looked at my clock on the TV stand. 6:21 a.m. This was the best sleep I had gotten since coming back from Arizona.

"Everything okay?" I asked.

"I just wanted to give you a heads-up," she said. "It hasn't been officially announced yet, but they found something strange with Alicia's bloodwork."

"Strange in what way?"

"I don't know all the particulars, but there was something about the blood cells that wasn't right."

"Did she have some kind of illness?"

"Alicia was the healthiest person I knew. She called in sick only one time since I've worked with her. She had the flu and could barely get out of bed. That's the only time I've known her to be sick."

"Are they saying she has some type of blood disease?"

"The ME hasn't declared the cause of death yet. They just found this abnormality yesterday, and they're looking into it."

"How did you find all this out?"

"Are you forgetting what I do for a living?" She laughed softly. "We're the press. We have sources everywhere."

"Understood. If you find out what exactly was wrong with her blood, let me know."

I sat there for a moment staring at my closed blinds trying to digest what I had just heard. I couldn't make much of it, but it was definitely peculiar that a healthy thirty-two-year-old woman who rarely got sick suddenly died from a blood disorder. I opened the search engine on my phone to see if there was any official announcement of what Martin had just told me. After fifteen minutes of searching and not finding anything, I gave up and dozed off.

I wasn't sure how long I had been asleep, but I woke up to my phone buzzing again. This time it was Burke.

"Late night?" he said.

"Had an early call," I said. "Something's wrong with Alicia Roscati's blood."

"I didn't know they had announced cause of death."

"They haven't. They're still investigating, but there's a problem with the blood."

"That's not what you called me about yesterday."

"No, I need some help. I could use your weight. Figuratively, that is."

I explained to him the missing video card from Reece's DVR and the cameras on the building that might've captured the mysterious lady cop and the management company that had control of the security footage. I left out the part about the video from the Cooper camera that Rayshawn was working on.

"Jesus Christ," he said. "Why is it every time I talk to you things seem to be getting worse instead of better?"

"That would depend on your perspective," I said. "I don't know if Reece's family or people in the community would see it the same way. For them, this would be progress. Confirming the evil they already know."

"Not all cops are bad," Burke said.

"Very true. I wore the uniform too. But I don't anymore, so I need you to make a call to that management company so they'll let me see the video."

I spent the next hour sitting in bed thinking about Reece Williams and Slim Henderson, two vibrant, innocent men who joined a growing list of victims who had been chewed up and eaten by a flawed system of justice that constantly revealed it was anything but blind.

I STOOD ON A SMALL patch of turf inside Hole 19 taking full cuts at the golf ball sitting on a rubber tee. This was my first time here, and even in the middle of the day, it was packed with fellow golf addicts trying to get their fix as the approaching winter quickly extinguished any hopes that we would get one more day on the fairways. So this is where my fellow degenerates and I found ourselves, men and women, bankers standing next to plumbers, retirees swinging beside college students, all of us trying not to lose that touch. The warehouse was pleasantly silent except for the constant smack of the metal club faces smashing the golf balls.

I had gone through my first bucket of balls when my phone rang. I stepped back from the tee box and answered it. Kurtis Lewis was on the other end.

"I have mixed news for you," he said. "Not sure if it will help or not, but I've done all I could do."

"I'll take any help I can get right about now," I said.

"I think I can tell you the general area of the city where the letter was mailed, but I can't tell you if it was mailed at a drop box or pickup location."

"What do you mean by a pickup location?"

"Like an apartment building. Carriers drop off the day's mail and pick up the outgoing mail that was left in the mailroom. So I can't tell you how the envelopes entered the system, but I can tell you they were likely mailed somewhere in the River North or Gold Coast area. That's all I can say with any certainty."

"Is it possible to find out how many stand-alone boxes there are in that area?"

"I already did. Thirty-five."

"But then you have all the apartment buildings. There have to be a couple hundred."

"That's the real problem," he said. "With so many buildings down there, you'd never be able to figure out the exact location."

"So what you're basically saying is there's no real hope beyond identifying the general area."

"Not with the limited information in the postmark. Letters mailed like that are virtually untraceable."

I thanked Lewis and stepped back up to the next ball. This wasn't what I wanted to hear, but there was no doubt I would keep swinging. It was the only way to get better.

41

I finished my session at Hole 19 and decided a visit from Mechanic might help distract me from the disappointment of Lewis's call. We sat in my office debating classic Porsches and the location of the engines, arguing which design produced better driving performance—the engine located in the middle of the car or the rear. I was in the midst of making my case for the rear-engine placement when my phone rang.

"This is David Wilford from Hewitt Brothers," the caller said. "I just got off the phone with Commander Burke. He said you needed some help with video at one of our buildings on the South Side."

Burke complained and grumbled, but he never let me down.

"Thanks for calling me back," I said. "I was down there in the alley behind your building in the forty-five hundred block of South Indiana and noticed you had a couple of rear-facing cameras. One was on the north side of the building, second floor. The other was on the first floor adjacent to the fire escape."

"I have to be honest," he said. "It's been a while since I've been out to that building. We don't have much tenant turnover there, so very little comes up to rent or buy. I don't remember the cameras you're speaking of, but if you say they're there, I believe you."

"I'm certain. Both face east looking out into the alley. Then right across the alley is the rear of the apartment building 4415 South Prairie. Is it possible I can take a look at the footage?"

"Sure, if we have anything. We manage lots of buildings around the city, but they don't all have the same systems or video storage capacity. I don't know the specifics for each building, but I can look into it as soon as possible and try to get some answers. Is there something you're specifically looking for?"

"I'm trying to see if those cameras captured any of the cars driving down the alley or maybe entering and leaving the parking lot of 4415 South Prairie. I couldn't tell by the positioning of the cameras how much they might've picked up if anything at all, but I figured it's worth a try."

"You looking for footage from both cameras or just one?"

"Both if possible."

"We had all of our surveillance systems overhauled a couple of years ago, so I know the cameras are relatively new."

"Do you know if the video is stored on the premises or offsite?"

"Definitely not on premises," he said. "We don't have supers in our buildings, so there aren't any recording devices or servers in the individual buildings, just the cameras. All of the South Side buildings are monitored by a service out of our central hub over on East Randolph. Do you have the exact days you need to check?"

"That's a little bit of a problem," I said. "I don't have the specific dates, but I have a range. I'll take anything from four to ten months ago."

"Wow. Like I said before, I'm no kind of security expert, but that's pretty far back. I'm not sure how long the video is held before it gets taped over. Let me check on it and get back to you."

"I'm not sure what Commander Burke told you," I said. "But this is really urgent, so anything you can do to expedite things would be greatly appreciated. This investigation is very delicate, so I'd also appreciate your discretion. You have my number."

"I understand," he said. "I'll make some calls right away and see what answers I can come up with."

TODAY WAS ONE OF THOSE breakthrough October days when the temperature suddenly climbed back up in open defiance of the calendar. The unexpected warmth prompted a taste for Cajun, so Mechanic and I decided to walk over to Wabash and grab a table at Lowcountry. Their shrimp and snow crab platter with cornbread and Cajun waffle fries was calling my name. We were halfway to the restaurant when Carolina called.

"You have a few minutes?" she said.

"For you, I have the rest of my life," I said. Mechanic shot a quick glance in my direction and rolled his eyes.

"You always know the right thing to say." She laughed.

"Practice makes perfect."

"I've done some more research on Hakeem Jefferson," she said. "And unfortunately there wasn't much there."

"I'll take whatever you found."

"As you know, he was never a detective, and he never worked out of the Sixth. He graduated from the Academy nineteen years ago. He worked patrol way up north in the Sixteenth. Jefferson Park. Was there for a little more than five years, then he transferred to Harrison and worked tac."

"I forget what district Harrison is."

"The Eleventh. Around Garfield Park before you get to Austin. You catch it off the Eisenhower or take Madison all the way west."

I had been to that district a couple of times on a bad carjacking case where a fifteen-year-old kid ended up killing a mother and two-month-old baby. It was one of the city's hot spots for violent crimes and drug dealing.

"Anything notable in his file while he was working tac?"

"He was injured many years ago chasing a drug dealer who ended up shooting him in the leg. He went out on medical for eighteen months, then returned to Harrison and got promoted to sergeant. A year later, he moved to street ops. He's been there ever since."

"Any disciplinaries?"

"Nothing. And no suspensions. Five complaints his entire career, and they go back to when he was on the streets working patrol in the Sixteenth. None of them were substantiated. Other than that, he's completely clean."

I still couldn't make any sense of this. Why was a sergeant in street ops fielding calls about the chain of custody for missing evidence? This was like a homicide detective writing a ticket for an expired parking meter. It just never happened.

"Did you read the investigations for those five complaints?" I asked.

"I didn't pull them, but I can if you want me to," Carolina said.

"How about his personals?"

"Married, two kids, lives down near Pullman. Grew up on the West Side. Went to Robert Morris University on a basketball scholarship. Majored in criminal justice. Joined the Academy right after he graduated. All straightforward stuff."

I thought about it for a moment. What had him so interested in this case? Was it possible he knew Reece? Did he know the officers involved?

"Partners," I said. "We need to take a look at his former partners in the Eleventh and Sixteenth. Maybe there's a connection."

"I'll add partners to my search list," Carolina said. "Anything else you want with your order, sir?"

"Absolutely," I said. "But it's not on the menu."

42

Rayshawn Jackson had taken his tiny university room and converted it into a makeshift office with monitors and electronic equipment covering every available surface except the bathroom. It was quite an impressive arrangement. I took a seat next to him in a chair that looked like it belonged on a spaceship. He had the video cued up.

"You're really lucky," he said. "The camera that shot this footage was really good quality. A lot of these residential security cameras are garbage, but not this one. I've loaded the video on both monitors. The one in front of me is in the format you sent me. The one in front of you is magnified so you can see better detail."

He tapped a couple of buttons, and the video began playing on both monitors. We watched quietly. The magnification made the images seem like they would jump off the screen.

"Damn," Rayshawn said as Mankovich's gun fired and Reece crumpled to the ground.

Anyone who saw this video would find it disturbing to watch.

"Back it up to where they get out of the car," I said.

Rayshawn tapped a few keys, and the tape rewound to the point just before the cops got out of the car.

"Now put it in slow motion from here," I said.

He tapped a couple of keys, and the video started playing in slow motion. Mankovich exited the car with his gun out. Nettles and Knight definitely had their guns still holstered as they got out of the car.

"Pause it," I said.

I thought my way through the scene. An officer usually gets out of the car with his gun out when he knows for certain the target is armed or there's been a report of a shooting. The officer must have reasonable suspicion the target poses a deadly threat. Mankovich had his gun out, and the other two did not. What was it that Mankovich knew that they didn't? The other possibility would be that Mankovich was the first or only one to see Reece with a gun, which is why he left the car with his drawn. But that wouldn't make sense either because if he was in the back seat and saw a gun, how did the officers in the front seat not see the same gun? And if they did see Reece with a gun, why didn't they exit the car with their guns unholstered like Mankovich?

"Okay," I said to Rayshawn. "Play it."

The tape continued. Mankovich took the lead. Nettles and Knight hung back. They drew their guns a couple of seconds later. Then I noticed something I hadn't seen before.

"Take it back just before the shots are fired," I said. "Can you go back frame by frame?"

"Yup. Give me a sec."

He played with a couple of buttons and changed some settings, then the video crawled back one frame at a time.

One second before Mankovich fired, both Nettles and Knight began lowering their guns. They were at their sides when the shots rang out.

"That explains it," I said aloud.

"Explains what?" Rayshawn asked.

"I couldn't figure out why only one of them fired if they all had their guns out and they all said they saw Reece reach for a gun in his waistband. It's clear the first two officers had lowered their guns. Not only did they not fire, but they had no intention of doing so. Their statements didn't match the video. An officer would never lower his gun if he saw the target reach for a gun."

"They lied," Rayshawn said. "They must've dropped their guns because they saw he didn't have anything."

"Exactly. Can you zoom in on Reece's hands while they're in the air?"

Rayshawn slowly dragged the cursor across the screen and tapped a few keys. These adjustments caused Reece's hands to enlarge on the monitor. His hands were empty. No gun and no phone either. What happened to his phone?

"Go back to when the car pulls up, then slow it down so I can see everything Reece does. I don't know what happened to his phone."

Rayshawn dragged the video back several frames, then we watched. The car jumped into frame. Reece backed up against the fence, then he turned and looked as if he were about to jump over the fence. He placed both hands over the top rail.

"Slow it down a little more," I said.

"Where do you want the tape to start?" Rayshawn asked.

"Just as he's about to turn around toward the fence."

It became clear that Reece had the phone in his hand as he turned toward the fence, but when he went to grab the rail, he dropped the phone over the fence and onto the lawn. When he turned back, his hands were empty. He had them raised before the officers exited the car.

"Freeze the video where we can see his hands are empty," I said. "Print a still of that frame."

"Right away," Rayshawn said.

Seconds later, his printer spit out the photograph. I held it in my hands and stared at it for a moment. This image could turn everything upside down. Now I needed a closer look at those eight seconds when Mankovich was alone with Reece's body.

"Let's go back to the point where Reece gets hit and falls to the ground," I said. "Then put it in slow-mo."

We watched once the video was cued up. Reece fell to the ground. Mankovich approached his body with his gun still out, then holstered it once he stood over Reece.

"Freeze right there," I said. "Zoom in on Reece."

A couple of key strikes brought us in closer.

"A little more," I said. "I want to clearly see there's no gun anywhere near him."

Rayshawn zoomed in a little closer. It was a perfect shot. We had a full view of Reece's body and the area around it. There was no gun, only Mankovich's feet.

"Print a still of that," I said. This marked the beginning of the eight seconds. Once the image had printed, the tape rolled again.

Mankovich knelt down with his back to the camera. It wasn't clear what he was doing, but his arms were definitely moving. After four seconds, his body moved enough where you could then see him reach forward and put his right hand on the left side of Reece's neck. He stood up at the eight second mark as the other two officers approached.

"Go back and pause it when he stands," I said.

Rayshawn ran the video back and stopped just as Mankovich stood.

"Push in on Reece," I said.

The image expanded without losing much clarity. I stared at the screen and took a deep breath. The gun was there next to Reece's left hip.

"Sonuvabitch," I said. "Mankovich threw the gun down."

Rayshawn stared at the screen. "Ain't this some shit," he said.

"Print this screen," I said.

The printer came to life and the image slid out. I held them next to each other. The evidence was clear and indisputable. There was no gun when Reece hit the ground and then a gun suddenly appears eight seconds later after Mankovich had been kneeling next to the body. Morgan Shaw just won the overnights.

PART III

43

OCTOBER 28
FIRST DAY OF NOVEMBER SWEEPS

Burke and I were seated at the small counter at West Egg working on enough food to feed an entire elementary school. At least I had an excuse, having just finished a five-mile run. Burke, however, was just a bottomless pit and the only person I had ever met who ordered two entrees and asked for the first to be served as an appetizer. His bacado omelette, a house specialty of bacon, jack cheese, guacamole, and salsa and every bit the size of a frisbee, was already half demolished. I had taken him through the video, the nefarious activities of Officer Garrity, and the suspicious involvement of one Hakeem Jefferson.

When I had finished my briefing, Burke said, "I should've known from jump street this wasn't good news. You only offer to pay when you have bad shit to tell me and you wanna soften the blow."

"You're less likely to bite when your mouth is full," I said. "And this is more than bad shit. This is an entire sewer that's gonna stink like hell when Morgan runs that story in a few days."

"Jesus fuckin' Christ," Burke said. "The city's gonna explode. The last thing we need going into holiday season."

"Look at the good side," I said. "It would be a lot worse if all this came out in the middle of a scorching summer."

"Protests, looting, vandalism, street closures. It's gonna start all over again like it was a few years ago during the George Floyd stuff."

"Two men are dead for no apparent reason," I said. "We live in a world where all actions have consequences. What happens next shouldn't be blamed on the people. The blame squarely falls on those who unnecessarily brought us to this point."

"What was the motivation?" Burke asked. "It's pretty obvious Mankovich set out to do this, but why? What was it about Williams, who you say was an honest, straightforward guy, that made him a target? It's not like Mankovich just randomly picked his name out of a hat and went and killed him."

"I don't have that answer," I said. "Yet. But the truth needs to come out."

"And you won't stop until it does."

"Am I that predictable?"

Burke finished the omelette, wiped his mouth, and leaned back to give his jaws a rest. "You're more than predictable," he said. "You're a fuckin' relentless pain in the ass. And that's why you're one of the best in the game."

Had melanin not been my birthright, I would've blushed.

THAT NIGHT, CAROLINA AND I sat in my living room watching the first round of a battle that looked like it would go the distance. I had moved the kitchen TV and placed it next to the big screen so we could see both prima donnas at once. A bowl full of hot, buttered popcorn sat between us.

"Who gets the big screen?" Carolina said.

"The one writing the checks," I said, smiling.

"Sometimes you're so easy."

"Only when it doesn't count."

Almost to the second, both newscasts opened up with their respective station logo and a short video preamble teasing what was coming up next. Then both Morgan Shaw and Giselle Burgos stared out at the city, and the first round had officially begun.

"They're both so beautiful," Carolina said. "I'm trying to listen to what they're saying, but I can't stop looking at them. It's distracting."

"Agreed," I said. "It's good for you to finally experience what I feel like sometimes when I'm sitting across the table from you."

Carolina turned and looked at me. "Only sometimes?" she said.

I smiled. "You just said I was so easy." I reached over and kissed her softly at first, then pressed fully into her as Morgan and Giselle went to commercial break, bringing round one to a close.

OCTOBER 29
SECOND DAY OF SWEEPS

I had just arrived at my office, not because I had anything in particular to do, but sometimes simply being there made me feel more productive. I stood at the window and looked over Grant Park. Soon the Christmas lights would be up, and the decorations would bring life to the otherwise barren cityscape. The retailers in the Gold Coast suffered impatiently through Thanksgiving so they could get to the bonanza of Christmas. This had always been my favorite time of the year since I was a child. I called it the holiday corner, starting with Halloween, then running straight through New Year's. The mood of the entire country palpably transformed as everyone shared in the festivities, and the differences that kept us at odds at other times of the year no longer mattered as we focused on the merriment that united us. I was contemplating what was in store for me in the coming year when my phone rang. David Wilford from the management company.

"I'm really sorry it took so long," he said. "But I don't have good news."

"I figured as much," I said.

"The cameras are operational, but they're only motion activated so they aren't constantly running. That other building's parking lot is a little too far for the cameras to pick up all of the movements. Occasionally they do, but more often than not, they don't. The other problem is the dates. The way the storage is set up, once the recording drive is full, it starts taping back over the older video. The dates you're looking for are just too old. That video is long gone."

"Are you sure?" I asked, already knowing the answer.

"Very. I actually went over there myself and took a look at it. There's nothing left from those dates. Unfortunately, the furthest back we still have on the drive is about three months."

"And those were your only cameras facing east?"

"Yes. Our other cameras are out front facing west. I'm really sorry. I wish I could be more help."

"You tried," I said. "I appreciate the effort."

"Anything else I can do, feel free to give me a call."

I hung up the phone and continued staring out the window. This was common in almost all investigations—getting so close to an answer only to have it just suddenly disappear. I left the office, jumped in my car, and drove to Reece's apartment building. Every time I visited his home and saw his personal belongings, I learned something new about him, understood some of the mundane activities of his life. But I always left wondering about the simplest of things, like which direction he approached his building when he came home from work, or where in the back parking lot he liked to park. Which neighbors did he get along with, and which ones did he avoid? Sometimes in these challenging cases when there wasn't much to go on, learning a person's routine could help explain how other pieces in the puzzle might fit.

I pulled into the alley behind Reece's building, and as I slowly traveled south, I scanned the buildings to see if there were any others that had surveillance cameras. When I reached the end of the alley, at least twenty yards from Reece's parking lot, I saw a garage with a camera mounted on the roof, but as I got closer, I realized it was pointing in the wrong direction.

I turned around and parked behind Reece's building. I looked up to the second floor and his back window. This must've been her route. She parked back here, walked up the steps, and he let her in through the back door. Entering back here meant she was shielded from view of the busier traffic passing in front of the building. Why didn't she want to come through the front door? Where was she now, and how did she feel knowing one of her fellow cops had shot the man whose bed she shared? Their relationship was exactly that—*their* relationship. She was a complete mystery, and without that missing memory card, she would most likely remain one. I would have to accept that. I took a last look at Reece's kitchen window, then started the car and rolled slowly out of the alley with Pop Smoke on the radio rapping "What You Know Bout Love."

As I drove back to the South Loop, my phone never stopped ringing. First was a text from Julia. Finally. She apologized for getting back to me so late. Her business out of town was going to keep her another week, but she would definitely be back that weekend. We agreed to meet a few days later at my apartment. I felt both relieved and anxious at the same time.

Morgan called next.

"You looked amazing last night," I said. "We watched you on the big screen."

"We?" Morgan said.

"I had company."

"So there is more to your life than another round of golf. I thought all that handsomeness might be going to waste."

"Not anymore," I said.

"Well thanks for watching," she said.

"Sometimes I forget how good you are," I said.

"Tell that to the hundred thousand viewers we lost to her last night. We got beat badly. Management is freaking out. Then Leeder featured her in his column today and made her out to be the second coming."

"I didn't read it yet."

"That man has no loyalty," she said. "One minute you're his flavor, the next minute you're not."

"Why even bother reading his column?"

"Everyone in the business has to read his column. Whether he pulverizes or applauds you, making his column is still a big deal."

"Don't feel so dejected," I said. "It was just the first night. Plenty of time to turn it around."

"Tell that to my bosses. We're having a big strategy meeting this morning. They're trying to figure out when to air my story. They're praying it'll give us some real numbers."

"You worked really hard on it."

"Hopefully hard enough."

Carolina called next.

"From one beauty to the most beautiful," I said.

"Did you just call another woman beautiful to my face?" she said.

"Well, not exactly to your face. On the phone."

"And you think you can get away with calling both of us beautiful?"

"I didn't. I called her beautiful and you *most* beautiful."

"That one word saves you. Now I can give you the information on Jefferson. He had two partners when he worked in the Sixteenth and one when he worked the Eleventh."

"You have their names?"

"Yup. I also have where they are now."

"Okay. Text that to me. Anything else?"

"That's all I have for now."

Within seconds, I got her text message. McGrath and Ramundo in the 16th. Barnwell in the 11th.

44

That night when I arrived home, my doorman handed me a large envelope. I knew right away it was from Burke. I popped a Sam Adams out of the fridge, sat on the couch, and opened the flap. A copy of the case report awaited.

Slim Henderson had been flashed and instructed to pull over his vehicle. Officers noticed he had a broken right taillight. Once he had pulled over, they ran his tag through the computer and found there were several violations on the car. As both officers approached the vehicle, Henderson shifted the car into gear and sped away from the scene. The officers ran back to their vehicle, gave chase, following him through the busy streets, trying several times to overtake him and make him stop. Attempts at neutralization were unsuccessful, and Henderson increased his speed to dangerous levels, almost hitting pedestrians and other vehicles both parked and moving. Henderson ran a red light at the intersection of South Lafayette Avenue and Eighty-Third Street. At that point, he crashed head-on into a concrete barrier and was immediately neutralized. The report went on to explain the life-saving methods employed at the scene and the eventual extraction of Henderson's lifeless body from the car. The report listed officers Keenan Garrity and Marco Francetti as the pursuing officers.

I read the report a second time, angered by every sentence and the omission of key information Henderson's cousin had shared, such as them initially approaching his car with their guns drawn and them hitting him from behind during the pursuit. In fact, given their own admission that they had pulled him over for just a broken taillight, it had long been departmental policy not to give chase at excessive speeds for those types of minor infractions, as these chases not only endanger the lives of the target and officers but innocent citizens. I could think of only one plausible reason why they were so aggressive in their pursuit of a target who had committed no crime. They wanted Slim Henderson, and they were going to do whatever it took to get him.

My phone rang. It was Tyra Martin.

"We just got word from someone in the ME's office," she said. "They think Alicia was poisoned."

"They're making an official announcement?" I asked.

"No, because they haven't confirmed it. They're adding more blood tests, but they're running out of possibilities, and they think this might be it."

I wasn't really sure what to think. It was bizarre in so many ways. One of the city's most high-profile journalists was targeted and poisoned by a lunatic stalker. There were so many questions. Why her? Why now? If it was the same person going after Morgan, why did they kill Alicia first? How did they get close enough to poison her? Was it someone she knew? My head was spinning.

"Can you think of anyone who might've wanted to hurt her?" I asked Tyra. "Ex-boyfriend, jealous wife, angry family member?"

"Nobody," Tyra said. "Alicia didn't have enemies. She was universally liked inside and outside the newsroom. She never let the lights or the money get to her head. The only thing I can think of is that it was some deranged psycho who just flipped out."

"I agree, but it's not easy poisoning someone you don't know or you can't get close to. When she called out sick that day, did she say anything about getting stuck by anything?"

"What do you mean?"

"Like a pin stick or needle stick. Anything like that?"

"No. Why do you ask?"

"Sometimes poison can be introduced through the skin through a prick. Russians do it all the time. Tap an unsuspecting person with an umbrella or shoot a small dart into their leg. They feel a prick but ignore it and keep moving. Then the poison gradually seeps into their blood and takes over."

"She didn't say anything about feeling pricked," Tyra said.

"Had she been with anyone that day or the night before?"

"I really don't know. I talked to her for only a few minutes. She said she was feeling really bad. She didn't have any strength, and her legs felt weird. That was it. I told her to get some rest and call me in the morning."

"The more I can find out, the better I can protect Morgan. Anyone you can think of who might know what she did?"

"Her best friend was Rhonda Braumgarten, who anchors the morning show over at WVN."

"See if she'll talk to me," I said. "I just wanna ask her a few questions."

"I'll get back to you tomorrow. But I have to tell you, Rhonda is a tough customer. She doesn't take shit from anybody."

45

OCTOBER 30
THIRD DAY OF SWEEPS

It had been against my better judgment, but Morgan was not to be deterred. She insisted on attending the Bulls game against the LA Lakers, and she wanted to be on full display. Giselle Burgos had widened the ratings gap, and all anyone could talk about was this beautiful Hollywood couple that had brought new glamour to the Midwest. The falling numbers on the overnights had management at WLTV panicking, which meant they were putting more pressure on Morgan and her producers. But to her credit, she remained cool and methodical. She had the Reece Williams story in her back pocket, and she was confident it would put her back over the top. Tonight she wanted her fans to see her, and there was no better place than a jam-packed United Center on a Saturday night with LeBron James in town searching for yet another ring.

Mechanic and I had a one-hour conference call with the security team at the United Center. Every minute of her visit would be planned and secured. We would enter through the heavily restricted tunnel the players use, then be taken to the owner's box to meet with the Meinsdorfs, who had owned the team since the mideighties, a year after Michael Jordan joined the team. Mechanic, Rox, and I would all be on duty, and we had been granted permission to carry.

I drove Morgan's G-Wagon with Mechanic seated next to me. Rox and Morgan sat in the back. The narrow streets surrounding the United Center were jammed as cars impatiently queued and fans, yelling and cheering, poured in from all directions. We pulled up to the long driveway where only the players and visiting teams entered, and after the security guard finished checking under the car with a mirror and bomb-sniffing dog, we descended toward the back of the arena. Another cluster of guards stood outside an enormous garage door that rolled up as we approached and closed just as quickly after we entered. Mechanic and I exited the car first, scanning the chaos as vendors pushed carts and carried boxes. There was a heavy security presence as VIPs mingled and made an effort to look more important than each other.

I opened Morgan's door, and she exited in her skin-tight jeans, red-bottom heels, and a low-cut silk shirt with fur trimmings. She wore a pair of yellow diamond earrings surrounded by blue sapphires big enough to blind you fifty yards away. She had not come to play. Tonight was all about making a statement.

After several autographs and a couple of pictures with employees, we pushed our way from the car to the tunnel and joined the stream of players casually walking onto the floor for their pregame shootaround. I was amazed at how big they were in person. Tall, lean, muscular racehorses. TV didn't do them justice. Many of them stared at Morgan and smiled as they walked by. She pretended not to notice, but I knew she caught every single utterance and extended glance. After all, this was why we were here.

We walked toward the players' locker room to a private elevator that would take us up to the owner's suite. Rox walked in front, I stood on Morgan's right, an arena security guard to her left, and Mechanic brought up the rear. We slowly walked in that formation, and as we passed the visiting team's locker room, LeBron walked out dressed in a deep purple Lakers warm-up suit, earbuds in, his head bopping side to side. Two assistants walked with him as he looked straight ahead, relaxed, focused, and in complete control. I had never been prone to celebrity admiration, but seeing him in person did get the adrenaline flowing a little faster. Morgan looked up at him and flashed a smile. He gave her a subtle nod, then continued looking straight ahead.

The wood-paneled elevator controlled by a uniformed operator deposited us on the mezzanine level, and a few quick steps brought us to an unmarked door guarded by two armed security guards and a police officer. They opened the door as we approached, all three of them trying their best not to stare but failing miserably.

We walked into a luxuriously decorated suite that had the coziness of someone's living room. The low lighting combined with the dark walls were offset by a long bar stationed against the back wall with a row of contiguous monitors perched above broadcasting different sporting events. The room had an unmistakable air of quiet power as small clusters of people huddled over drinks at the bar, while others sat at a long oak table eating off of formal china and polished cutlery. I had been to many boxes and suites before but nothing like this.

An attractive woman with long brown hair and casual dress made a beeline toward us. She didn't wear any makeup, but when she curled her hair behind her ear, an enormous diamond earring sparkled like a firecracker on a hot summer night.

"So good to see you, Morgan," she said.

The two embraced like old friends. Mechanic, Rox, and I slid back a few feet to give them their space.

"Nancy, it's been way too long," Morgan said. "I haven't seen you all season."

"Mike and I have been all over the place with the kids," she said. "Two of them are in college on the East Coast and the other one is out in Hollywood interning at a production company. Sometimes I don't even know what city I'm in."

Rox looked up at me and mouthed the word *owner.*

"Let's get something to drink," Nancy said. She grabbed Morgan by the arm, and they walked over to the bar.

I looked around the room. A table had been set up along the left wall full of hot plates. Steak, burgers, polishes, steamed vegetables, and fries. A woman tended to the food, freshening up the trays and setting out new bundles of silverware wrapped in linen napkins. A glass wall with a door to the left of the room led out to several rows of boxed seating within the arena that overlooked the basketball court below.

"Helluva way to watch a game," Mechanic said to me quietly as the door opened and Chicago's most famous hip-hop singer, Chance the Rapper, donning his signature cap with an embroidered 3 on it, walked in with a security guard the size of Mt. Olympus and a beautiful young girl with gold fingernails that matched the gold highlights in her hair. He walked up to Mike Meinsdorf, who embraced him immediately.

After the guests had eaten, had plenty to drink, and took a few pictures among themselves, it was time to watch the game. Everyone filed out into the arena seating area on the other side of the glass partition. Three rows of chairs had been walled off from the other suites by a tall concrete barrier. Each chair had been assigned to a guest whose name had been formally inscribed on a laminated seating placard that sat on the ledge fronting each chair. The fans seated below and next to the owner's box stood and cheered and turned on their cell phone cameras as the VIPs filed to their seats. Morgan was seated next to Chance the Rapper, and they made quick conversation. Mechanic, Rox, and I fanned out to the upper corners of the box, trying our best to disappear into the background but vigilantly scanning the crowd. There were thousands of people around us, all of them a threat, the target possibly hiding in plain sight among them.

Minutes later, the lights turned out for the opening video presentation of the starting lineup announcements, and all eyes turned up to the glowing jumbotron as a stampede of bulls raged down the Chicago streets on their way to the United Center. We kept our eyes down on the crowd. Once both teams had been announced and they jumped and skipped and clapped their way onto the court, the lights came back on, and the place erupted in cheers, making it impossible to hear anything but the roar of the crowd. A man dressed in ripped jeans and a leather blazer stepped to the center of the floor after being announced as a son of Chicago who now anchored the number-one morning news show in Detroit. He belted out a soulful version of the National Anthem that was met with a thunderous applause and approval even from Chicago's own Jennifer Hudson seated courtside along celebrity row.

Tonight's game was the hottest ticket in town and for good reason. The Lakers were in first place and predicted to win another championship, but the Bulls had put together several key off-season trades that brought in a couple of veterans along with some promising upstarts. The Bulls were leading their division, though it was early, and the last few seasons had not been banner years.

The game was a battle right from the opening tip-off with LeBron scoring his first two points on a monster dunk off a fast break. The lead changed several times the first few minutes of play, and both teams competed with the intensity usually reserved for playoff games.

Even during the timeouts, the arena remained electrified as the crowd enjoyed performances from the dancing Luvabulls and drummers beating on plastic buckets with uncanny rhythmic precision. During the third timeout, the cameras flashed along celebrity row, capturing the Bears' quarterback sitting next to an actress from *Chicago Fire* and one of the Jonas brothers. The camera finally froze on Giselle Burgos and her husband, the fans cheering as Giselle smiled seductively into the camera. I watched Morgan staring at the image of her rival on the jumbotron. Totally aware that others might be watching her reaction, she smiled calmly and clapped softly.

The fans spent most of the game on their feet as the first half ended with a last second three-point shot from the Bulls' point guard that just beat the buzzer and put them in the locker room up by a point. A dessert cart rolled into the suite as everyone filed out of their seats and back into the lounge to sample the decadent desserts. Mechanic and I were putting in our order for a slice of the rainbow cake when Morgan walked up to us.

"I'm going down at the beginning of the fourth quarter," she said.

"Going down where?" I asked.

"To the floor. I'm gonna sit courtside for the entire fourth quarter."

I looked at Mechanic whose eyes conveyed my thoughts.

"Not a good idea," I said. "There's no way in hell we can protect you down there."

"You won't need to. There're tons of security guards down there, and besides, there are lots of celebrities already there. I wouldn't be alone."

"I still don't think it's a good idea. The only way to protect you is containment. It's bad enough you're out there in the open arena with thousands of people who have a line on you."

"Ashe, I appreciate you being cautious," she said. "But I wasn't asking you if I could go down there. I was telling you that I'm going."

She turned and walked over to an older woman with steel gray hair and enough diamonds on to fill a vault. They smiled at each other and embraced.

"What do you suggest?" Mechanic said.

"We need to talk to the security team right away," I said.

We asked Nancy Meinsdorf's assistant to radio security. They met us outside the suite a few minutes later. We devised the best strategy possible, but it also meant there would be many agonizing minutes she would be vulnerable. All three of us with the help of security would get her to a seat, then Rox would go back to the box and keep a look-out from across the court while Mechanic and I took seats a couple of rows off the floor behind her. Once the game was over, we would leave through the tunnel with the players and team officials to go back to the car.

The third quarter of the game started off with the same intensity as the previous half. The teams exchanged baskets and leads, and the crowd hung on to every pass and shot. The timeouts kept the fans entertained with shooting contests for free tickets to Hawaii and a man with a tiny dog performing an acrobatic routine to one of the worst soundtracks I had ever heard. With five minutes left in the third quarter, Morgan stood from her seat and signaled she was ready to go down to the court. She kissed and thanked the Meinsdorfs, then walked toward the door. We assembled a protective formation around her, then proceeded toward the elevator.

"I'm taking the stairs," Morgan announced.

"What do you mean 'the stairs'?" I said. "The elevator to the tunnel is right there."

"I don't want to take the elevator. I want to take the stairs and walk down to the court like everyone else."

"I don't recommend that," the arena's security guard said. "There are thousands of people in the concessions corridor. We'd have to go through them, then through the arena gate and down the stairs."

"That'll be fine," Morgan said.

Shaking her head, Rox looked at me. Before I could say anything, Morgan set off away from the elevator and toward the stairwell.

"Are you trying to get yourself hurt?" I said.

"These are my fans," Morgan said. "I'm trying to let them know I walk with them too."

Mechanic rolled his eyes. She kept walking. We scrambled to keep the protective formation around her. We got down the steps leading from the suite without incident, but then we entered the main concessions hall, and it was absolute pandemonium. People were everywhere walking, running, yelling, eating, laughing. It was one big sprawling party.

"Tighten!" I yelled.

We closed in on Morgan. She was completely unfazed, stopping to pose for selfies, kissing a baby on the cheek, signing autographs on the back of Jordan jerseys. I couldn't understand how the same woman who had come to my office weeks ago, afraid she was on the brink of being killed, could think it was all right to be here in this moment at this place completely vulnerable to any number of attacks. My instinct had been to grab her by the arm and move her back toward the suite, but we were too far downstream to turn around.

We squeezed our way down the hall and through the mass of bodies, trying to keep her moving as we struggled to block arms and hands coming from all directions trying to touch her.

"We're halfway there," the arena security guard announced.

We continued our march slowly but steadily. As we walked by a popcorn booth, there was a sudden flurry of activity. All I saw was a guy lunge at Morgan from the right side as she was waving at a group of fans on her left. Rox broke formation and threw a quick left jab to his jaw followed by a right uppercut under his chin. She then burrowed her shoulder into his chest and sent him sprawling to the ground. It happened so fast that by the time Morgan heard the disturbance and turned around, we were already on the move. She appeared completely unbothered by it all, as the smile never left her face.

We finally made it to our gate, squeezed our way through, and headed down the steep steps that led to the floor. The fans screamed her name as we passed, and she slowed down for them to get out their phones and snap pictures. She slapped hands with those sitting in the aisle seats and winked at several men who whistled at her. She soaked up every ounce of adoration as we made our way to the floor, the cheers and commotion reaching a crescendo the farther we descended.

When we got to the bottom of the steps, a police officer immediately unlatched the rope protecting the long row of courtside seats. They had emptied what was considered the number-one seat that was closest to center court and adjacent to the scorer's table. All of the opposing team's players had to walk by that seat to check in before entering the game. She sat next to the Chicago-born actors John Cusack and major Cubs fan Bill Murray. Mechanic and I fanned out and sat several feet behind her in a couple of house seats they had quickly made available to us. I could see Rox up in the owner's box scanning the crowd with her binoculars.

The fourth quarter began with the Lakers ahead by five points. Like most NBA contests, this was the real quarter where the game was decided. Players tightened their games, coaches got up and pranced on the sidelines barking orders, and the tension around the arena was palpable. LeBron was already one rebound away from a triple double, and many in the hometown crowd wanted to see him get it.

The Bulls, however, were not backing down from the higher-ranked and much celebrated team from Tinseltown. They were scrappy and resilient, answering the Lakers' charges with exceptional runs of their own. Up close, the action was fast and the display of physicality and athletic prowess akin to hardcourt ballet.

Then it happened. During the second timeout of the quarter as the teams huddled and the arena quieted for a break in the action, a roving cameraman walked onto the court and stopped in front of

Morgan. The entire arena stared up at the jumbotron, which played a short video of Morgan sitting at the anchor desk delivering the news. Once the video ended, the theme music to her show blasted throughout the arena, and a live image of Morgan sitting courtside smiling lit up the screen to the roar of twenty thousand fans. She might've been locked in a ratings war with the Hollywood transplant sitting on the other side of the court, but they made it noticeably clear who was their number one. Morgan stood and waved to the crowd, and the place went absolutely nuts. This was the single moment she had planned, and it went off with seamless perfection. She took her seat, and the cameraman finally cut away, and even I had to admire how strategically brilliant the whole performance had been.

The teams released from their huddle, then LeBron walked by her, stopped, and said something to her that made her smile as he headed back onto the court.

My cell vibrated in my coat. It was Rox.

"Diggs is here," she said.

"Where?"

"Section 211 on your right. He's wearing a red jacket."

I turned and located the section. I couldn't see his face clearly from where I was, but I spotted a couple of red jackets.

"Are you sure it's him?"

"Hundred percent."

"Is he alone?"

"Looks to be."

"Keep an eye on him. I'll call you back."

I had to make a decision. The safest thing would be to grab Morgan and leave the arena without incident. But after what had just happened with the jumbotron, I knew there was no way she was going to leave before the last buzzer sounded. I walked over to Mechanic's seat and explained the situation to him. He didn't say anything, just got up and walked up the steps. I returned to my seat and kept my eyes on section 211 and the red coats. I called Rox.

"What's his status?" I asked.

"Still sitting there eating popcorn," she said. "He made a call on his phone for a few seconds, then started watching the game."

"Mechanic is on his way."

"I hope he behaves himself."

"Depends on what Diggs wants to do."

"I just spotted Mechanic," she said. "He just walked through the gate."

I saw him also. He stood there and scanned the crowd. He then walked forward a little and took an empty seat against the aisle.

"I'll call you back," I said to Rox. I hung up and called Mechanic.

"What's going on up there?" I said when he answered.

"Looks like he's alone," Mechanic said. "He's two rows beneath me on the other side of the stairwell."

"Has he seen you?"

"Negative. He's busy stuffing his face with popcorn."

"Rox is watching also," I said. "Don't do anything prematurely. We don't want a big scene. Just stay on him."

I looked up at the game clock. There were four minutes left, and the Bulls were up by three points. Bill Murray leaned over and said something to Morgan, and she laughed. I hung up the phone. The Bulls were on offense and up by a point. The center took a shot and missed, which led to a Lakers fast break going toward the other end of the court. The point guard for the Bulls was alone on defense but waited for the last second and anticipated the pass to LeBron and intercepted it. Now in control of the ball, he headed back down the court, and the crowd got to its feet.

Rox called in. "He's on the move," she said. "He's walking down the row away from Mechanic's position."

"Is Mechanic moving?"

"He is, but he's having a hard time getting by people."

"Keep on Diggs."

I quickly got up and motioned to the security guard who had walked with us. I explained to him what was happening and that we needed to move Morgan out immediately. He opened the rope, knelt down beside Morgan, and gave her my message. She turned and looked at me, then quickly got up and followed the security guard. We flanked her and moved quickly.

"What's happening?" I asked Rox.

"Diggs made it out the gate. He's in the concessions hall. Mechanic is just getting there. Diggs has about a seven-second jump on him."

"We're on the move to the car, but it's gonna take us some time," I said. "We have to walk through the tunnel and all the way around the arena to get there. Go ahead and get to the car and get it running. We'll meet you there and get out."

"What about Mechanic?"

"I wouldn't worry about Mechanic. It's Diggs that I'm worried about."

I hung up and grabbed Morgan's arm. People kept screaming her name and trying to take pictures as we passed. This time, she smiled but kept moving. It was the first time I had seen traces of fear in her eyes. She moved as fast as she could in those heels, but at one point, we practically lifted her off the ground to quickly get through the bends of the tunnel.

We could hear the scorer's horn and roar of the crowd, but unlike the experiences in the open arena, down here it was muted and distant. We walked even faster as the security guard yelled for clearance from the arena employees carrying out their end-of-the-night preparations.

"About thirty yards away," the security guard called out.

Suddenly, a forklift moved across our path and blocked us in. The operator jumped out and started walking to the front of the machine. The hood of his dark gray sweatshirt covered his head. We were about sixty feet away from him.

"Move it!" the security guard yelled.

The operator looked up, startled.

"Get it out the way," the security guard yelled, frantically waving his hand.

I don't know why I did, but I looked at the operator's shoes. They were clean and very white. Something didn't seem right. They didn't match the drab uniform. Then he looked up. Our eyes locked for only a moment before he went in motion, running toward us at full speed. I pushed Morgan and the security guard to the side and stepped into the center of the hallway. Morgan shrieked. He kept coming. I looked at his hands. They were empty. I kept my gun holstered. I knew I'd be at a disadvantage if I just stood there and accepted his charge. These types of confrontations were all about momentum and who made the best calculations at the right time. I had a plan. It was more reflex than anything else, but it would avoid me pulling out my gun, which would lead to a certainty that Diggs would leave the arena that night in a body bag.

I started toward him, not at full speed but enough that I could control my next move. He had just closed within a few feet of us when out of the corner of my eye I saw a moving object and the flash of metal. Mechanic emerged from a side corridor and slammed his gun against the side of Diggs's head. I heard the loud crunch of bone and saw the immediate cascade of blood. Diggs went sideways first, those white sneakers flying in the air. Mechanic was on top of him before he hit the ground. There would be no fight. Diggs lay motionless as blood poured out the large gash in his face.

Mechanic felt his neck for a pulse.

"Is he breathing?" I asked.

"Unfortunately," Mechanic replied. "I missed my mark by half an inch."

46

Everyone made it out of the arena alive, including Haley Diggs, who was recuperating in a jail cell not too far from the United Center. Morgan rode the entire way home in a trancelike state, gazing out the window not saying very much. Rox had offered to spend the night with her, but she declined, insisting she was fine and wanted to be alone. Now that Diggs was locked up, she felt safe and confident nothing would happen. I called Detective Torres once she had gotten out of the car and filled him in on the night's activities. He was on his way to visit Diggs. I scrolled through several text messages I had received during the game but hadn't read. The next morning, I had a confirmed meeting with one of Alicia Roscati's best friends.

OCTOBER 31
FOURTH DAY OF SWEEPS

Rhonda Braumgarten had agreed to meet me at the station after her tour of duty on the city's most popular morning show. WVN occupied a rambling low-sitting building in an out-of-the-way part of the city that few had reason to visit. The morning show team had become local icons as they delivered the news tongue-in-cheek, almost subversive at times, never taking themselves or the constant barrage of city mishaps too seriously. Viewers loved Braumgarten for her sarcastic wit and tough demeanor. She only knew one way to tell it—just like it was.

After walking through double security doors and being met by an intern who escorted me to a vacant cafeteria, I found Rhonda sitting at a circular plastic table with a tall mug of coffee in front of her. She was reading something on an iPad. Unlike many of the other anchors I had seen, she wore little makeup and didn't seem fussed over. She had the sober countenance of a Catholic high school principal. Tyra's warning had been spot on.

"Ashe Cayne," I said, extending my hand as I approached. The intern left the two of us alone.

"They didn't lie," she said. "You are very easy to look at."

"'Rather than love, than money, than fame, give me truth.'"

"Haven't heard anyone quote Thoreau in a while," she said without smiling. "I was warned you were smart too."

"Did they also tell you that I can spin a basketball on my fingers for ten minutes straight?"

"They didn't."

"Good, because I can only do it for nine minutes and thirty-five seconds."

Rhonda laughed easily. The ice had been broken.

"I like you already," she said. "And that's saying a lot because I don't really like a lot of people."

"You liked Alicia," I said.

"Correction. I loved Alicia. She was like a little sister to me."

"So what happened?"

"For the life of me, I wish I knew. I've heard all types of things, but none of it makes sense."

"Such as?"

"For starters, there was that pervert who was harassing her with those nasty letters. He finally found a way to get her. Then I heard she had some health problem no one knew about, which is strange since she never mentioned it to me and was never sick. Last I heard was she might've been poisoned. I don't know what to believe."

"Is it possible she just died of natural causes?"

"Not for a minute. Alicia was the healthiest person I've ever met. Seriously. She ate like a rabbit. Everything was green and organic. I used to tell her that it wouldn't hurt for her to gain a few pounds so the rest of us working girls wouldn't look so bad." Rhonda smiled softly.

"Do you know anyone who disliked her enough to kill her? Maybe an ex-boyfriend or scorned lover? Someone she really pissed off?"

"No one I can think of," Rhonda said, shaking her head. "Alicia didn't have enemies like that. She had this remarkable ability to get along even with people she didn't like. Me, on the other hand, totally different story. Either you love me or hate me. I could give two shits either way. I don't lose a second of sleep over what people think about me or what I say to them. This is a tough, cutthroat business. There's a whole lotta shit behind what people think is the magic of TV. But everyone liked Alicia. She was just a sweet midwestern girl who made it big in the city. She could be a little naïve, but that's just who she was. Heart bigger than Lake Michigan."

"When was the last time you talked to her?"

"The morning a few days before she died. She called me to see if I wanted to grab lunch, but I couldn't because one of my daughters had volleyball practice. We agreed to get together in a couple of days."

"How did she seem when you talked to her?"

"Normal," Rhonda said with a shrug. "She was excited because she was going back home to Iowa right before sweeps to see her family. Her parents were celebrating their fortieth wedding anniversary." Rhonda's eyes moistened.

"Did she mention anything that maybe at the time seemed normal but when you look back at it now might've been a little strange or different from things she typically said or did?"

Rhonda shook her head. "Nothing at all," she said. "It was like any other conversation we've had over the years. She was in a great mood. Everything seemed completely normal."

"Did she mention any of her other plans for that weekend?"

"She said she was gonna do a little shopping on Sunday then go to dinner at Sushi Ishiyama in Wicker Park."

"Did she say who she was having dinner with?"

"She said it was gonna surprise me, and I wouldn't believe it when she told me."

"Did she tell you?"

Rhonda shook her head. "She said she would call and tell me everything on Monday."

"Did she?"

"We never spoke again. She died three days later."

When I got to my car, I called Detective Torres.

"Diggs isn't saying much," Torres said. "He claims he was at the game minding his own business having a good time."

"Until he jumped on a forklift, blocked our exit, and started running at us," I said.

"When I mentioned those minor details, he stopped talking. Said he had nothing else to say until he had his lawyer."

"He's in violation of his parole," I said. "He's gonna need more than just one lawyer to get out of this mess."

"And a whole case of lube because he's definitely going back in."

"Anything new on the Roscati case?"

"I talked to the lead, Vreeland, a couple of days ago. They hit a wall. No motive. No suspects until now. They're working to connect Diggs. Checking surveillance footage, his credit card transactions, anything that puts him near her."

"Any closer to cause of death?"

"Not yet. Still waiting on the ME's final determination. All the tests aren't back yet."

"What about this poison rumor that's going around?"

"Right now it might be just a shot in the dark. ME is considering everything. You know how it goes. Nothing at the top of the list has stuck, so they're working their way to the bottom."

"Were they able to track her last twenty-four hours?"

"I'd assume so," Torres said. "I didn't ask."

My instinct was not to tell him what Rhonda had just told me. I would work it on my own first to see if anything came of it.

"Let me know if you hear anything," I said, then hung up.

I opened up the browser on my phone and searched for Sushi Ishiyama. It was less than ten minutes away. Before I jumped on the expressway, my phone buzzed, and a text message popped on my screen. It was Julia.

I'm back in Chicago. Let me know when you want to meet.

Saturday at 5.

Location?

Since you already have the key, my apartment.

Should I bring dinner?

Not necessary. I'll take care of everything.

See you then. ♥

I was definitely ready, and I knew what I wanted to say. There were a finite number of opportunities in life, and I was determined not to let this one slip away.

I pulled up to Sushi Ishiyama located on a trendy section of Division Street. It was squeezed between a shiny redbrick town-house that had a fancy florist on the bottom floor and a tire shop that looked completely out of place on this chic block of pricey boutiques and scrubbed sidewalks. I jumped out of the car and walked up to the front door only to learn that they didn't open for lunch service for another hour. I walked over to the tall dark windows and pressed against the glass. I saw a small woman moving diligently behind a shiny oak L-shaped sushi bar. I'd come back another time.

47

NOVEMBER 3
SEVENTH DAY OF SWEEPS

The next couple of days were filled with anticipatory energy for all of us. Morgan remained solely focused on her big night. The station ran splashy promos teasing a breaking news story that would rock the city. Leeder ran daily accountings of the ratings war and hinted that while Morgan was on the losing side of things so far, she was not to be counted out.

Diggs remained in custody after being hit with several charges including criminal trespass, parole violation, and stalking. Investigators worked around the clock to connect him to Roscati's death but so far had come up empty-handed. Regardless, the new charges would send him back south for many more years.

The first night of Morgan's explosive series had finally arrived. We sat in her apartment looking out over the northern part of the city as the lake's shoreline curved its way up toward Wisconsin.

"It's been a long time since I've been nervous," Morgan said, gazing out the window. Her reflection in the glass looked like a painting.

"Why are you nervous?" I asked. "You've done the work. You have the elements. Now the viewers will decide."

"There's just so much at stake," she said. "I haven't had butterflies during sweeps since I first got to Chicago."

"Sometimes it's good to be a little nervous. It can actually sharpen your senses, keep you focused, bring out the best of your competitive instincts."

"Giselle has a big lead on me right now."

"I read about it in Leeder's column."

"But if this series performs, I can overtake her."

"You're off to a good start. I've seen the promotions everywhere."

"So has CPD. They threatened our legal department yesterday. A bunch of really nasty emails and phone calls."

"What did they say?"

"The usual bullshit. We were exploiting the case for ratings. We were recklessly tainting an ongoing investigation. They would go to court to get an injunction to stop us from airing the series. You name it, they threatened it."

"They're testing you to see if you'll blink."

"Snowball's chance in hell. We're going even harder."

"Just to be extra cautious," I said. "And I personally want to see it live as you blow this case wide open. They murdered two men. They should pay for it like any other criminal. Their uniforms shouldn't protect them."

"I wouldn't have been able to finish this story without you," she said. "I want to properly thank you for all your help."

She reached down to the small table behind her chair and pulled out a narrow box wrapped in gold paper.

"No client has ever given me a gift before," I said, carefully opening the paper. "A simple thank-you would've been more than enough."

I pulled the lid off the box and sat there staring at a beautiful stainless steel and gold Rolex.

"Wow," I said. "Thank you. This wasn't expected or necessary. You're already paying me very well. This is beyond."

"You've gone beyond too," she said. "If everything works out, your help with this case might be the single reason why I remain number one."

FATHER FLAGGER AND I SAT in the shadows behind one of the robotic cameras in the studio as Morgan and her co-anchor took final looks at their scripts and the producer gave them last-minute instructions. A tall man who had gone soft at the shoulders and had eaten too many prime rib dinners stood on the other side of the studio with the news director Rebecca Karlson watching everything quietly but intently. He had been introduced to us as the station general manager—the big boss. He spent most of his days tucked away in an office in another part of the building while most of the news staff rarely visited unless something had gone wrong and was significant enough to cross his desk. Tonight, however, he found his way to the studio, as this was no ordinary night and this newscast was no ordinary newscast. His star anchor was going to charge headfirst into the Chicago Police Department, and it was going to send shockwaves across the city.

"Who are those two over there?" Father Flagger asked, pointing to a slender, nervous-looking man in an ill-fitting suit and lopsided glasses talking to a portly woman in an unflattering pantsuit holding a briefcase.

"Morgan told me they were the lawyers," I said. "All hands on deck tonight."

A young woman who looked to be barely out of college carried a stack of different colored pages to the news desk and quietly slid them to Morgan and her co-anchor. Neither of them looked up from their laptops or acknowledged her.

"Two minutes to air!" a woman wearing a heavy-looking headset yelled from across the floor. No one seemed to notice her or react except Father Flagger and me. The robotic cameras came to life and started moving across the floor as everyone stepped over their thick cables tangled on the floor.

"Tonight, the bear will be poked," Father Flagger whispered to me with noticeable excitement in his voice.

"He's not gonna be poked," I said. "He's gonna be hit with a sledgehammer."

"Sixty seconds to air," the floor director yelled.

A young, attractive woman with a large bag of makeup and accessories scurried up to the anchor desk and quickly went to work on Morgan's face, blotting and powdering, then teasing her hair. Morgan kept her eyes on the laptop the entire time. Her co-anchor reached under the desk and pulled up a mirror, raked his fingers through his hair, then took a small powder puff and tapped his face a few times before returning to his laptop.

"They don't even talk to each other," Father Flagger whispered. "It's like they're in their own world."

I admired their preshow routine, like professional athletes going through their pregame rituals to focus on the work ahead of them. Right now, they were in their own world, but when the light came on, they would be a well-rehearsed team.

"Thirty seconds!" the floor director yelled. She took her position between two of the cameras facing the anchor desk just feet away. She pushed some buttons on the control pack clipped to her waist. She said something into her headphone, then announced, "Morgan, we're coming out on a two shot after the open, then a single on camera three."

Morgan nodded, still not looking up.

The floor director said, "Standby," and the intro music started playing. Finally, Morgan looked up. She had a smile on her face that could light a thousand fires. The music stopped, the cameras went live, and she spoke confidently to the city. Right from the top of the show she mentioned her special investigative report about new and disturbing information concerning the shooting of a South Side man earlier that summer.

"The die has been cast," I said.

Father Flagger tapped me on the leg and smiled.

For the next twenty minutes, Morgan and her co-anchor tag-teamed on stories whose only purpose seemed to be to shock and scare. Shootings, car jackings, political investigations, hit-and-runs—one bad news narrative bled right into another. Then Morgan announced that coming up next, she would share exclusive new information learned about the controversial shooting of Reece Williams. They went to commercial break. Morgan looked down and quickly typed something into her computer.

"Thirty seconds," the floor director announced.

The image on the large monitor behind the anchor desk changed. The station logo had been replaced by a large picture of Reece Williams, a cell phone, and yellow police tape wrapped around Reece's torso. The floor director gave Morgan instructions and then pointed to a camera whose red light went on simultaneously. Show time.

Morgan looked into the camera and told the city that the shooting of Reece Williams was not only suspicious but likely part of a larger coverup to avoid the truth of what really happened that summer night. Her investigation uncovered the questionable actions of one Chicago police officer who since the shooting had been transferred to another district on the North Side and had yet to be disciplined for his role in the shooting that many are claiming was the equivalent of an execution.

The piece started, and everyone in the room had their eyes glued to the monitor as Morgan told the backstory of Reece Williams. Father Flagger's interview was key to this part of the story as were interviews with Earl, Gina, and several people who had known Reece, some of whom had been with him that night at the basketball game in Mahalia Jackson Park.

When the taped portion of the segment ended, the camera came back to Morgan, and she explained that repeated requests had been made to CPD for comment, but they never responded. She also said that sources confirmed that Mankovich, Nettles, and Knight were subjects in an internal affairs probe looking into whether their actions that night violated departmental policy. She teased tomorrow night's story that would take a look into firsthand accounts from those who were at the scene of the shooting and the story of one eyewitness who suspiciously died in a police chase on the same day he was supposed to sit down for an interview and tell all that he knew and had seen regarding the shooting.

As programming went to commercial, I watched the general manager and news director. They nodded emphatically and acknowledged Morgan's superb work. The lawyers were still huddled together, relief finally visible on their faces. Morgan looked over at Father Flagger and me and winked. Game on.

48

The first thing I did the next morning was open my phone and scan the newspaper websites, first the *Sun-Times*. Leeder prominently featured the story on the front page, heralding Morgan not only as a much beloved anchorwoman but also a gifted investigative journalist whose skills as a reporter had not been diminished by her many years at the anchor desk. He compared her to a queen who could descend from her throne and still walk with her people. The piece couldn't have been more laudatory had Morgan written it herself. He ended the column predicting that Morgan's series would likely attract even more viewers to the upcoming segments and potentially reverse the ratings momentum Giselle Burgos had brought to rival WMTQ.

The *Chicago Tribune* had not only one but two stories dedicated to Morgan's report. The first piece talked about Morgan and how she had deftly turned a story that few had given much attention to into an explosive investigation. Similar to the Leeder column, it spoke about her award-winning investigative skills and how she was not going to simply relinquish her number-one ratings spot to a rival anchor whose time in town had been shorter than a Chicago Bears lead in a football game.

I had just finished reading the second story, which focused on the allegations and interview, when Morgan called.

"Congratulations," I said.

"For what?" she said, her voice fully awake.

"Okay. I'll play along. Let's pretend like you haven't read all of the articles this morning."

She laughed. "I really haven't read all of them," she said. "I have about five more to go."

"How do you feel?"

"Relieved. Determined."

"What about the overnights?"

"We don't get them for another couple of hours."

"Any early signs?"

"We heard from CPD last night. They weren't happy. They warned us to make sure we had our facts right."

"Leeder loved you this morning."

"I've read every word three times already."

"What's in store for tonight?"

"Bring your popcorn," she said. "Yesterday was just a teaser."

I SPENT MOST OF THE morning looking at the articles and social media stories about Reece Williams and Morgan's investigation. Several organizations were already promising protests and Mayor Bailey, always quick to respond to anything that came close to dulling the luster of his office, uncharacteristically had nothing to say when questioned by reporters. I looked over the case reports again—first Reece's, then Slim Henderson's. Something was bothering me, but I couldn't put my finger on it. I put them away, convincing myself that another read at another time might help me see things more clearly.

My TV had been on in the background and turned to the Cooking Channel. As I got up from my desk and walked into the kitchen to look for something I could put together for lunch, I just happened to look at the screen. A Japanese chef was being featured for his elaborate and meticulous sushi presentations. Not only did that give me a taste for sushi, but it reminded me that I hadn't followed up with Sushi Ishiyama, the restaurant where Alicia was supposed to have dinner with a surprise companion two nights before she died. I grabbed my keys, jumped into the Defender, and headed up to Wicker Park.

Today was warmer than a typical November afternoon, which brought lots of people outdoors jogging, shopping, and walking through the trendy neighborhood. Wicker Park was a shining example of Chicago's constant transformation, a neighborhood that had been the seat of the Polish migration and then Puerto Ricans before becoming the original home of the notorious Latin Warlords gang. Reinvestment and development and its proximity to public transportation made it a popular place to live for those working in nearby downtown and the South Loop.

The parking spots in front of the restaurant were all taken, so I turned the corner and found a spot on a quiet, residential side street. As I got out of the car and walked past the quirky boutiques and darkened nightclubs, I had flashbacks of my college years when my friends and I would come home for break and visit this hipster neighborhood mostly to party at Double Door, one of the hottest nightclubs and concert venues in the city.

I walked into Sushi Ishiyama and a thin, attractive Asian girl showed me to a table along the perimeter of the room closer to the window. A little more than half of the tables were occupied, including most of the chairs at the long sushi bar. The restaurant was a minimalist affair of polished oak and dark leather. Light instrumental Japanese music piped in from above. I promptly ordered some veggie tempura, a cucumber salad, and eight pieces of the spicy crispy tuna rolls.

I looked around the room and noticed two cameras—one next to the host stand near the door and the other behind the bar. If Alicia had been here that night, she definitely would've been captured on camera.

My phone rang. It was Morgan.

"You're not gonna believe this," she said. "We didn't just win last night. We killed them."

"I'm not surprised," I said. "I already knew what was in the story and still got caught up in it."

"Rebecca wants to try to extend the series for another night."

"Do you have enough material?"

"Not yet, but I'm digging around to see if I can get maybe a former police officer on camera to say something and add any kind of per-spective from someone who's been on the inside."

"Good luck with that," I said.

"I know it won't be easy, but the math is in my favor. More than two thousand former police officers live in the city. All I need is just one of them to speak up and talk about some of the internal problems they feel need to be fixed."

"There are lots of ex-cops who know the problems, but whether they're willing to go on camera and speak up about it is something completely different. They still live in the city. They still have friends in the department. They still get certain perks being a former cop. You're gonna have to find the right person."

"Maybe I'm talking to him."

I laughed. "I should've known that's where all this was heading."

"You'd be perfect," she said.

"Exactly the opposite," I said. "They'd say I was nothing more than a disgruntled cop who was insubordinate and got a very generous settlement when I left the city."

"But you stood up to them when they were doing wrong," Morgan said. "That means something to a lot of people."

"I haven't been inside for years," I said. "You need someone closer to the action."

"You know anyone?"

"I know plenty. Question is if they're willing to talk."

"Will you talk to them? I only need one."

"I'll do my best."

My food arrived, and I wasted no time diving in. I started with the large pieces of tempura, then attacked the salad. I had plenty of room for the tuna rolls, and they definitely didn't disappoint. The flavors were fresh and rich, and the sauce brought it all together. It was worth a return visit.

The server brought my bill.

"Is the manager here?" I asked him.

"Sure," he said. "Is there a problem?"

"Not at all. The food was amazing. I just wanted to ask him a question about your security."

A look of confusion registered on his face, but he was polite and told me he would get the manager right away. He walked back toward the kitchen then emerged a couple of minutes later with an older woman dressed in a long white chef's coat and matching hat. She walked with great purpose.

When she reached my table, she nodded and said, "Good afternoon. How can I be of help to you?" I heard traces of a British accent. She looked stern but was still polite.

"This might sound like a strange question," I said, "but are your security cameras operable?"

She looked at both cameras, then turned back to me and said, "Yes, of course. Why do you ask?"

"I'm an investigator, and I'm trying to find out if someone had dinner here a couple of weeks ago."

"You are police?" she said.

"Not exactly."

"What are you investigating?"

"A woman who had dinner here and died two days later."

"Who is she?"

"The evening news anchor at WMTQ."

"I don't know her," she said. "I don't watch the news. Do you know the date she was here?"

"October tenth."

She said something to the server standing behind her, who raced off toward the bar. Once he was gone, she turned back to me and said, "Did something bad happen?"

"I don't know. That's what I'm trying to find out."

The server returned with a pad and pen and handed it to the manager, then walked away.

"What was this woman's name?" she asked.

"Alicia Roscati."

She wrote Alicia's name on the pad, and I repeated the date for her.

"What's your name?" she asked.

I gave her one of my cards. She looked it over carefully, then slid it in the front pocket of her jacket.

"I need to talk to my husband about this," she said. "He went to New York for a couple of days. He'll be back tomorrow. I will have him call you."

"Please tell him it's urgent," I said.

She nodded.

"And tell him this is some of the best sushi in the entire city."

Finally, she allowed a smile to turn up the corners of her tiny mouth.

49

Mechanic and I had agreed to meet at Hammer's for a quick sparring session, so I headed in that direction, taking the streets to avoid the midday traffic on the expressway. I was halfway there when Burke called in.

"Your client is quickly making a lot of enemies on Thirty-Fifth Street," he said.

"That's not too hard to do," I said. "What's the word?"

"We've been given our marching orders. No one is to talk to the press about anything related to this case."

"Which means they're hiding something."

"You can read it as you wish."

"Do you know something that I should know?"

"I know that you need to be careful. This might be bigger than Mankovich."

"What about the IAD investigation? Can you get anywhere near it?"

"No chance. You know how they operate. Their firewall can't be breached, and if it is, there's no way to do it without leaving prints."

"How high might this go?"

"I have no idea, but Mankovich is lawyered up and, as of an hour ago, just went out on a four-week furlough."

"How about Nettles and Knight?"

"They're off the streets. Desk duty."

"They saying anything?"

"Only to their union reps."

"There's more coming out tonight," I said.

"The brass is well aware of it."

"Are they gonna do anything about it?"

"I'm not in on the conversation, but my advice to you is create distance and grow some eyes in the back of your head."

MECHANIC AND I HAD A tough session. Hammer stood in the corner yelling at us as we went a couple of extra rounds to make up for not being in the gym for almost a week. I was a little sluggish at first, but my legs held up, and my punches found the gaps. Mechanic was not himself. He was missing badly and getting frustrated. He finally pushed me off and said he'd had enough. We bumped gloves and headed to the locker room.

"You okay?" I said.

"Late night," he said.

"Take tonight off," I said. "I'll do the shift."

"I watched," he said. "She did a good job last night."

"Maybe too good."

I took a long hot shower and spent most of my time thinking about Julia and what I'd say to her when we met. My biggest concern, however, was Carolina. I wasn't sure what she'd say or how she'd react. I was almost dressed when my phone rang. I didn't recognize the number.

"This is Earl," the caller said.

"You watched the story last night?" I asked.

"Everybody did. She did good."

"It's just a start. There's more tonight."

"That's why I'm calling," he said. "I have the lady cop's picture."

"Are you serious?" I said. I had all but given up on identifying Reece's mystery lover.

"Dead serious," he said. "And I'm a hundred percent sure it's her."

"How did you get it?"

"Reece went to the Essence Fest in New Orleans almost every summer. Usually he went by himself and met up with a group of our boys. Nobody wants to bring sand to the beach, so the ladies stay at home. Last summer for the first time, he decided to bring a little honey. I don't know why he changed his mind, but he took the cop with him."

"Did you go?"

"Ain't never been. Not my scene. But I know a lot of fellas who went down there. When Reece was with the cop, he ran into a guy he plays hoops with in the Forty-and-Under League. Darnell. He was down there with his girl too. So all four of them hung out a little and grabbed dinner one night."

"And Darnell had the picture?"

"Yup. The four of them went to the Beyoncé concert. Reece loved him some Beyoncé." Earl laughed softly. "All four of them took a picture on Darnell's girl's phone. They texted it to me."

I wasn't sure this would turn out to be anything, but I felt a sudden surge of excitement. Just being able to identify her, even if it meant nothing to the case, was a small victory.

"What's her name?" I asked.

"Now that's one thing I don't have," Earl said. "Darnell said they only saw them a couple of times. He and his girl, don't remember her name, but they remember she was a cop."

"I'll track her down with the picture. Text it to me when you can."

"Already done," he said.

"Good work, Earl. This might not amount to anything, but in cases like this, you can't count anything out."

"When all this is said and done, you think those cops are ever gonna pay for what they did?"

"Not a single doubt in my mind."

"What makes you so certain?"

"I've seen the receipts. And in a few days, the entire city will see them too."

I opened my text messages as soon as the line disconnected. The picture was high quality. I recognized Reece right away. He wore a light blue tank top and gold chain, his muscles showing as proudly as his smile. He had his arm around the shoulder of a woman standing to his right. She was light-skinned with straight shoulder-length hair. She wore a red dress with a plunging neckline and small gold hoop earrings. She was extremely attractive and fit. The muscles in her bare arms were long and nicely defined. She looked happy with both of her arms wrapped around Reece's waist. I had never seen her before, which didn't mean much given the department had over thirteen thousand officers. But looking into her face, I was definitely intrigued.

I dialed Carolina's number.

"Your ears must've been burning," she said. "I was just talking about you."

"Good things I hope," I said.

"Depends on your perspective," she said laughing. "I was just telling one of my girlfriends that I had a taste for Mexican and you always knew the best places to find it, but you had abandoned me."

"Nothing could be further from the truth," I said. "Tonight at seven."

"Which restaurant?"

"Mi Tocaya Antojeria in Logan Square. I'll pick you up at six thirty."

"Dress?"

"Comfortable."

"I saw Morgan's story last night," she said. "Everyone around here is talking about it, wondering what she'll air tonight."

"I think tonight is Slim Henderson, the witness who died in that car chase the same day he was to be interviewed by Morgan."

"The bosses have been in meetings all day over this. They're trying to figure out some way to respond. The community leaders are already calling for protests. The family is threatening a lawsuit. The alderman of the ward he died in is calling for all the names involved to be made public."

"Speaking of names, I could use your help identifying a picture Earl just sent me."

"Who's in it?"

"It's a photo of Reece and the cop he was seeing. They were together at last year's Essence Festival in New Orleans."

"Text it to me. I'll have one of my friends run it through the facial recognition database and see if there's a match."

"Can you trust your friend will keep this quiet?"

"Have I ever let you down before?"

"Never."

"Then why would I start now and jeopardize a free Mexican dinner?"

50

I was planning on going back to the office, but I was too tired and felt like I needed a nap. It was going to be a long night again—first, dinner with Carolina, then back to the studio afterward for a ringside seat for round two of Morgan's exposé. When I got back to the apartment, I took Stryker for a quick walk, then grabbed some salami and saltines. I turned on the Golf Channel and grabbed Reece's and Slim's case files to read them over again.

I read Reece's file first, then I read Slim's. As I circled all of the names in both files to see if there was a connection, an idea struck me. I picked up my phone and dialed the old number I had for Pam Rigby.

She picked up right away.

"Riggs, it's Ashe," I said.

"AC," she said. "This is a nice surprise."

"Hope I'm not bothering you."

"Not at all. Just about to get off shift. What's going on?"

"Remember when we were at the car accident a couple of weeks ago and you pointed out the two tac guys talking to the street deputy?"

"Sure. Garrity and Francetti."

"I was trying to recall the name of the deputy, but I totally forgot.

You know how it is when you get something on your mind, and you can't let it go."

"Happens to me all the time. Hate to admit it but seems like my memory is getting worse with every birthday. His name is Deputy Palmer. Grant Palmer."

"How could I forget that?" I said. "I knew his first name was Grant but couldn't recall the last name."

"Palmer's been around for a while. I think he's about to hit twenty-five years. You need to talk to him or something?"

"Not at all," I said. "Just one of those things where your mind gets stuck on something, and the more you think about it, the more frustrated you get. I'm all good now."

"Glad to help," she said, laughing. "Too cold for you to play golf, so let's get together soon and catch up."

"You still a big fan of Japanese?"

"More than ever."

"Perfect. I have a new spot you're gonna love. My treat."

"You got my number," she said. "I'm always ready for good food, especially when it's free."

After we disconnected, I picked up Reece's case file. At the bottom of the third page I found where I had circled Grant Palmer's name. He had been at both Reece's shooting and Slim Henderson's deadly car crash. Why had his name not been listed in the Henderson case report, especially since he was the responding deputy? Was it a co-incidence that he had been at both scenes? I leaned back and closed my eyes, picturing Slim's wreckage and the deadly Reece shooting caught on the Cooper security camera. Deputy Grant Palmer's appearance at both locations wasn't sitting well with my gut.

CAROLINA AND I HAD A dinner full of enchiladas made from fresh masa and stuffed with fried beans, queso ranchero, cabbage, and salsa.

While it was difficult not ordering a second, I limited myself to one drink of Manzana Borracha, which perfectly combined tequila, apple cider, and vermouth. Carolina stuck with bottled water declaring she had consumed enough calories in the collection of small plates that had been wiped clean. I dropped her off at home, then headed to the station. The security guard escorted me back to the studio as soon as I arrived.

Father Flagger and I returned to our same seats from the previous night. The same cast of characters were present in almost the exact positions, except there was now an older African American woman dressed in a royal-blue skirt suit and lots of large colorful jewelry. Morgan had introduced her to us as the director of special projects and community relations. She stood with the lawyers who looked even more anxious tonight.

Morgan wore a black suit with a silk pink blouse and a pair of matching pink diamond earrings. The floor director went through the same drill of counting them into the show, then the music started, and the newscast went live.

"One thing for certain is they have this drill down," Father Flagger whispered to me. "Everything turned to the second."

It felt like we were watching a movie we had seen before—the makeup artist running in for last looks, the young woman bringing out the colored scripts, Morgan and her co-anchor glued to their computers, not acknowledging any of the commotion around them. Right before each commercial break, Morgan teased her special report, promising viewers it was something they didn't want to miss.

After the third commercial break, they came back with Morgan on a single shot. This time, the large wall monitor behind her that had shown a photo of Reece last night now displayed a smiling Slim Henderson, his mangled car, and the yellow police tape wrapped around it all. Morgan looked into the camera and told viewers that new information had come to light possibly connecting the death of a South Side man in a car crash to the shooting of Reece Williams.

The story started with Slim Henderson's mother sitting in a small but tidy living room recounting how her youngest son had always been the spark in the family, a young man who went to work every day stocking shelves at Walmart and went to school at night trying to earn his college degree. She then recounted how she had gotten the call that he had died in a car crash and how her entire world suddenly turned upside down. Through her tears, she insisted the crash was no accident. She believed her son had been targeted and chased by the police.

Slim's cousin, the one I had talked to at the scene, was up next. She looked much different than the afternoon I had seen her. She wore a light blue sweater, makeup, and her hair had been done nicely and pulled back from her face. She spoke confidently, even defiantly, about the conversation she had with Slim as he was being pulled over by the police. Her voice was firm and steady, and she came across as extremely believable.

The next interview was Slim's older sister, who explained what happened the night Reece was killed and how Slim had seen what happened but snuck back in the house and denied seeing anything when the police officers came to their door asking questions. Slim was certain that Reece didn't have a gun, and the police officer from the back seat got out with his gun already drawn. He said that within seconds of the officers getting out of the car, he saw the one officer fire his gun and Reece fall to the ground. He crawled low along his porch to avoid being seen, opened the front door, and slid into the house. Once the door was closed and locked, he ran to the back of the house to his bedroom and closed the door. A photograph of Mankovich in street clothes filled the screen as Morgan explained that this was the man who had shot and killed Reece Williams. The screen then showed a photograph of Officer Keenan Garrity next to Mankovich, and Morgan explained their partnership and how it had been broken up after Mankovich was transferred to a district up north while Garrity stayed behind. The taped piece ended with a photograph of Garrity at the crash scene talking to Deputy Palmer.

When Morgan came back live on camera, she went for it all. She calmly told viewers that Slim Henderson had been scheduled to sit down with her for an interview and for the first time reveal all that he had seen the night of the shooting. He never made it to their interview that night because he had been crushed to death after a police chase by the former partner of the officer who had shot and killed Reece Williams. Neither Mankovich nor Garrity had been disciplined or reprimanded and continued to work for CPD, and the department still had not responded to her request for an interview or official statement. Henderson had been chased to his death over a broken taillight. The camera faded to black.

The others in the studio applauded as Morgan let out a sigh and fell back into her chair. She knew she had delivered, and so did everyone else.

"She really has the stuff," Father Flagger said. "Brilliant piece of reporting. Unflappable."

I knew what she was planning for tomorrow night. It was going to be the crowning moment, not just with the story but the overnights too. I could feel the entire city watching that newscast and following every detail Morgan had laid out with the meticulousness of a seasoned investigative journalist. I watched as the management team and attorneys huddled together, smiles being exchanged amid a lot of head nodding. There was no doubt in anyone's mind that this was going to be a victory, and new headlines for tomorrow's papers had just been written.

Before the newscast was over, I had gotten three text messages. The first was from Carolina. Riveting!

The next was from Tyra Martin. Your girl just killed it! How the hell does she top that?

The last was from Burke. I can spot your work a mile away. You're a relentless sonuvabitch.

If he thought what he had seen so far was relentless, what would he think after tomorrow night's finale?

51

NOVEMBER 5
NINTH DAY OF SWEEPS

I was awoken the next morning with my phone buzzing on my nightstand. It was barely seven o'clock. I opened my text messages. It was Tyra Martin.

> Just heard from our source inside ME's office. They can't figure out cause of death. None of the tests have shown anything. I guess it will just be a mystery.

I texted her back asking if she could talk. My phone rang seconds later.

"What are you doing up so early?" I said. "Don't you work evenings?"

"I do, but it's crazy right now. Morgan killed us in the overnights that first night of her series, and everyone's regrouping to see what we can do to stop the bleeding."

"What were the results from last night?"

"Too early to tell. They usually come out a little after nine. We're expecting the worst."

"I have bad news," I said. "Last night was probably not the worst. There's a lot more hurt in your future."

"Are you speaking this from knowledge or speculation?"

"I'll let you figure that one out."

"Fuck. Management is gonna have a stroke."

"What's going on with the autopsy?" I asked.

"More bad news. They can't figure it out. They've tested and tried everything. Nothing is making sense."

"When will they release the official results?"

"We're hearing the next couple of days."

"If they haven't found anything, what will they say for cause of death?"

"Hold on for a sec," she said. "I have the exact wording written down." I could hear her rifling through papers, then she said, "Cannot exclude external causes."

They were hedging. I knew exactly the person who could help me sort through it, but it was too early to call him.

"Good luck tonight," I said.

"We're gonna need more than luck."

"You're right," I said. At this point they were gonna need an act of God.

I hung up and decided to go for my run before looking at the day's headlines. The temperature had dipped below freezing, so I bundled up in my cold-weather gear and headed out the door. The running path was virtually empty except for a hardy few. The wind was strong but not too harsh. It felt good against my face. The water rolled in violently, crashing loudly against the rocks along the shoreline. The gray sky looked threatening and determined. Snow would be in the forecast soon, and I had visions of Scottsdale and the lush fairways culminating in those elevated greens.

Halfway through my run, my watch vibrated. I hit the screen and saw that Carolina left a message. I kept running, not wanting to break stride. My breathing and heart rate settled into a nice rhythm that would carry me to the end of the run. I looked over to Lake Shore Drive and the morning traffic slowly starting to build as the city woke up and tens of thousands of residents moved about in those luxury high-rises preparing themselves for yet another day on the grind.

I finished the last eighth of a mile with an all-out kick that scorched my lungs and gripped my muscles. My watch gave me the good news that I had completed the five-mile run in under thirty-five minutes which meant a sub-seven-minute average mile. Not my best but definitely not my worst either. I'd take it.

Once I caught my breath, I opened my text messages and read what Carolina had written. I have the cop's identity. Call me ASAP!

I couldn't dial her number fast enough.

"Did I wake you?" she said.

"Nope. Just finishing my run."

"It's so cold out."

"Good running weather."

"I just got an answer on the girlfriend cop. Her name is Lieutenant Eboni Markham. She works out of the Second. Did you see the photos I sent?"

"I don't have my phone with me, just my watch. I'll be home in a few minutes."

"Are you sure this was the same woman Reece was seeing?"

"Positive. What's the problem?"

"Eboni Markham is very married. Her husband is Dominic Colacchio."

That stopped me. "Dominic Colacchio as in the first deputy of police?"

"Yes, that Dominic Colacchio."

"You sure this isn't some kind of mistake?"

"When you see the photographs, you'll see there's no mistake."

I had to take a moment for this to settle in. I believed Carolina knew her information to be correct, but I still couldn't believe what I had heard. None of it made any sense. I had never met Colacchio, but I had seen plenty of photographs. He was in his late fifties, maybe early sixties, bald, overweight with a ruddy complexion and a long mustache that earned him the nickname "The Walrus." Eboni had to be at least twenty years younger and attractive enough to have her pick of men. Why the hell would she get locked up with Colacchio of all people?

"Can you pull anything on her?" I asked.

"Already did. Born and raised on the West Side. Ten years on the force. Has an eight-year-old daughter from a previous relationship. She and Colacchio tied the knot four years ago, and she got promoted to lieutenant six months later. Works out of the Second District. Colacchio has two grown children from his first wife who moved back to St. Louis after they divorced."

"I'm just trying to make all this work," I said. "And right now it's just not making much sense."

"Which part?"

"All of it. Her being married to Colacchio and her having an affair with Reece."

I thought about what Earl had said about Reece telling him that she liked to keep things on the low. They never went out and only met at his apartment, never hers. Damn right she wanted to stay off the radar. Her husband was the second most powerful cop in the city and rumored to be the next superintendent once Fitzpatrick stepped down in a couple of years. Now it made sense why she only used the back stairs to get in and out of Reece's apartment.

"What are you going to do now?" Carolina asked.

"Talk to her," I said.

"You sure that's a good idea?"

"No. But it's the only idea I have right now."

"Colacchio is not the nicest of men. And he's obsessed with power. Very cutthroat."

"I wish you were here right now."

"Why?"

"So you could see me shaking in my sneakers."

"This isn't funny, Ashe," she said. "Confronting Colacchio or his wife is not a laughing matter. This is a real mess."

"These days the kids are calling it an *entanglement*."

"I'm worried about you."

"I'll be fine."

"What makes you so sure?"

"Because I have Mechanic and they don't."

After calming Carolina down, I squeezed a glass of apple juice and started reading the headlines. Morgan's story was everywhere and not just the local papers. She made it into a couple of national papers and wire services, her beautiful picture plastered in full color. The praise was endless as was the collective fury that yet another police department had murdered an unarmed man for no good cause. Morgan Shaw had become a journalistic hero overnight, and viewers were anxiously awaiting what she would reveal in the next and final installment of the series. A protest had already been set for later that morning in front of police headquarters with Father Flagger and several other prominent community activists leading the charge.

In several of the papers, the department had finally issued a statement. It was exactly what I had expected. They refused to comment on an open investigation, nor could they comment on personnel matters until a complete vetting of accusations had undergone a full internal review. That was as far as they were willing to go, but it was telling that they didn't deny something worthy of a review had occurred. The real statement in these comments had always been hidden in what wasn't said.

I dialed Burke's number. He picked up after the first ring.

"I saw it last night," he said. "Is this an 'I-told-you-so' call?"

"Nope. It's a fact-finding mission. Off the record, of course."

"I'm listening."

"How well do you know Colacchio?"

"If you're asking whether we sit back on Sunday and watch a Bears game together, then the answer is not well at all. But I've had my dealings with him through the years. He's tough. Mostly fair. He wants the big office."

"What about his personal life? Wife? Kids?"

"Don't know much more than what I've heard. He's married to some really pretty cop that he made a lieutenant after they got married. She's really young and has a little girl from a previous relationship."

"And this doesn't strike you as an odd union?"

"Because of the mixed-race thing?"

"The entire situation. A young, attractive Black cop who's a single mother hooks up with an old, cranky, fat, white deputy whose only focus is snagging the top spot in a big-city police department. He's not rich. He's not good-looking. I can't even bring myself to think about what he can and can't do in bed. Why the hell would a woman like that choose him?"

"Power is an aphrodisiac."

"I know, but it's not a damn immaculate conception either."

"What the hell do I know?" Burke said. "I'm not some damn psychotherapist or a marriage counselor."

"And neither am I. But I know strange when I see it."

"Are you gonna tell me why you're asking me all these damn questions about Colacchio and his wife?"

"I will but not now."

"What the hell is that supposed to mean?"

"I need to do some more homework, make sure I've connected some dots, then get back to you."

"Does this have anything to do with the Williams story?"

"We still off the record?" I said.

"Of course," Burke said.

"Reece Williams was sleeping with Colacchio's wife."

"Say that again."

I repeated myself.

"Jesus fuckin' Christ!" Burke growled.

"Much more eloquent than how I would've put it."

"Are you a hundred percent sure?"

"Is your name Rory Seamus Burke?"

"Does this have something to do with that surveillance footage you wanted from that building across the alley from Williams?"

"It did."

"Goddammit! My fingerprints are on this. I'm the one who made the call to get them to give you access."

"Don't worry," I said. "You're clean. They didn't have any footage, so there was nothing for me to see. They have no idea who or what I was looking for. There's no way anyone can connect you to this."

Burke's relief was audible.

"Now what are you gonna do?" he said.

"What I always do. Keep digging around."

"Knowing you, I guess it would be a big waste of breath to tell you to just leave this shit alone."

"It would."

"What's your end game?"

"Same as always. The truth."

"You know you're mixing it up with some big leaguers," Burke said. "They have real big bites."

"And sometimes you just have to bite back harder."

52

It took a couple of hours and several calls, but I finally found an old ally who knew the backstory of Eboni Markham. Liz McPhee had been a senior detective when I got my promotion. I spent a couple of months working under her tutelage before she got promoted to sergeant and transferred to another district. She was a no-bullshit cop whose family came first and who had little tolerance for the political warfare that too often consumed the inner workings of the department. I had only seen her a couple of times since she had been transferred, but those two months I had spent with her had made a lasting impression.

"It's Ashe Cayne," I said when she answered the phone.

"Whoa," she said. "How the hell are ya?"

"Life is good," I said. "What about you?"

"On the countdown," she said. "Two more years and I'm gone. I've done what I needed to do. Time to turn the page and ride off into the sunset. What about you?"

"Golf mostly," I said. "Then I take on a private investigation here and there."

"Ya know, I never got a chance to tell you how proud I was of what you did," she said. "We all heard what happened, and I just thought it was amazing that a young officer would stand up like that for what was right. Everyone knew it was a bad shooting, but you had the courage to say something."

"Feels strange to think that doing what's right means you're courageous. That was a tough time for me. I loved being a cop. I believed I could make a difference. I knew my career would be over if I did the right thing with the Peyton shooting. But my father always says, 'Sometimes in life, there's no other option than playing the hand you're dealt.'"

"You played it well."

"Thanks. Means a lot coming from one of the best. I wanted to ask you about something discreetly."

"Of course. What's on your mind?"

"Lieutenant Eboni Markham."

Liz groaned. "What about her?" she said.

"What can you tell me?"

"Where do you want me to start? Eboni is an interesting person. She comes across as this really sweet girl who just goes along with the program, but she is anything but that. She's extremely ambitious and strategic. We both worked out of the Second before she was suddenly promoted to lieutenant and transferred. There were a lot of officers with much more experience who got passed over, but when you're sleeping with the boss, you get certain perks. A lot of us were pissed about it. I've been up on that lieutenant list several times and never made it off. I have friends who've spent their entire careers serving the city and playing by the rules. They literally took bullets for the city. They never got promoted."

"Did you know she was seeing Colacchio?"

"No one knew. We were shocked when it all came out. Eboni acted very single. Have you seen her? She's stunning. She flirted with a couple of guys in the district, but we knew she was seriously dating some white guy who worked in real estate. They used to tease her because his first name was Ivory, so the guys would joke around and sing that Paul McCartney and Stevie Wonder song, 'Ebony and Ivory.'"

"When did you find out she married Colacchio?"

"One day she just came into the station with a wedding band on. No announcement or nothing. One of the girls on the desk asked her about it, and she simply said she was married. We thought she and Ivory had gotten hitched, but turns out it was Colacchio."

"And no one knew she and Colacchio were dating?"

"We didn't have a clue. She never mentioned him. Colacchio never came by the district. It was the most bizarre situation. One minute she's dating Ivory. Next minute she's married to the number two in the department."

"Do you know Colacchio?"

"Not personally, but I've heard things like anyone else."

"Such as?"

"Is there something going on, Ashe?"

"Can we keep this conversation between the two of us?"

"Absolutely."

"I'm following up on a case, and her name has come up. I knew she was a cop, but I had no idea she was married to Colacchio."

"What kind of case is it?"

"I'd rather not say right now. I'm still trying to get everything together."

"I understand. Well, I have to warn you to be careful."

"Careful about what?"

"I don't trust her," Liz said. "She's very cunning. She's laser-focused on what she wants, and nothing will get in the way. And Colacchio is a real brute. I've heard bad stories. Really bad stories. He's not someone I would mess around with."

"You think they have a normal marriage?"

Liz laughed softly. "I've been married for thirty-five years. I don't know if there's such a thing as a *normal* marriage, but if you're asking me do I think they're head over heels in love with each other, the answer is no. They're a strange couple. From what I know about her and from what I've heard about him, I think they both are just getting what they want out of the relationship. I'm not passing judgment. It's just a guess."

"This is really helpful, Liz. I appreciate it."

"Anytime," she said. "I don't know what kind of case you're working on, but promise me you'll be safe. You're a good guy, and the city is safer with you around."

"Eyes in the back of my head," I said.

THE REST OF THE DAY had been relatively quiet. Rox worked the morning shift and reported that Morgan was in a great mood. The overnights had come in, and the numbers had been even better than they expected. They went shopping on Oak Street, and after buying an entire rack at Prada, Morgan went to lunch with some philanthropist who had donated a new wing to the Art Institute.

I sat in my office reading over my case notes from the Williams and Henderson files, trying to see what connections I might've missed. I kept coming back to Palmer. What was he up to? Was someone pulling his strings? I had the important dots, but I just couldn't figure out how to connect them. I called Carolina and asked her to look into Eboni Markham's personnel file. She assured me she would be able to do that without leaving a trail.

It's strange how the mind works sometimes. You can be totally focused on one thing when all of a sudden you see or hear something that distracts you and takes your thoughts in an entirely different direction. I was reading an old article about the rise of Dominic Colacchio within CPD when I looked up for a moment and my eyes settled on a framed print Mechanic had given me for my birthday several years ago. It was a black-and-white still of a stack of one-hundred-dollar bills sitting on a gun that was resting on a Bible. I had stared at this print thousands of times. I had positioned it so that whenever I sat at my desk, I would see it. The money and the gun made me think of Moneygun, which made me think of my meeting with Tyra Martin, which made me think of our last phone call, which made me think of her saying the words "cannot exclude external causes."

I picked up the phone and dialed retired pathologist Barry Ellison, who was an old friend of my father's and critical in helping me crack my previous case involving the suspicious death of the former president of the Chicago Board of Education.

"How are you, Ashe?" Ellison said.

"Cold," I said. "Searching for about forty more degrees and lots of sunshine."

"I have that for you and more," he said.

"Where are you?"

"Naples, Florida."

"Thanks for rubbing it in."

"I'll be here through the end of March. Plenty of room and plenty of tee times. You have an open invitation."

"I might have to take you up on it," I said. "But I wanted to ask you a question about a case I'm working on."

"Shoot."

I told him about Alicia Roscati being found dead in her bed with no signs of physical trauma. I shared with him all the relevant details that Tyra Martin had told me.

Then I said, "So my question is, what exactly does it mean when they say, 'cannot exclude external causes'?"

"That means they didn't find anything on autopsy that gave them a definitive cause of death. There was nothing physical they could see, like brain injury, heart damage, anything like that. However, when they look at her age, previous good health, and the factors surrounding her death, they are still suspicious that something other than natural causes is the reason why she died. They just can't prove it."

"Do you think they have a theory of what might've caused it but can't find the physical evidence to confirm it?"

"Most likely. I ran into that problem many times with my cases. Any good pathologist has at least one working theory even if all the evidence isn't there."

"What would be yours in this case?"

"Poisoning."

"Based on?"

"Her symptoms prior to her death and how quickly she died after reporting those symptoms. Someone who is completely healthy with no known medical problems does not typically complain of weakness, nausea, and extremity paresthesia."

"Paresthesia?"

"Feeling of pins and needles. It happens when there's lots of pressure applied to peripheral nerves or they're actually damaged. Lots of conditions can cause it. Diabetes, stroke, infection, multiple sclerosis, even sitting on the toilet too long can restrict blood flow and cause it temporarily."

"If she was poisoned, then wouldn't they find something wrong in the blood or tissue samples?"

"Sometimes they can, sometimes they can't. Depends. Many poisons break down very quickly and unfortunately can make our job as pathologist even harder. When the poison breaks down, often our standard tests can't detect them, but there are times when they leave a trail."

"What do you mean 'a trail'?"

"Even if you can't isolate and identify the poisonous compounds, you can look at the full picture of the death. In this case, you look at the symptoms, what kind of health the person was in prior to dying, and what they might've been doing within twenty-four to forty-eight hours before death. Much like what you do, medical examiners sometimes have to be detectives and put together all the clues to figure out what really happened and how it went down."

That's when I remembered Sushi Ishiyama and the callback I was expecting but never received.

53

I called Sushi Ishiyama and, after three attempts, finally got through. I was told by a young woman who answered the phone that Mr. Ishiyama was not in yet, but she took my name and a message for him to return my call. Then I called Morgan.

"Are you coming tonight?" she said.

"Sitting courtside with a bucket of popcorn," I said.

"We're crushing them. The overnights are some of the best I've ever had."

"I've read all about it. They're even talking about you in Des Moines, Iowa."

"Jackson, Mississippi, too." She laughed softly.

"There's something I need to tell you," I said.

"Please tell me it's good news."

"For you, really good news. For someone else, maybe not."

"I'm listening."

"I have a positive identification of the cop Reece was seeing. Her name is Lieutenant Eboni Markham. She was and still is the current wife of First Deputy Dominic Colacchio."

"You're kidding."

"Not about something like this."

"Colacchio's wife was having an affair with Reece Williams?"

"That's correct."

"You have proof of this?"

"I have the photo and eyewitnesses."

"When did you find this out?"

"This morning."

"And you're just telling me now?"

"I didn't want to interrupt you emptying out Prada."

"This is next-level stuff. Can you get me someone who can confirm the relationship to me?"

"I can get you a name and number. What they're willing to say is up to them."

"Text it to me," she said. "I have to go talk to my news director. If I can get this confirmed, this series will get a fourth night."

I called Earl and told him about Eboni Markham. He sent me Darnell's phone number, which I quickly texted to Morgan. Minutes later, Carolina called.

"Are you sitting down?" she said.

"And reclining," I replied.

"I found something very interesting about Markham. She graduated from the Academy ten years ago. Mankovich also graduated the same year."

"And so did a couple of hundred other cadets."

"But it gets better. Mankovich and Markham were not just in the same class but also the same cohort."

That sat me up.

"Eboni Markham connects to Mankovich," I said. "Mankovich connects to Garrity, who chased Slim Henderson into that concrete barricade. Two connections down, two more to go."

"What are they?"

"Palmer, the street deputy, and Hakeem Jefferson, the paper pusher working in street ops."

I went back to the reports when Mechanic opened my door.

"You hear about the protest?" he said, taking a seat on the other side of my desk.

"I read it was happening sometime today."

"It's in full swing."

"You drove by it?"

"On my way here. Your priest is front and center."

I smiled. Father Flagger might've been slight in stature, but he was tough as they come and relentless.

"Let's go on a field trip," I said. "See what's going on with the people."

We got into the Defender and headed over to Thirty-Fifth Street. We hadn't even made it to Thirty-Third Street when we saw the huge crowds spilling onto Michigan Avenue. The large, bright placards bobbed in the air like horses on a merry-go-round.

"Damn," I said. "Must be over a thousand people down there."

I tried to drive closer, but police had set up wooden barricades to block vehicles. I pulled over and parked. As soon as we got out of the car, we could hear the noise. It sounded like kickoff at a football game. Mechanic and I walked around the barricades and made our way through the mass of bodies. There were people of all ages and races holding signs and chanting, "No justice. No peace." I was impressed by the racial diversity, something that had increased since the George Floyd protests spread throughout the country and attracted a broad spectrum of people unified in their demands for equality. The protesters were peaceful, but they were loud and angry. They hoisted blown-up photographs of Reece and Slim into the air. A long line of officers stood behind the barricades. Father Flagger stood facing the officers with a cluster of other community leaders, including a couple of aldermen and several ministers. Flagger yelled into a bullhorn, leading the protesters in defiant slogans as they raised their fisted right hands in solidarity.

I noticed Horace Robinson in the crowd. He and my father had gone to college together and had moved to Chicago after he finished law school and my father finished medical school. Robinson had worked many years as a partner at one of the city's most prestigious law firms. He retired several years ago a very wealthy man and now volunteered his efforts doing pro bono work for social justice issues. He was a member of COPA, the Civilian Office of Police Accountability, which was charged with conducting investigations of police misconduct brought against members of CPD. Twisting and bending my way through the crowd, Mechanic and I finally reached him. He embraced me before I introduced him to Mechanic, and I asked him to speak privately with me. We walked to the perimeter of the crowd.

"Bad stuff," Horace said once we were alone. "The whole thing smells rotten to the core."

"What do you know?" I asked.

"We've been looking into this for some months now," he said. "Lots of complaints about several of the officers involved, specifically Mankovich and Garrity."

"Have you talked to them yet?"

Horace hesitated then said, "Everything's in process."

"How deep?"

"Very."

"I'm working with Morgan Shaw," I said.

Horace lifted his bushy eyebrows. "I wasn't aware of that," he said.

"Tonight's not going to be a good night for some of the finest men in blue."

"Can you give me anything, or do I have to wait to see it like everyone else?"

"There's tape of the shooting."

He tightened his eyes slightly. "Who has it?"

"Morgan does."

"Are you certain it's authentic?"

"I'm the one who got it for her."

"I'm going to share something that must stay between us."

I nodded.

"We got a complaint that the only available video had been taken by officers and never returned to the source. Several attempts had been made to collect it, and no explanation of its whereabouts or what happened to it have been offered. So I'm not sure how it's possible you got your hands on the video card when no one else seems to know where it is."

"Do you know who took the missing card?"

"We do."

"Can you tell me the name?"

"I can't."

"How about I throw out a name."

"I can't stop you from doing that."

"Grant Palmer."

Horace gave me a confirmation with his eyes.

"Do you know Hakeem Jefferson in street ops?"

Horace nodded slightly.

"Have you talked to him?"

Horace nodded again.

"I think Hakeem, acting on orders, either destroyed the tape or knows what happened to it," I said.

"I can't comment on that specifically," Horace said.

The crowd roared as several officers started pushing protesters back with the steel barricades. The horse-mounted officers moved

closer to the front lines, a clear show of force. The protesters refused
to back down.

"Give me something," I said once the noise had settled a bit.

"Way off the record," Horace said. "And this can't go any further."

"Understood."

"Hakeem Jefferson was one of the people who actually lodged one
of the misconduct complaints."

MORGAN TOOK OFF HER MIC and pulled me to the side when I walked
into the studio that night. She wanted me to know that minutes ago she
had just gotten tentative approval for a fourth night based on the Eboni
Markham information. The team of lawyers had spent most of the day
combing through everything and finally gave the final segment their
blessing with the stipulation that Morgan stick to the script without
any ad-libs. Every word had been meticulously parsed.

Father Flagger and I took our seats while the rest of the viewing
team assembled in their customary positions. It was the same routine
as it was every night. Morgan and her co-anchor sat next to each other
totally absorbed in their laptops with all of the activity swirling around
not fazing them for a second. The music began, then when it ended,
the camera opened up on a two shot. Morgan read something about
changes in the mayor's office, then her co-anchor talked about snow in
the forecast. When Morgan took the camera on a solo shot, the large
background behind her changed from the station logo to video of
the protest earlier that day in front of police headquarters. She briefly
explained what provoked the protest, then a reporter spent the next
two minutes showing images from the earlier scene and asking several
police officers for comment as they ignored her. Father Flagger and the
community leaders then appeared on screen rallying the crowd through
the bullhorn.

Once the reporter's story ended, Morgan came back on camera and the video wall changed. This time it showed an enlarged still photo from Mrs. Cooper's video. Mankovich stood there with his gun drawn and Reece with his hands in the air.

"What you're about to·see might be extremely disturbing," Morgan said. "You will see actual footage of the shooting of Reece Williams. This footage was not taken from police bodycams because, conveniently, they were not turned on until after Reece Williams was already on the ground with two bullets in his body. This is footage recorded by a nearby security camera."

The tape rolled without sound for the next four minutes. No edits, just the raw footage as it was recorded. The lack of sound or narration made the tape even more chilling, and those of us in the studio were as mesmerized as the those watching at home. When the footage stopped, Morgan then explained that Mankovich got out of the car with his gun drawn and Reece only had a cell phone in his hand. As she made these statements, still photographs to back them up appeared on screen. She then made the claim the lawyers approved at the eleventh hour. Reece had no gun in his hand. The gun that appeared next to his body did not come from him and only appeared once Mankovich was kneeling beside him alone for eight seconds. The camera came back to her live, and she concluded by saying that tomorrow night would be the final installment of the series and the most damning as they would examine a possible motivation for this otherwise unexplained and tragic shooting.

After the newscast, I drove Morgan home.

"How do you feel?" I asked as we rolled down the empty streets.

"Exhausted and excited at the same time," she said.

"Your bosses seemed happy."

"Of course they are. If the numbers hold tonight and tomorrow night, we'll be too far ahead for them to catch us and hold on to the top spot. That means more money in ad dollars and a big bonus for the GM."

"He gets a bonus when you do all the work."

"I get a bonus too, but not as big as his. That's how it works. I get the best seats at restaurants and ball games, while they make themselves feel better by taking a little bigger bonus. Still shakes out in my favor."

"How's everything shaping up for tomorrow night?"

"Coming along. Our lawyers had a big fight with the city lawyers. CPD won't put anyone on camera, so they just reissued another say-nothing statement. I'll read it at the end of the story."

"Do they know you have Markham and Reece as a couple?"

"Not yet."

"Do they know Colacchio is implicated?"

"We requested to speak to him about his involvement in the shooting. Our request was denied."

"What else do you have to connect Colacchio?"

"We have a source that says Colacchio has his own infidelity issues. He's been sleeping with a sergeant out of the Twenty-Third. But our lawyers won't let us touch that without the sergeant going on record."

"Do you know who it is?"

"Yup. And we've asked her about it. She hung up on us after sharing a few choice words."

We pulled up to a stoplight. A woman walking a tiny dog crossed the street. An unmarked pulled up next to us on Morgan's side. The driver rolled down his window just enough to show his face. It was difficult to tell if he was white or Latino. His eyes were dark, and it looked like he hadn't shaved in days. He wore a bulletproof vest. Morgan waved at him. He just stared at her menacingly. The light turned green. I drove straight as the unmarked rode next to us, making sure to let us know they were still there.

"What's that all about?" Morgan said.

"Supposed to be intimidation," I said. "They want you to know they're watching."

Morgan smiled. "I'm shaking like a leaf."

"I know you're tough, but we shouldn't take any chances. The next few days it would be better for you to keep your head down a little. Mechanic and Rox will stick by you, but we need to minimize your exposure."

We arrived at her apartment building. I noticed the unmarked in my rearview mirror. It had stopped at the end of the block and was just sitting there. Morgan was about to get out until I grabbed her arm.

"Wait a second," I said.

I drove about ten yards down the street and turned into the driveway.

"Let me have your key card," I said.

She rummaged through her purse and pulled it out. I swiped it against the reader, and the garage door opened. We rolled in, and the door closed behind us.

"Mechanic is with you in the morning," I said, pulling up to the rear entrance. "No shopping or going out to lunch tomorrow. Low-key for a few days."

"If tonight's story brought on all this, what's gonna happen after tomorrow night? They're gonna try to break into my apartment?"

"They've done a lot worse."

54

NOVEMBER 6
TENTH DAY OF SWEEPS

That evening's show not only gave Morgan and the station another big win in the overnights, but it was the highest number they had posted since Michael Jordan and the Bulls won their first of six titles in 1991. I don't even know what you call the person who analyzes and charts these ratings, but they had concluded that one more victorious night and their lead would be so insurmountable, the top spot would be secured yet again. I thought about the general manager leaning back in his swivel chair, feet on his desk, thinking about how he was going to spend that large bonus.

Today was the day I would finally sit down with Julia and get everything worked out. I was nervous, and I had done everything I could up to that point to avoid thinking about it. For the next several hours, I needed to stay busy to make the time go by faster. Mechanic's call interrupted my thoughts. He was downstairs and ready to go. It was time to pay Officer Hakeem Jefferson a little visit. We had it on good intel that every Saturday morning before going to work, he liked to eat breakfast at a chicken-and-waffle restaurant in Bronzeville on South King Drive. We walked into the busy restaurant and spotted him right away. He was in uniform, seated against the back wall, flipping through the *Sun-Times*. He looked up once we approached his table.

"Officer Jefferson," I said. "Apologies for intruding on this gastronomic excellence. My name is Ashe Cayne, and this is my colleague Mechanic."

"I know exactly who the hell you are," Jefferson said, closing the paper and resting it on the table. "How can I help you?"

"I was gonna ask you the same question."

"Take a seat," he said.

Mechanic and I pulled up nearby chairs and sat down.

"Reece Williams," I said.

"What about him?" he replied.

"Gaynell and Rodney Cooper," I said.

"You've mentioned three names since you sat down. Is there a question in there?"

"What happened to that missing video card?"

Jefferson took a sip of his coffee, then said, "Who are you working for?"

"The truth," I said.

Jefferson looked at me, then Mechanic.

"Off the record," he said.

"This conversation never happened."

Jefferson looked at Mechanic, who nodded his agreement.

"I had nothing to do with that shit," Jefferson said. "I work in street ops. I'm an administrator just trying to ride out my days. I get a call one afternoon from one of our deputies who says I might be getting a phone call about a video card that was surrendered from a home at the scene of a police shooting. He told me the date and location of the shooting. I asked him why they would be calling me. I didn't know anything about it and had nothing to do with it. He said it was better to have all questions from the district routed to me, and I'd be given instructions on how to respond."

"You didn't find that suspicious?" I asked.

"Of course I did," Jefferson said. "You know how it works. Those were the orders I was given. I pushed back a little, but my superior gave me instructions. I carried them out."

"What were the instructions?"

"If someone called looking for the memory card, lose the number. If they called again, take my time calling them back. When I did call them back, don't give them any real answers."

"How much longer before you plan on returning the call?"

"I don't like lying to people. I'm an honest person. If I don't return the call, then I won't have to lie."

"Do you know what happened to the card?"

"No idea. Never saw it myself, and no one has told me what happened to it."

"Grant Palmer was the deputy who gave you those orders," I said.

"You said that, not me."

"Since you're such an honest person, do you want to deny it?"

Jefferson shifted in his seat. "Listen, man. This shit is way above me. I didn't ask to be involved. I don't wanna be involved. I just wanna mind my own business and do my job."

"What's Palmer's relationship to Colacchio?" I asked.

"Did you just hear what I said?"

"I did."

"Then you of all people understand where I'm coming from. This is the kinda shit that ruins careers."

"It's also the kind of shit that kills innocent people," I said. "Reece Williams was executed by a police officer. He didn't deserve it. His friends and family are owed answers and justice. You're an officer of the law, but more than that, you're a human being. How can you sleep peacefully at night knowing what happened and remaining silent?"

An expression of resignation fell softly on Jefferson's face as his shoulders relaxed. "I'm not being silent, man," he said. "COPA is conducting their own investigation into what happened. I'm cooperating. Confidentially."

That confirmed what Horace Robinson had already told me.

"One more question," I said. "Who gave the order to kill Williams?"

Jefferson moved his eyes quickly between Mechanic and me, and I was sure he wouldn't answer. Then he calmly said, "Colacchio."

I GAVE MECHANIC AND ROX clear instructions to keep Morgan in her apartment, then drive her to the station and not let her out of their sight. Morgan tried to appear unfazed by my insistence on the heightened security, but I knew she was nervous. Tonight was the series finale, and the entire city was speculating about what more she had to say regarding the deaths of Reece Williams and Slim Henderson.

My phone rang as I sat down to my computer. It was Tyra Martin.

"She pulled off a miracle," Tyra said. "Caught us completely off guard."

"She's a real fighter," I said. "I guess you have to be to get to number one and stay there as long as she has."

"Management over here is going crazy. They can't believe we missed this story, and they can't believe how deeply sourced she got. I'm sure your investigative expertise had nothing to do with it."

"I'm trying to think back to what you told me at Moneygun. 'You're very charming and very nice to look at. But that's something I can't tell even you.'"

"Touché. Well, I tip my hat to her. She's done it again. Anyway, I wanted you to know they're officially concluding Alicia's autopsy results. What I told you before will hold. They don't know the cause, but they can't say for certain something or someone didn't cause it."

"Gonna be tough on the family not to have a decisive answer."

"It only makes the pain worse. But there's nothing that can be done. We'll just never know what really happened."

"I know it probably doesn't bring any comfort saying this, but this is not uncommon. Plenty of young people die, and the ME has no idea what happened. Sad but true."

"Has Morgan had any blowback from her reports?"

"Besides a few cops giving her some hard looks, she's been fine. No more letters or calls. All is quiet."

"Good for her. Well, if you ever wanna grab a drink sometime, let me know. You're fun to talk to."

"Feeling's mutual."

I got off the phone thinking about how uneven life could be. On the one hand, here was Alicia Roscati, a beautiful, talented rising star who flamed out way too early, unexpectedly, and without any answers as to what caused it. Then you had Morgan Shaw now having the time of her life, vibrant and reinvigorated, celebrating yet another ratings success and her confirmed status as queen of Chicago media.

I had cleaned my apartment and burned some candles so that it smelled good. Julia was arriving at five o'clock, and I wanted everything to look presentable.

I took out a bottle of wine my father had given me for my birthday and told me to only open for a worthy occasion. I shaved, got dressed, then headed into the living to open the blinds. The front door opened. Julia walked in looking more beautiful than I had ever seen her. She walked toward me, and we kissed on the cheek, though at first, I felt her leaning in for a kiss on the mouth.

"You look great," I said. "Thanks for coming."

"I'm so glad you wanted to see me," she said. "I've been waiting for this moment for a long time."

I poured a couple of glasses of wine, then we walked to the sofa and sat down. Stryker settled near the patio door and looked at both of us.

"I want to start by saying that I've forgiven you," I said. "I've realized that I need to do that first in order to heal properly."

"I know this hasn't been easy," she said. "And I know there's really nothing I can say now to take back all the pain you felt. But I want you to know how bad I felt knowing what you were going through."

"I appreciate that," I said. "But I'm not gonna lie. I've hurt every day since you left me. It got so bad there were times I felt like I couldn't breathe. But then I had a revelation when I was in Arizona. I realized my frame of reference was all wrong."

"In what way?"

"I kept thinking this was about me. I spent all this time trying to figure out what it was that made you run away from me. But that was the wrong perspective, and it kept me from healing. I had to accept that it really was about you and whatever was going on in your mind and life that I didn't know about. That perspective shift was a gamechanger for me."

She took a sip of wine. I looked at the clock. It was ten minutes after five.

"I don't know how else to say this other than I just lost my shit," she said. "You were as perfect as a partner could be. You gave me everything I could ask for. You loved me like no one has ever loved me. But I just lost confidence in myself and who I was. I was insecure, worried that I wasn't good enough for you, and I'd spend the rest of my life in your shadow."

"So your solution was to turn and run?"

"I thought the distance would give me space to reconnect with myself and find my confidence again. I never would've been able to do that if I stayed. At least that's what I thought."

"You could've sat down and talked to me. We could've gotten help together, figured this out. There were so many options other than you running."

"I was too scared and confused to think of anything else," she said. "And I was too selfish to consider what it might do to you."

I looked at the clock. It was a quarter past five.

"My actions might've said something else, but I never stopped loving you," she said. "Not for a single day."

"Which is why you were with that stockbroker?"

"Being with him made me love you even more."

"And my pain almost unbearable. How could I not think that there was something wrong with me when you ended up being with someone else?"

She lowered her head, then said, "I'm so sorry. I was searching for answers in the wrong places. Being with him helped me see that."

"Love is amazing in so many ways," I said. "All the hurt you caused and anger I felt, and still I never stopped loving you."

I moved closer to her.

"And I love you right now," I said. I kissed her softly and briefly on the lips. "But not like I did before."

"Give me a chance," she said, resting her hand on mine. "I'm in a much better place. I know we can make this work. I'm ready."

I heard the door open and close softly.

"So many nights I fell asleep alone wishing for just one chance to say those words to you," I said. "My heart is gone, Jules."

"Do you remember that long night at the Sixty-Third Street beach house? The waves were crashing onto the rocks beneath us, and the air was so clear we could see the skyline all the way across the darkness of the lake."

"Like it was yesterday," I said. "I told you that love was like the tide. Sometimes it comes on in vast powerful surges, and sometimes it just slowly slips away so it can return even stronger."

"Well, I've returned and so can the power of our love," she said. "I want to fight for us."

I heard her footsteps on the hardwood floor. She was making her way down the hallway.

Julia looked up as Carolina stood at the entrance of the living room. I saw the tears immediately swell in Julia's eyes. I felt for her. I knew the pain too well.

I stood.

"You will always mean something to me, and so will the time we shared together," I said. I walked to Carolina, kissed her on the lips, then turned back to Julia. "This is Carolina Espinoza," I said. "The woman I've fallen in love with, who can finish my sentences and make that tide roar when it comes rushing back."

Carolina smiled. Julia stood and looked at her. She looked at me, her eyes now leaking. Both of us knew it was finally over. She gathered her handbag and walked down the hallway.

"Please leave the keys," I said.

I heard them jingle as she placed them on the table on her way through the door and out of my life.

55

That night, I arrived at the station early. Morgan was still in her office making last-minute changes to her scripts when I walked in. She wore a fuchsia suit that perfectly matched the traces of rouge on her cheeks. The office lighting had been dimmed, which made her face glow even more.

"You ready?" I said, taking a seat next to her desk.

"As ready as I'll ever be," she said.

"Nervous?"

"I'd be lying if I said I wasn't. The lawyers are nervous too."

"They're paid to be nervous."

"They rewrote the script thirty times before they let me track it for the piece. They went over every single word."

"There's a lot riding on tonight."

"You're dramatic. We're gonna expose these killers, and they'll pay for what they did to those two families."

"One can only hope," I said. "But we both know it doesn't always work out that way."

"We can't control the justice system," she said. "But we can influence the court of public opinion. That's what we'll do tonight."

A woman came and tapped on the office window. Morgan got up, ran her fingers through her hair, and departed for the studio.

I called Mechanic, who was standing by in the garage. He reported that everything was good. I then called Rox, who was stationed outside of Morgan's apartment building. "All's quiet in the Gold Coast," her report came back.

The same cast assembled in the studio as it had the previous nights. Father Flagger smiled as I sat next to him. He was giddy with anticipation.

"This is the night we nail those sons-a-bitches," he said.

His language sat me back.

"Don't worry—I'll confess later," he said, still smiling.

The tension in the studio was more palpable than it had been all week. Everyone knew the stakes and all that rode on the next thirty minutes. Unlike the other nights, the production assistant delivered the scripts to the team of lawyers first, then once they had read through them, she delivered them to Morgan and her co-anchor.

The floor director made her series of announcements. Just before the music started, Morgan closed her eyes, took a deep breath, then turned directly to the camera. She had the goods and was ready to share them with the entire city.

They held her story for the B block so that viewers would stay through the first commercial break, something that was important for how they calculated the ratings. The news director walked up to the anchor desk during the break and said something to Morgan. This was the first time I had seen her do that. I couldn't hear what they were saying, but Morgan smiled and nodded. The floor director counted down, and when the on-air light flashed, Morgan sat perfectly framed in the camera.

For the next eight minutes, Morgan's taped piece laid out the timeline like a prosecutor making a closing argument to the jury.

She carefully strung together all the elements from the arrival of Mankovich and his tac team on South Eggleston, to witness accounts, Mrs. Cooper's critical video, and tonight's pièce de résistance, the connection between Reece Williams, Eboni Markham, Mankovich, and First Deputy Dominic Colacchio. She showed the photo of Reece and Eboni at Essence Festival with a sound bite from Darnell who confirmed that Reece and Eboni were romantically involved. She even found a photo of Eboni and Mankovich together as cadets in the academy. Morgan didn't directly accuse Colacchio of ordering the hit, but the way she connected the dots left little to the imagination. Once the tape had finished, they came back to Morgan live in the studio. She took a pause for effect, then told the audience that in a democratic country governed by the rule of law, no one was above it, and those who swear an oath to enforce it must especially be held accountable when they run afoul of it. The screen faded to black, and everyone in the studio vigorously applauded.

56

The reaction to Morgan's story had been swift. Protests raged and swelled across the city for weeks even as the temperatures dipped below freezing. Colacchio, Markham, and Palmer were placed on immediate leave pending an internal investigation, then Colacchio and Palmer abruptly retired so they wouldn't lose their pension and benefits. The Cook County State's Attorney brought several charges against Mankovich and Garrity, who had quickly been terminated from the department.

Morgan still sat on her throne every night and delivered the news to a city that had fallen in love with her all over again for breaking open the sad and twisted story of Reece Williams. The Williams family had finally hired an attorney, and rumors had the settlement figure well above ten million.

Giselle Burgos had gone back to covering red carpet arrivals in LA. Julia had gone back to Paris. Rox had gone back to selling flowers. And Mechanic was still Mechanic. In two days, I was heading back to Scottsdale to finish my golf vacation that had been cut short. Carolina had agreed to join me for a long weekend at the end of my stay, then we'd return home in time for Christmas. I had taken a quick run along the lake that morning, then rushed home to get changed so I could meet my father for breakfast. My phone buzzed as I got out of the shower. I dried my hands and picked it up.

"This is Barry Ellison. I hope it's not a bad time."

"Not at all," I said. "Getting dressed to meet my father for breakfast. How's the weather down there?"

"About fifty degrees better than where you are," he said, laughing.

"Not for long," I said. "In two days, I'll be in Scottsdale hitting five irons under the sun and sleeping under central air."

"The temps in Arizona this time of year even make us look chilly. Anyway, I don't mean to take up too much of your time, but I was just wondering if you're still working on that case with the possible poisoning."

"It was never solved."

"Well, I've been giving it some thought. Are they still saying the cause is indeterminant?"

"Last I heard, nothing changed."

"Well, I've narrowed down some potential agents that you might consider. Carbon disulfide, dioxin, and tetrodotoxin. They all can cause neurological symptoms, and if given in high enough concentrations or over a long enough period of time, they all can cause neurological problems and the other symptoms she experienced like fatigue and weakness. A lot of investigators and examiners miss them at autopsy because they don't suspect them, or they don't have the right lab equipment to detect them."

I grabbed a pen and piece of paper and asked him to repeat the agents again, then I asked him to explain the differences.

"Carbon disulfide is a colorless liquid," he said. "Smells like ether, and if it's really pure, it smells sweet. Can hurt your eyes, kidneys, blood, nerves, skin—you name it. But it's not something you can just buy off the shelf, so it's not commonly used or looked for during autopsy unless someone worked in an industrial plant where it's available."

"But it could be detected?"

"Yes, but the key is you have to look for it. It's one of those things if you don't expect it, then you won't find it. Dioxin is different. It's the stuff that made Agent Orange so dangerous. Not very common at all. Really difficult to get ahold of the stuff. You can find it in the blood if you're fast enough, or you can find it in the fat if you're careful enough to look there. But you have to consider the circumstances. If you have a healthy young woman who appeared to die in her sleep, some might not think to look at the fat. They should, but you never know."

"What about the last agent?" I asked.

"Tetrodotoxin is very interesting," he said. "That's really one you have to be looking for from the start. I've never seen it in my career, and it's not really all that common anymore, but it's a possibility."

"What does it do?"

"It's a neurotoxin that's commonly found in marine animals. We eat some of them like octopus, snails, and pufferfish."

"Pufferfish as in sushi?"

"Yes. You don't hear about it much these days. Most of the cases are in places like Japan, Taiwan, and some Southeast Asian countries. Very rare here in the US. Lots of precautions are taken to make sure the seafood is treated properly."

I immediately thought of Sushi Ishiyama.

"How long after eating sushi would someone experience symptoms?"

"It really depends on how much toxin is in the food. We all respond differently. But I would say as quick as thirty minutes up to twenty hours. Within that time frame, someone will start seeing their first symptom. Usually the paresthesia and numbness around the mouth start first, and then they might have the gastrointestinal symptoms you mentioned like nausea or vomiting or abdominal discomfort."

"How long does it take someone to die from it?"

"Once again, that's hard to say. So many variables involved. It could be as fast as a few hours to as much as twenty-four or forty-eight hours depending on the toxin concentration."

"Is it possible for someone to go to dinner, have pufferfish sushi, experience some of the symptoms the next day, lie down in bed, then die in their sleep within twenty-four hours?"

"It doesn't happen very often, but yes, that's theoretically possible."

"And what would a medical examiner find at autopsy?"

"Depends on how much time lapses between ingestion and the autopsy. One of the first things you'd look at is gastric or stomach contents and see if there's anything there to sample. You take blood and urine samples and get them tested, but it has to be done within a certain time frame, or it's difficult to extract the toxin and make a diagnosis. But the most important thing in all this is that you need to have a suspicion for what the agent might be. You can't find what you're not looking for."

"Once again, you've been a big help, Dr. Ellison," I said.

"Hope it makes sense," he said. "And if you ever want to come down here and escape the freezing cold, that invitation still stands."

"I appreciate it."

No sooner than I was off the phone, I jumped in the truck and headed toward Sushi Ishiyama. I wasn't going to wait any longer for someone to return my call. They were already prepping the restaurant for lunch service, arranging tables while the chefs worked diligently on the fresh fish that had just been delivered. I asked the hostess if I could speak to Mr. Ishiyama. She told me to wait up front while she went back and got him. Minutes later she was followed by a tall, thin man with small oval glasses and a mound of gray hair. An easy smile settled across his narrow face.

"How can I help you?" he said with an accent similar to his wife's.

"My name is Ashe Cayne," I said. "I've left several messages for you to call me back."

"Is this about the video of the news woman?"

"It is. Do you have video of her from that night?"

"Not anymore."

"What happened to it?"

"It's been erased. We only keep video for two weeks, then it gets recycled. I didn't call you back because your request didn't make sense."

"What do you mean?"

"You said the woman you were looking for on the video is dead. She's not dead. She's very much alive. I figured you had the wrong restaurant, so I didn't bother calling you back."

"I'm not sure what you're talking about. The woman who was here that night died two days after she had dinner at your restaurant."

"With all due respect, you are mistaken, sir," he said. "I saw her on the news last night. She comes here often. I watch her every night when I'm not here."

None of what he said was making sense. I thought he was joking at first, but he looked very serious. Maybe he was right, and I had the wrong restaurant. I took out my phone and pulled up a picture of Alicia Roscati and showed it to him.

"This is the woman who was here, and right now she's buried in a cemetery in Iowa," I said.

Ishiyama smiled and shook his head. "That's not the woman I'm talking about," he said. "The woman I thought you were talking about is Morgan Shaw. She was here for dinner that night. She comes often. Very quietly. She always enters and leaves through the back door. That night she asked to sit over at that table." Ishiyama pointed to a table out of the way in a small nook near the kitchen. It was almost totally hidden from the rest of the room. "That's the first time she ever asked to sit there," Ishiyama said. "She didn't want anyone to recognize her and make a fuss."

I just stood there and stared at him. After I was able to process what he said, I pulled up a photo of Morgan and showed it to him.

"Yes, that's Morgan," he said. "She's on TV every night and very famous. She had dinner that night with a friend of hers who was very beautiful like the woman you just showed me."

"Was it the same woman in the picture?"

"Could've been, but I can't say for sure. They both are very pretty. Morgan was happy to eat with her. She even brought in special fish for them to eat."

"She brought in her own fish?"

"Yes. We normally don't allow that, but Ms. Shaw is a very good customer, and we like her, so we accommodated the special request. She had very expensive fugu imported for their dinner. We just plated it, added some garnish, and served it."

Absolutely genius, I thought. She'd played me the entire time.

57

We had agreed to meet for lunch at Piccolo Sogno, an Italian restaurant in the River West neighborhood. They had set me up at my favorite table against the last of a row of windows with a perfect view of the expansive dining room. I knew she had arrived because I could hear the increasing commotion and murmuring of the other diners. I looked up and saw her confidently striding across the room in long boots, tight jeans, and a creamy-white cashmere sweater that looked soft enough to sleep on. Half the room ogled and pointed and whispered as she sauntered by. She never acknowledged the admirers, instead making a beeline for my table. She kissed me softly on both cheeks as I stood to pull her chair out. She smelled expensive.

"I haven't been here in years," she said. "I used to order a black pasta with mussels, clams, and shrimp. It was out of this world."

"They still have it," I said. "Spaghetti neri."

"Then that's what I'll have," she said, pushing her menu aside. "So you're heading to play golf again?"

"Two more days and I'll be soaking up the sun. My escape comes just before that big storm hits us."

"I'm so dreading it. Our weatherman says it'll dump close to a foot, then we'll get hit with a polar vortex a few days later. And you'll be sipping margaritas next to a cactus while we freeze our asses off back here."

"I'll raise one for you."

The waiter came and took our orders and refilled our water glasses. We talked about nothing for the next fifteen minutes, then our food was served piping hot.

"So how's it going at the station?" I asked.

"Couldn't be better," she said. "Everyone's happy. We averted disaster. Giselle and her Ken-doll husband are back in LA where they belong. The experiment failed, but at least they made it interesting."

"Do you think Alicia would've beaten you if she hadn't been killed?"

"It's hard to say . . . Wait, did you say killed?"

"Yes. Killed."

She dropped her fork. "What do you mean? Did they change the autopsy results?"

"Not yet."

"So why are you saying she was killed?"

"I think you know the answer to that."

"Are we playing some kind of guessing game?" she said, smiling. It was a nervous smile.

"I've been doing that a lot the last few weeks," I said.

"What are you guessing?"

"Exactly how you pulled it off. I have most of it put together but not all of it."

"Ashe, you have a couple of drinks before you got here?" she said, shaking her finger at me.

"I know that you had dinner with Alicia shortly before she died," I said.

"Really?"

"I talked to Mr. Ishiyama. He's a big fan. He remembers you coming in that night."

She didn't say anything.

I leaned forward. "This is how I think you did it. You used a burner phone and sent yourself a threatening text message that night. The threat gave a reason for you to ask Mechanic to come up and spend the night in a guest bedroom in your apartment. He was a perfect alibi. If you ever got questioned, you could say he was with you all night in the apartment. So when he was all settled, you went downstairs, snuck out the door, took the service elevator down, and walked out the back of the building. If the video footage still exists, I bet you can be seen entering and leaving the elevator and walking out the back door. You caught a taxi or rideshare to Sushi Ishiyama and either you already had it in your apartment, or you picked it up along the way, but somehow you got the puffer sushi to the restaurant."

I paused, giving her a chance to help me connect the dots. She just smiled.

"Mr. Ishiyama told me that you had a special fish that you brought with you, and while they normally don't allow outside food, he made an exception and served it to you and Alicia. I don't know how you did it, but somehow you made sure she got the sushi loaded with toxic levels of tetrodotoxin."

Morgan took a shallow sip of wine, then said, "Sounds like you should try your hand at screenwriting. The best screenwriters in Hollywood couldn't make up this plot."

"And any actress who could pull off what you did and how you did it would win an Oscar."

"You're making some really wild allegations," she said. "You have proof to back all this up?"

"If I did, we'd be having this conversation on a jail phone looking at each other through plexiglass."

"So what's the purpose of all this?"

"To let you know that I know what you did."

She nodded softly. "Any other great discoveries you want to share before dessert arrives?"

"You played me hard," I said. "That's not easy to do."

"I hired you to protect me," she said. "And I appreciate your professionalism and the job you did."

"No, you hired me for cover, and for good measure, you lied about your relationship with the majority leader to distract me while you carried out your plan."

She raised her eyebrows.

"You and Schmidt never broke up. You completely fabricated the story about it being an acrimonious split. But you needed that narrative so that when you sent yourself those floggers in the mail, it would look like he or someone else was extorting you. All subterfuge, including the vandalism to your truck with the fish on your windshield and the slit tires. I always felt something was wrong about that. Who would take that kind of risk in a garage that they had to assume had cameras and plenty of people around who might see them? Only you because you knew the holes in the surveillance camera coverage. You knew the few locations the cameras missed, so you parked in one of them, messed your car up, then called and fed me a line that one of the new cameramen had accidentally parked in your regular spot, which forced you to park in the surveillance gap. I must admit that was pretty damn genius."

"If this wasn't so outrageous and implausible, I'd be angry enough to reach across this table and slap you," she said. "I'm one of the most recognized faces in all of Chicago. Why the hell would I plan something so elaborate and depraved as this and risk everything I've worked so hard for?"

"Because in your mind you were in jeopardy of losing it all, and you were willing to do whatever it took to win and hold on to that number-one spot."

"And be stupid enough to hire one of the city's best investigators just to give me cover? I could've hired anyone."

"You could've, but you hired me so you could kill two birds with one big stone. Not only would I give you cover, but you did your research and discovered I'm also the kind of person who would help you solve Reece's case and turn it into a blockbuster story for your sweeps ratings. Well played, Morgan."

"I wish I was worthy of such platitudes," she said.

"You deserve them and then some. Beautiful, smart, tough—you're as smooth as they come. And a ruthless killer."

"You can think whatever farfetched ideas you want, but be very careful what you say. I have a team of hungry lawyers always waiting for flesh to be thrown into their pit."

I smiled at her. "Of course you do." I pushed back from the table and reached for my coat. "All of this because Alicia Roscati was going to finally beat you in the overnights. And to think I really had come to like you."

"There's a lot to like," she said. "I admire you. Formidable."

"And the most determined man you'll ever meet," I said. "You're a cold, calculating murderer who deserves to die alone inside four drab walls of a dank prison cell."

"I'm sorry you feel that way," she said. "It's very sad you're so wrong about me."

I stood, dropped some money on the table, pulled the Rolex she had given me out of my coat pocket, and set it on top of the money.

"This isn't the end," I said. "Every night you go to sleep in that mansion, and every morning you wake up to that view of the sun rising behind the lake, know that I'm out here, and I know what you did, and I sure as hell won't stop until you pay for it."

I walked away, then turned back just before leaving the dining room. She sat there calmly sipping her wine with that million-watt smile lighting up her gorgeous face as if she hadn't a single care in the world.

Acknowledgments

Creating story and character arcs is one of my favorite parts of writing. Every time I sit down to my computer to release my imagination, I am in awe of how lucky I am to have the opportunity to do so. But creating is just one of my joys. Being able to share and bounce around ideas and talk story and be supported are right up there as far as motivating me to keep pushing. I give thanks to my cousin Damian, who loves the Ashe Cayne series more than anyone else except me. Right beside him, always hungry for the next install-ment, is Evrod Cassimy, who hounds me on a weekly basis about the arrival of his next advanced copy. Thanks to my agent, Mitch Hoffman, who has believed in me and this series from day one, and who continues to cheer and advise and fight for us with a sagacity and intellectual muscle that seems infinite. Lynn Cherry, my aunt and voracious reader, you inspired me to love books. Maureen Arsenault, my high school English teacher, you helped me fall in love with the magic of storytelling. Michael Lieteau, who will read no other novels than mine. Michael and Nancy Reinsdorf, generous friends who don't mind serving as muses now and again.

My brother, Dana, a courageous and endless story creator who inspires me to keep stretching my creative muscle and believing that good content will always be in demand.

Tristé, Dashiell, and Declan, the A-team. Thanks for allowing me to slip away into the corners of my imagination, even in the middle of African safaris. Your grace and space allow the fire to keep burning. *Besitos.*

About the Author

Ian K. Smith is a #1 *New York Times* bestselling author. His Ashe Cayne series is currently in development to become a TV series, and his novel *The Ancient Nine* has been optioned to become a motion picture. His acclaimed novel *The Blackbird Papers* was a Black Caucus of the American Library Association fiction honor award recipient. Many of his books have been number one bestsellers and have been translated into more than ten languages.

For more information, you can visit:

www.doctoriansmith.com
Instagram: @doctoriansmith
Twitter: @DrIanSmith
TikTok: @theofficialdrian